# HIGHLAND SECRETS

## SECRETS OF THE HEART SERIES - BOOK 1

## ELIZABETH ROSE

ROSESCRIBE MEDIA INC.

Cover created by Elizabeth Rose Krejcik
Edited by Scott Moreland

ISBN-13: 978-1720892458
ISBN-10: 1720892458

TO MY READERS

Secrets of the Heart is a series about the eldest daughters of the bastard triplets from the Legendary Bastards of the Crown which is followed by Seasons of Fortitude. This series can be read as standalone books, but if you prefer to read them in chronological order, I have listed the series below.

Watch for more books in the Secrets of the Heart Series coming soon!

**Legendary Bastards of the Crown:**

**Destiny's Kiss – Series Prequel**
 **Restless Sea Lord – Book 1**
 **Ruthless Knight – Book 2**
 **Reckless Highlander – Book 3**

**Seasons of Fortitude Series:**
 **Highland Spring – Book 1**
 **Summer's Reign – Book 2**
 **Autumn's Touch – Book 3**

Winter's Flame – Book 4

Secrets of the Heart Series:
   Highland Secrets – Book 1
   Seductive Secrets – Book 2
   Rebellious Secrets – Book 3
   Forgotten Secrets – Book 4

*Enjoy!*

*Elizabeth Rose*

# PROLOGUE

ENGLAND, JUNE 1377

"*H*urry, my lords, the king is dying and has called for you." The messenger of King Edward III waved his arm, urging the small traveling party down the corridor of Sheen Palace. King Edward III was at his life's end and had called for his bastard triplets, Rowen, Rook, and Reed to be at his side. He also summoned their eldest daughters, Maira, Willow and Fia. The girls and their fathers had traveled for two days to get here from Whitehaven Castle where they were celebrating the birth of Rowen's new baby boy, Michael.

Ten-year-old Fia Douglas followed behind her father, Reed, and her uncles. Nearly having to run to keep up with their long strides, she held tightly to the hands of her cousins, ten-year-old Maira and eight-year-old Willow. Fia's long red braids bobbed up and down as she hurried through the corridor. She'd inherited her vibrant hair from her father. Willow's ebony tresses were dark like her father, Rook's, while Maira had strawberry-blond hair that was a combination of her father, Rowen's blond hair and her mother's auburn locks. The girls' fathers were triplets and identical in every other way. Triplets were considered a curse and the brunt of many superstitions. When they were born, the king ordered them killed. But that was long ago, and things had changed since then. Fia's father and uncles told her that they no longer raided the king or wanted vengeance against him.

"Hurry lassies, move yer wee legs faster," Reed called back over his shoulder, speaking in his Scottish burr. Reed wore the dark green Douglas plaid. The triplets had been raised in Scotland by Annalyse and Ross Douglas, as well as with their four sisters all named after the seasons. For the first twelve years of their lives, the boys had no idea that the king was their father and Annalyse's late sister was their mother. Reed embraced the Scottish dialect and customs since he had always idolized Ross Douglas. Rowen and Rook, on the other hand, spoke and acted like Englishmen, taking on the ways and customs of their aunt.

"We are hurryin', Da," Fia answered her father in a soft voice. Her eyes swept the corridor and the many people watching them curiously from the shadows. She noticed every detail of the castle from the height of the ceiling with the thick wooden beams to the swirls in the marble floor beneath her feet. She was the shyest of the three girls, but also the most observant. Nothing escaped Fia's attention, no matter where she went. She had a sharp memory and details were her strong point.

Being the eldest daughter and child of Reed, Fia felt special. Her father often doted over her, wanting to protect her and keep her close to his side. She liked her father's attention.

The men led the way to the dying king's chamber, their swords swinging at their sides with every step they took. The jingle of their chainmail and spurs filled the air, sounding twice as loud since everyone around them was quiet. Their heavy booted feet stomped down the corridor, making it impossible for anyone not to know they were there.

"I wonder what Edward wants with us," Rook mumbled to his brothers, speaking in a low voice, but still, Fia heard every word.

Her father let out a frustrated breath before he answered. "I dinna ken, but do ye think it's that important?" Fia's family lived over the border in the Lowlands of Scotland with her mother's clan, the Gordons. Reed only came to England occasionally to visit his brothers. It was no secret he had no love for the English and especially not for his father.

"You fool, of course it's important," growled Rowen. "If not, he wouldn't have summoned us on his deathbed." Fia's Uncle Rowen was the voice of reason between the three brothers.

"I'm scared," Willow whispered to the girls. Fia felt the same way. The corridor was crowded with knights, ladies, pages, guards, and even servants that now emerged, watching the procession headed toward the king's chamber. The way everyone stared at them made Fia very uncomfortable. As they passed by a boy who was a few years younger than her, he pointed at Fia's father and uncles, speaking to his mother in a loud voice.

"Mother, are they the king's bastards?" Someone in the crowd chuckled at the boy's question.

"Hush," the boy's mother scolded the child, pulling him closer as Fia and her cousins passed by them.

"What is a bastard?" asked Willow, almost tripping on her shoe since they moved so fast.

"It's a bad thing," Maira told her.

"Why did that boy call our fathers bastards?" Willow asked, much too loudly.

"Shh," Fia scolded, her eyes darting from one person to another. She didn't like it here. She wanted to go home.

"I'll bet he's finally going to legitimize us," Rook told his brothers as they continued to walk.

"I dinna want that," spat Reed. "I told Edward he is no' goin' to change my mind. I will never pay allegiance to him the way ye two do."

Fia was well aware that her father never totally reconciled with the king, refusing to pay him homage like his brothers. After all, the men were the illegitimate sons of King Edward – a man who once ordered them killed as babies.

Living in Scotland, Fia had never met her grandfather. Today would be the first, and probably the last time she would ever meet the English king. The man was dying, and it sounded as if he wasn't going to last long.

"In here." The king's messenger held open a door and motioned with a nod of his head. He wore a small cap that reminded Fia of a jester. His shoes were dirty and he had a small rip in his hose just under the knee.

Rook and Rowen entered the room, but Reed stopped at the threshold and glanced back over his shoulder.

"Stay close, lassies. The king has requested yer presence, but I dinna ken why. He is near death, but there is nothin' to fear."

"We're no' afraid, Da," Fia answered for all of them.

"Edward might no' be able to speak up, so listen carefully to everythin' he says."

"We will, Uncle Reed," Maira said with a nod.

After they entered the room, the messenger closed the door behind them. Fia squeezed the hands of her cousins, taking a good look around the king's chamber. The room was filled with people. Servants stood in the shadows, and important-looking men were in groups talking softly to each other. A man in a dark robe that looked to be a healer leaned over the bed, checking the king. A woman wearing a jeweled headpiece over her wimple studied Edward with a sour look on her face, standing close to the king's bedside. The queen was dead, so Fia guessed this woman was Alice. She had heard her father and uncles say Alice was a shrewd woman and also the king's mistress.

There was even a young boy that looked to be about her age, watching curiously from the other side of the room.

King Edward III lay on his bed in the middle of the vast

chamber. His thick, overstuffed pallet was positioned atop a small dais of three steps that led to the dying man's resting place. Tall, ornately carved, wooden spindles two lengths the height of a full-grown man rose up from each corner of the bed. Above the spindles were iron rods holding long, burgundy, velvet bedcurtains that were half-closed on one side. Fia observed the curtain rings that were made of iron and shaped into claws. Each one gripped the bedcurtain as tightly as the dying king seemed to cling to his life.

The aroma of evergreen and exotic spices from beeswax candles filled the air, intermingling with the stagnant scent of death. The candles burned brightly in the circular iron holder hanging from chains connected to the beams overhead. Colorful tapestries and banners with the king's crest lined the walls. The area behind the bed was filled with crossed swords, battleaxes, and weapons of all kinds.

At the far side of the room was a large window. And to her surprise, it wasn't an open hole covered by a shutter but, instead, it was embedded with glass. It wasn't just any glass, but expensive, beautiful, stained glass depicting a scene of a royal joust. The early morning sunrays shone through the window, projecting a multitude of orange, blue, and red hues into the room. The light splashed across the wooden floor in colorful blotches, bathing her soft slippers, making them look magical. Fia drank in every little thing that made the king's chamber so exquisite.

"Stay close, lassies," Reed instructed moving forward to join his brothers. A good dozen people surrounded Edward now, trying their best to make him comfortable in his last minutes of life.

"He's looking at us," Maira whispered, keeping her bright blue eyes fastened to the man on the bed as she spoke. She was a small girl, but afraid of nothing.

Indeed, the king was watching them through his dark, sunken

eyes. The man was old and gaunt and had a long white beard trailing halfway down his chest. With his head propped up on a pillow, it looked as if it took all his strength just to keep his eyelids from closing. Fia had seen people die before, and this man had the same look of death that she'd witnessed on those that had left this world before him. His open mouth formed a hollow O, seeming as if his spirit were getting ready to flee his body. A shiver ran up Fia's spine. Death loomed here, throwing shadows of the grave over King Edward's pale, pasty skin.

"Father," said Rowen, stepping up to the bed while Rook and Reed lingered behind him. The buzz of conversation in the room softened as everyone watched intently when the king's bastard son approached him. "We are here at your request."

"Aye," answered Rook, moving forward eagerly now. "You wanted to speak to us?"

"I did," said Edward, not able to lift his head. His face was as white as a ghost, and his thin body looked bony beneath the covers. Frightening was the only way to describe what Fia saw. His long fingers of one hand gripped the bedcovers while his other arm lay limp next to him. Two ornate gold and jeweled rings on his fingers winked at her in the light.

"I'm scared," said Willow, the youngest of the three girls. Maira and Fia were the same age, but Maira was by far the bravest. Nothing seemed to rattle her nerves. Maira always stood up for her cousins and had even physically fought off their brothers when they teased the girls too much. She sometimes acted like a boy. Willow, on the other hand, was very feminine and probably the prettiest of the three girls and she knew it. She had a little button nose on a heart-shaped face. Her skin was smooth, her hair wavy, and her cheeks rosy. Even at her young age, she often used her looks to her advantage. She smiled at the boys to get them to do her bidding.

Fia, being the most observant of the three, noticed not only things around her, but what was inside a person as well. She noticed now the way the king looked fondly at his bastard triplets from his deathbed.

"Dinna be scared," Fia whispered, feeling her knees knocking together as she spoke. Then her father pushed his way to the king's bedside to stand beside his brothers.

"Edward, if ye're finally goin' to legitimize us on yer deathbed, my answer is still the same," Reed spat. "I dinna want it."

"Good," said the king in a weak voice. "Because that is not why I called you boys here today."

"Wait. What did you say?" Rook pushed his way in front of Reed, leaning closer to the king to make sure he heard the man's faint voice correctly. One of the king's guards took it as an act of aggression and drew his sword and pointed it at Rook.

"Step away from the bed," the guard commanded.

"God's eyes, Rook, get back," scoffed Rowen, pulling his brother away from the king. "We're not here to cause trouble. Our father is dying."

Rook spun around and scowled at Rowen. "You heard him. He's on his deathbed and, still, he refuses to legitimize us. I can't believe it." He threw his hands in the air.

"I can't . . . do it," said the king, his words sounding slurred. His eyelids flickered open and closed. One side of his face twitched while the other drooped. Only one side of his mouth moved when he spoke. "There is too much history . . . in your defiant acts against me. No one will ever forget it." He struggled to breathe. The healer put one hand on the king's chest and the other on his shoulder.

"My king, you must conserve your strength. Do not talk," the healer told him.

"Nay." The king used his left hand to push the healer's hand away. Fia noticed that the entire right side of his body never moved. "I need . . . to tell them. I'm sorry, boys, but I'm not going to legitimize you . . . even if I am dying."

"Then why did you call us here?" growled Rook, his quick

temper flaring. "Did you want pity from us after you tried to have us killed, just because now you're the one about to die?"

"Rook, stop it," warned Rowen, taking a step closer to the bed, trying to intervene. "It's all right," he said with a nod to the guard. "We are not going to hurt our father."

The guard's eyes traveled from the men to the king. Only when the king nodded slightly did the man lower his sword and step away.

"Your king is dying, and you mustn't upset him," said the woman standing next to the bed. Her voice was haughty, and she didn't seem friendly at all. She was also much younger than Edward. "You must leave now."

"Nay, Alice," said Edward, raising his shaky hand and holding it out toward the triplets. "I called them here. They will stay."

"Then don't upset him again!" snapped Alice, lifting her nose in the air before leaving the bedside to go over to talk to the young boy. The boy's clothes were made of velvet and silk and were very regal. It made Fia wonder if he was one of the king's dozen legitimate children.

"Father, why did you call us here?" questioned Rowen.

While Fia's uncles called the king father, she never heard her own father call him anything but Edward.

"My granddaughters," said Edward, reaching out his bony fingers, pointing to Fia and her cousins. "Come here, girls."

Fia gripped the hands of her cousins, too frightened even to move. Her heart beat furiously in her chest, the drumming sounding louder and louder in her ears.

"Go on, lass," said her father, giving her a slight nod of his head.

"Maira and Willow, you too," added Rowen, stepping to the side.

Fia walked forward with her cousins, slowly approaching the side of the dying man.

"Healer, leave us," commanded Edward, sending the man to the other side of the room. "Come closer, girls. Let me see you."

When the girls didn't move, Rook reached out and put his hands on their shoulders, gently guiding them closer to the bed.

"Go on, girls. He isn't going to hurt you," Rook explained.

"Just the opposite," said Edward. "You three are the eldest daughters of my sons, are you not?"

Fia nodded without speaking a word. So did Maira. Willow stared at the ground.

"What are your names?" asked Edward.

Rook spoke up. "My daughter's name is –"

"Nay," said the king, coughing slightly. "I want to hear it from them. I want to talk to my granddaughters."

"Go ahead, lassies." Reed gave a slight nod.

"I am Maira, and my father is Rowen," said Maira bravely, taking the lead as usual.

"I am Fia," answered Fia softly.

"You must be Reed's daughter with that bright red hair." The king attempted to smile but since only one corner of his mouth lifted, it looked more like a sneer.

"Aye. I am his daughter."

"What about you?" the king asked Willow. Willow's gaze fastened to the ground and she didn't look up or speak at all.

"Answer him," Maira told her, nudging Willow with her elbow.

Slowly, Willow looked up with her big, brown eyes. "I am Willow," she squeaked out in a breathy whisper.

"Aye, Rook's daughter," said the king with a slight chuckle. "With eyes like yours, you will have men falling at your feet when you get older."

"She'd better not," said Rook in a deep, warning voice.

"I have never taken the time to know my grandchildren," continued the king. "Now, I regret not trying harder as Philippa once begged me to do. My sweet, Philippa. I miss her dearly."

Fia heard a sniff from behind her. Glancing over her shoulder, she saw Alice's disgruntled face at having overheard the king's last comment.

"Ye summoned us here just to get a look at yer granddaughters before ye die?" asked Reed.

"Nay," said Edward. "Sir Simon, please approach the bed." The king nodded to a knight standing nearby, holding a box. The man walked over to join them. "I have something for my granddaughters." Edward looked directly at the girls and tried his hardest to smile. It was a lopsided grin, and his lips quivered. "It is a gift Philippa wanted to give you girls just after the youngest of the three of you were born. However, I wouldn't let her."

"A gift for the lassies?" asked Reed, perking up at the thought. "I have another daughter, too. Her name is Morag. She is the same age as Rook's daughter, Willow."

The king looked up at Reed and shook his head. "I am sorry, Reed, but this gift is for each of your eldest daughters only. You see, Philippa was a strong woman, and was convinced that my bastard sons would have daughters someday that would be strong as well."

"Shall I open the box now, Your Majesty?" asked the knight.

"Yes, Sir Simon. Please do. Each of the girls is to choose one."

The knight set the long, wooden box on the ground and removed the lid so the girls could see the contents.

Fia stretched her neck curiously, peeking over the rim. Maira and Willow did the same. Inside were three of the late queen's ornate jeweled crowns.

"What are you doing?" snapped Alice, rushing over to look into the box. The young boy followed. "Those crowns should be mine. Edward, you can't give them to children. Especially not the children of bastards!"

"These are my granddaughters, Alice . . . I will do what I want." The king started coughing, barely able to catch his breath. The healer rushed over, bringing him a cup of wine.

"Lady Alice, you seem to be upsetting the king," stated the healer. "Perhaps you'd better leave for now."

"I will not! I belong here, but these bastards and their children don't."

"Everyone, out!" shouted the king in aggravation. "All except for my sons and granddaughters."

"Grandfather," said the small, ten-year-old boy standing next to Alice. "You don't mean me, too."

"Yes, Richard, you, too," said Edward, seeming very drained of any energy at all.

"But I am going to succeed you on the throne. If I'm to be the future king, I should be here as well."

"And we're your legitimate sons," said one of two men who hurried over to the bedside. "Surely, we can stay."

"John, Thomas, take Richard and wait on the other side of the room. I want to talk to the triplets and my granddaughters alone," Edward commanded.

"Yes, Father," said one of the men, taking the boy with them, not at all sounding happy about the situation.

"Rowen, bring the box here, atop the bed." The king nodded slightly. "Girls, gather around me. Reed and Rook, close the bedcurtains so we can have some privacy."

"Come on, lassies," said Reed, taking the girls and plunking them down one at a time atop the foot of the king's bed. Rowen placed the long, wooden box of crowns in front of them. Then Rook and Reed proceeded to pull the bedcurtains closed, leaving them all inside the secluded area with the king.

"That's better," said the king. "Now, go ahead, girls. You all can choose a crown. Fia, you go first."

"Me?" asked Fia, not used to being first. "Mayhap Maira should be first instead."

"Yes, let me choose," said Maira, sticking her nose into the box.

"All right then," answered the king. "I can see Maira is the leader."

The three crowns were all beautiful but too large for the heads of children. Maira chose the one with the most gemstones. Then Fia took the tallest of the crowns, being attracted to the bright green stones. She picked it up in two hands, feeling the weight.

"That means, this one is yours," said Rook, taking the last of the crowns for his daughter. "I will hold it for you, Willow."

"I don't understand," said Rowen. "Why did the queen want to give these crowns to our daughters?"

"Aye," added Reed. "Ye canna think they can actually wear them."

"That's right," stated Rook with a curl of his lip. "The girls are naught but the daughters of bastards."

"It was my late wife's wish, and so I grant the girls permission to wear the crowns," Edward told them. "Your daughters will, from this day on, be treated like the granddaughters of a king. They will be introduced to the highest-ranking barons and earls, attend the celebrations of the nobles, and be respected in every way. They will be fostered by the Earl of Northumberland, Lord Walter Beaufort in Rothbury."

"Rothbury? Why there?" asked Rowen, not sounding at all happy at hearing this announcement.

"My castle in Naward isn't far from Rothbury," said Rook. "Why not let the girls stay with me to be fostered instead?"

"I'm a Scot and so is my daughter," spat Reed. "I dinna like the idea of Fia being fostered by a Sassenach on English soil. Nay, my daughter isna stayin' in England."

The king continued, although he seemed to be fading fast. "Lord Beaufort has been informed of my wishes and has been compensated accordingly. He will carry out my orders since it was the wish of Philippa that he would someday foster the girls. The queen had plans for your daughters. I will see them carried out if it is the last thing I ever do." The king squeezed his eyes closed in pain and swallowed forcefully.

"I dinna want my daughter being raised away from her only sister, Morag," Reed told him.

"Indeed," said the king. "I knew you would say that and it is why I made sure to tell the earl you will be sending him two daughters to foster as soon as the younger one is of age."

"By the rood, I willna hear of this nonsense." Reed crossed his arms over his chest. "Next ye will be tellin' me my daughters will be betrothed to Sassenachs as well."

"I don't know about the younger one," answered the king. "But my late wife was adamant that after what happened with you, not to mention your sister, Summer, that the girls wouldn't be betrothed until they felt they were ready. And the three girls will decide if they want to marry the men chosen for them. Surely, you can't disagree with that, Reed. After all, you wouldn't want your daughter to marry someone she didn't want to be with, would you? Remember, your wife, Maggie, almost had to do that."

"I suppose no'," said Reed, hanging his head and uncrossing his arms. "I will abide by yer decision."

"Well, I don't like the idea at all," said Rook. "I am Willow's father, and I will be the one, not her, to decide who she marries."

"Brothers, it was the queen's dying wish. Now it is the king's dying command," Rowen reminded them. "Our daughters will be fostered by the earl just as the king has ordered. And allowing the girls to agree or disagree with a betrothal will ensure they marry for love instead of alliances only."

"Father, I don't want to live with a stranger," protested Maira, being ever so bold to speak freely. Fia and Willow were terrified of the idea, but neither of them said a thing.

"We have no choice," said Rowen, laying a calming hand on his daughter's shoulder. "You will be well cared for and so will your cousins."

"Why are you doing this, Father?" Rook's face turned red as he glared at the king. "The queen is gone. You are soon to be gone from this earth as well. So what does it matter?"

"You are right," said Edward, half-closing his eyes. "I don't know the answer to that, as Philippa did not explain. She liked to keep her secrets." He lifted his good hand, dangling a small velvet pouch from his fingertips. "Philippa wanted the girls to have these as well."

Rowen took the pouch and slipped his fingers inside, pulling out three heart-shaped, metal brooches.

"What is it?" asked Rook, looking over at Rowen in question.

"Brooches," said Rowen. "Three heart brooches that are exactly alike. What is this all about?"

"Philippa said the girls . . . were to always wear them. When the time is right . . . they will . . . understand." Edward's eyes closed and his head fell to the side.

"I dinna understand," said Reed. "It makes no sense."

Edward didn't answer. Fia watched closely, but could not see the king's chest moving up and down anymore. He was no longer breathing!

"Edward? Answer me," said Reed.

"He can't," mumbled Rook.

"Why no'?"

"He's dead," Rowen said, slipping the brooches back into the bag. "Rook, pack up the crowns. There is nothing here for us anymore. It is time for us to go."

"I want to carry my crown," said Fia, clutching it to her chest. It meant the world to her and was the only memory she would have of her late grandparents.

The men opened the curtains and called to the healer. Everyone came rushing over in a frenzy when they heard their king had passed on. The women started sobbing. Alice put on the biggest show throwing herself over the body of Edward, laying her head on his chest and wailing loudly. Her hands covered the king's. Fia's eyes opened wide when Alice sat up, dabbing at her eyes and then folding something into the square of cloth and putting it into her pocket. The king's fingers were bare, when a moment ago, he had been wearing two rings.

As the crowd pushed and shoved, trying to get closer to Edward, Fia stood frozen, unable to move.

"Come, lassies, it is time to leave," said Fia's father.

As the men ushered the girls away, Fia glanced back over her shoulder one last time at the dead king. She would never again see her grandfather. Maira and Willow started crying, not wanting to be taken from their families and their homes to be fostered by Lord Beaufort.

As upset as Fia was, she didn't cry. She was busy taking in her surroundings and the people in the chamber. As she took a step, she barreled into the young boy named Richard.

"I want that crown!" He reached for it, but she only held it tighter. "It should be mine since I am going to be the next king," he said with envy.

Fia turned and ran toward the door, following her father and the others. But she stopped once again when she noticed a woman in a hooded cloak watching her. Something about her was mysterious and intriguing. The woman came closer, looked down at her and smiled. Fia's eyes interlocked with two-toned eyes of green and yellow. Then her gaze fastened to the brooch holding closed the mysterious woman's cloak. It was a heart-shaped, metal brooch just like the ones the queen had left for Fia and her two cousins.

"Your brooch," she said, pointing to it. "It looks like mine."

The woman, whose face was half-hidden in shadow, raised her finger to her lips to silence Fia from saying more. Her hand covered the heart-shaped brooch.

"It is not time yet," mumbled the woman. "You and your cousins will find me again when you are ready."

"Fia, hurry up before you are left behind." Maira ran back, tugging at Fia's arm. "We have to go."

When Fia looked back at the woman, she was gone. Little did she know that it would be five years before she once again saw the mysterious woman with the heart-shaped brooch so she could ask her what she meant.

## CASTLE ROTHBURY, FIVE YEARS LATER (1382)

"Go back to the keep and stop followin' us, Morag!" Fia hurried across the courtyard with her younger sister running behind her. Her cousins, Maira and Willow, were already in the stable, preparing the horses so they could sneak off before Lord Beaufort and his men returned from patrolling the border.

"I dinna want to stay here alone," Morag fretted. For a thirteen-year-old girl, she still acted very childishly at times.

"Ye have been at the castle for three years now," Fia scolded. "Ye should feel at ease by now. Besides, ye arena alone. Ye have an entire castle filled with people all around ye."

"I dinna ken why ye willna let me come with ye and Maira and Willow. Ye are always runnin' off without me."

"Ye're too young." Fia turned and continued toward the stables with her travel bag slung over her shoulder that held her crown. If they were going to sneak out of the castle and go to the woods, they would have to hurry. Nightfall would be here soon.

"I am no' too young," protested Morag, dogging her sister's heels. "I am the same age as Willow, yet ye take her with ye."

"Willow has been chosen by the late queen to wear the royal crown, just like Maira and me. Ye havena. We have a lot to discuss tryin' to figure things out, so stay here."

"Ye are mean, Fia. Ye all are. I am goin' to tell Faither the way ye treat me. He will come all the way from Scotland to punish ye."

"We are wards of Lord Beaufort now, Morag. Faither has nothin' to say about what we do here, so leave him outta this."

"Fia, hurry!" Maira rode out of the stable, holding on to the reins of Fia's horse. Willow was on a horse right behind her. They stayed in the shadows and would sneak out through the old, unused postern gate so the guards wouldn't see them. Lord Beaufort's guards usually played dice and drank a lot of ale while he was away and would not notice.

"Then I'll tell Lord Beaufort ye sneak outta the castle when he is away. It's goin' to be dark soon, and ye dinna have an escort," Morag reminded them.

Fia didn't want Morag to tattle because sneaking into the woods with her cousins was much too exciting and she didn't want it to end. She, Maira, and Willow had been sneaking away to play in the woods, wearing their crowns and pretending they were special ever since they came to live at Rothbury. It was their secret, and she didn't want her little sister to ruin it for them.

"Ye do that and I'll tell Lord Beaufort that ye were the one who stole the cook's pie before it even had a chance to cool."

"I was hungry. I love apples," whined Morag. "Please, Fia, let me come with ye."

Fia looked over to her cousins, but they were both frowning and shaking their heads. She didn't like denying her sister, but it was for the girl's own good. Morag was nothing but trouble. If she started coming along on their secret outings, she was sure to ruin things somehow or another. Fia loved Morag, but sometimes she wished her sister had stayed back in Scotland with their brothers.

"Mayhap next time, Morag. Now, go back to the keep and wait for me there."

Before Morag had a chance to protest, Fia took off on the horse. She and her cousins headed as silently as possible to the postern gate. It was dangerous leaving the castle unescorted, but they knew the woods better than anyone after all this time. They were in no real danger as long as they didn't wander far from Castle Rothbury.

The three girls rode through the forest, stopping only for a moment to put on their crowns as soon as they were out of sight of the castle. They liked to pretend they were queens. It was silly, but it was their way of entertaining themselves. It made them feel special. Lord Beaufort let them wear the crowns when he entertained other nobles, but they weren't allowed to wear them every day.

"Let's go to the river and walk in the water in our bare feet," suggested Willow.

"Willow, you like taking off your clothes way too much," Maira said in disgust.

"I do not," protested Willow.

"Aye, ye do," agreed Fia. "That's why ye rarely wear hose or even a shift under yer gown. If yer faither kent about it, he would have yer head."

"I don't like wearing hose," said Willow, removing the ribbon that tied back her hair. Her long, dark walnut tresses spilled out around her shoulders and lifted in the breeze. "I like the feel of freedom."

"Hah!" Maira blurted out. "We don't know the meaning of freedom. We are women, or did you forget? Women are naught but possessions of men. Men treat their dogs better than their wives."

"I don't ever want a husband," said Willow, fussing with her long hair.

"Ye dinna want to get married and have bairns someday?" asked Fia in surprise. "Every lassie wants that."

"Nay, not me. I would rather flit like a butterfly from flower to flower and never have to choose just one." Willow raised her arms in the air and threw back her head, smiling and closing her eyes. She took a deep breath and released it through her mouth.

"Willow, dinna say that," warned Fia. "Someone might hear ye and think ye mean to someday be a hoor."

"I am not a whore!" spat Willow.

"It did kind of sound that way," agreed Maira. "If you think you can tease men and then leave them without any repercussions, you are mistaken. You are going to get yourself into trouble someday if you act that way."

"Well, at least I like men even if I never want to marry," said Willow. "Maira, you act like a man. And Fia is so shy she wouldn't know what to do if a man spoke to her."

"Enough squabbling," said Maira. "I want to try out the new dagger my father sent me before it gets dark." Maira pulled out the dagger and held it up to admire it. It was a long and sharp weapon with a two-toned metal hilt. Only men owned daggers like this. Women usually had small daggers used for everyday things like cutting string or possibly meat at the dais table. They weren't meant to be used for protection. "Let's hunt for rabbits or perhaps some waterfowl or a polecat."

"Nay!" Willow wrinkled her nose, making a face at the disturbing thought.

"Maira, ye like usin' yer blade too much," said Fia. "Willow and I dinna want to kill animals."

"Don't make it sound like I'm an assassin. We eat everything I kill," protested Maira. "I do it for a purpose. Besides, I can't help it if I like the feel of a blade in my hand. Hunting is the only thing I have since I am a woman and will never be able to fight with a sword as our fathers do."

"It's not becoming of a lady," said Willow, smoothing the wrinkles from her gown with the palms of her hands. "What should we do today, cousins? Sit here idly and do nothing as usual?"

"I dinna consider our trips as doin' nothin'. I observe nature," Fia told them. "I'll bet ye dinna ken there is a nest in that black oak tree with three baby goldcrests that were born last week." She pointed up at the branches above their heads.

"That tree?" asked Willow, shading her eyes and pointing at a different tree altogether. It was appalling that Willow couldn't identify a simple tree. But yet, she could tell you the color of every nobleman's eyes and hair that had ever visited Castle Rothbury.

"Nay, that is a poplar tree," Fia told her with a roll of her eyes. "And I'm sure ye dinna even ken what a goldcrest looks like."

"I might not, but neither do I care." Willow ran her hands through her hair, pulling it to the side and quickly braiding it as she spoke.

"See that old hollow log?" asked Fia. "A big, brown rat lives in there."

"A rat?" repeated Willow with a squeal. She dropped the braid, and her hands covered her mouth. "Let's get away from here, anon!" She took off on her horse, directing it into a run. Maira and Fia followed. It wasn't long before Fia heard hoofbeats behind them.

"Stop," she called, out, bringing her cousins to a halt. "I heard hoofbeats. It might be bandits. We need to hide. Someone is following us."

"Hide? Where?" asked Maira, looking back and forth.

They had never encountered danger in Lord Beaufort's woods before, but they had been careless and traveled far today. It seemed they wandered off of the earl's land and crossed the line into the royal forest. Fia no longer recognized anything around them. Spotting some dense brush in the distance up against a hill, she pointed at it.

"Over there. That looks like a guid place to hide." Fia led the way. Her cousins followed. When they got closer, she realized it was more than just brush. "Look! There seems to be an old, hidden door, covered with tangled vines." Curious, she slipped off the horse, moving closer to inspect her new find. With one hand, she reached out and pushed open the door. The rusty hinges groaned as a secret place was revealed. Fia gasped in surprise when she saw what lie inside.

"What is it?" Maira rode closer, bending low atop the horse.

"What do you see?" asked Willow, glancing nervously over her shoulder and then back at her cousins.

"It looks like a secret garden," Fia explained. Excitement and intrigue coursed through her. There were rows of plants and flowers that she had never seen before. She had to get a closer look even though a tinge of fear ran through her, telling her to turn around and not to enter.

"Get inside, quickly," Maira urged her. "I hear hoofbeats approaching now as well. They are getting louder."

Fia quickly entered the garden with Maira and Willow right behind her. After dismounting, the girls stood in awe with their mouths wide open, not able to believe their find. What had looked like nothing but some shrubs against a hill to hide behind, turned out to be a beautiful hidden world of flowers, benches, trellises, and archways covered with climbing, flowering vines.

Fia took a deep breath and held it. Her senses tingled from the sweet smell of roses in colors of white, pink and red that were so large they were the size of her hand. Birds chirped happily overhead, flying from tree to tree and landing in arched trellises. Square, raised beds of plants filled the secret space. Taking a closer look, Fia realized they were herbs and vegetables. The patches of dirt were separated by fences made from branches woven together.

A carpet of bluebells spread out behind the raised beds and stopped at the foot of an enchanting cottage constructed of wattle and daub. Next to the cabin was a small shed with an open door that housed gardening tools. Attached to the house was a stable big enough for one horse. In it stood an old, black mare. Fia thought the surroundings looked like something out of a fairy tale.

"I feel like I'm in a dream world," said Willow, sniffing a rose and gently caressing the silky petals with her fingertips.

"I have never seen anything like this," replied Maira. She tied the reins of her horse to a tree and started down the winding stone pathway leading through the mystical garden.

"There is a cottage and a horse. Someone lives here," Fia told them in a voice no louder than a whisper. "How could this be here?"

"We never came this far into the woods before." Maira made her way over to a wooden swing big enough for two people and took a seat. The swing was suspended between two arches that had grapevines covering a trellis over her head. She pushed off slightly with her feet and giggled. Willow rushed over and plopped down on the seat right next to her.

"We shouldna be here," warned Fia. "We need to go."

"Quit fretting, Fia," scoffed her cousin, Maira. "I don't believe we are in any danger."

"Hello, girls," called out a voice from over by the shed.

"Fia's right. We had better go," blurted Willow, jumping off the swing and high-tailing it for her horse.

"Nay, I want to see who it is." Maira got to her feet and started in the opposite direction.

"Maira!" Fia rushed after her cousin and tried to stop her. "We dinna belong here."

"On the contrary, girls, I have been waiting for you to arrive for years now." An old woman stepped out of the shadows, smiling at the girls as she made her way over to them. She was tall and had graying hair pulled back behind her head. She wore a long, brown gown with a green kirtle. In her hands, she held a pair of work gloves covered in dirt.

Fia was getting ready to run when she noticed the heart-shaped brooch on the woman's bodice. "It's you," she said with a gasp, now knowing it was the woman she'd seen in the dying king's chamber. Her hand shot to the heart-shaped brooch pinned on her own chest.

"Do you know her?" asked Willow curiously, walking back to join her cousins.

"I saw her five years ago in the king's chamber on the day he died."

"Who are you?" Maira bravely stepped in front of her cousins protectively.

"Come and sit down, girls." The woman smiled and pointed to a small knoll of grass near the shed where the sun shone down warmly. Then she looked over the girls' shoulders as if something took her interest. "You might as well come join us too, Morag," she called out.

"Morag?" Fia spun around to see her younger sister sitting atop a horse, peering into the secret garden through the open gate. Fia groaned and shook her head. "Morag, I told ye to stay back at the keep."

"What is this place?" asked Morag, sliding off her horse and entering the garden.

"It's the queen's secret garden," the woman told them. "I am Imanie, the queen's keeper of secrets as well as her master gardener."

"Queen? What queen?" asked Maira in confusion.

"Why, Queen Philippa, of course," Imanie answered with a kind smile.

"But the queen is dead," stated Willow. "She has been dead since I was a toddler."

Fia noticed the look of wisdom in Imanie's two-toned green and yellow eyes as the woman answered. "She might be gone from this world, but her secrets live on." She settled herself in the grass and nodded for them to sit as well.

"Why should we believe you?" asked Maira, plunking down on the ground without even looking where she was sitting.

"Because it's the truth." Fia took off her crown and placed it on the ground in front of her as she sat crossed-legged next to Maira. "I believe this has somethin' to do with the crowns and the brooches and what the queen had planned for us, doesna it?"

"You are right," said Imanie.

"Did she have somethin' planned for me, too?" Morag squeezed in between Fia and Willow.

"Morag, ye are no' the eldest daughter," Fia reminded her. "King Edward told us on his deathbed that the queen left the crowns and brooches only for our faithers' eldest girls."

"That's right," said Imanie. "Philippa wanted the king's bastard triplets' eldest daughters to join her secret order, but you can stay and watch, Morag."

"A secret order?" asked Willow. "How so?"

Imanie's eyes twinkled with excitement. "Did you girls know that when your fathers were born, the king ordered them killed because they were triplets?"

"We do," said Fia. "Everyone kens that."

"Mayhap so." Imanie nodded in agreement. "But not everyone knows it was Philippa who saved their lives that day. She did it against the king's orders and in secret. He didn't know about it until many years later."

"That's true," Maira answered. "My father told me that story."

"Queen Philippa was a remarkable, strong woman," Imanie continued. "Many times it was her influence on the king that saved lives, such as those of the Burghers of Calais. She also filled in as regent while the king was away. When Philippa had to lead an army to war, she would. She and Edward traveled together often. Philippa gave birth to over a dozen children, the first when she was not even six and ten years of age."

"That's basically our age," said Maira, nodding to Fia.

"Queen Philippa was a remarkable woman, kind and fair and revered by all," Imanie explained. "Yes, she was strong in many ways, but not many knew exactly just how strong."

"Why are ye tellin' us this and what does this have to do with us?" asked Fia.

"Fia, you are very curious and in need of answers." Imanie chuckled. "That is the makings of a determined woman. But to answer your questions, I need to tell you that Philippa had a chosen group of women who she often met with in secret, right here in this garden."

"The queen used to come here?" asked Morag in amazement.

"She did. But no one knew, except for the women in the secret order."

"Even Lord Beaufort didn't know?" asked Maira.

Imanie shook her head. "This land was never his, but owned by the queen. He promised the queen many years ago that he would never come this far into the woods and would keep others from the land as well."

"We found it by accident," Fia told her.

"Nothing is by accident." Imanie gave them an all-knowing look. "You girls were meant to find this secret garden. I knew when the time was right, you would come to me, and you have."

"Why did you want us to come to the garden?" asked Willow.

"Let me tell you a story." Imanie crossed her legs and leaned forward. "I was once naught but a beggar with nowhere to go and nothing to eat. Queen Philippa pitied me and brought me to work in the royal kitchens. She befriended me, and we became close. One day when I killed a soldier who tried to rape me, I was sentenced by the king to be hanged to death."

"Oh, my. That's terrible," Morag shivered and made a face.

"Philippa felt more than pity for me this time. She told me the guard deserved it and that I was strong in defending myself. The queen saved me but banished me from her kingdom. However, she didn't let me go. Instead, she had me create this secret garden, living here in the woods by myself. Through the years she brought women here that she thought had potential to be inde-pendent. In secret, I trained them to be strong in many ways. And now, since it was her wish, I am going to train you three to be strong in secret as well."

"You live in this garden?" asked Morag. Her eyes widened.

"Yes. This is my home. I did it for the queen but, through the years, I realized it was my true calling to help other women."

"But you're old," said Maira boldly pointing out the fact. "What can you possibly teach us?"

"Don't let that fool you. I used to be a great warrior at one time. I had to be, to survive living on my own from the age of ten. I befriended an old bladesmith, and he took a liking to me. He taught me about weapons and how to fight like a man."

"He did?" The subject piqued Maira's interest. "Can you teach me to use a sword?"

"If that is where your strength lies, then I can teach you."

"What about me?" asked Willow. "I don't like to fight. What is my strength?"

"She only likes to dress up and bat her eyes at men," Morag told her, making the rest of the girls laugh.

"Don't laugh," scolded Imanie. "Even that can be a strength as well."

"It can?" asked Willow. "How?"

"It is by the persuasiveness of many strong women in the past that the queen was able to find out secrets that helped the king and his army to be successful."

"Persuasive? With enemies?" This interested Fia.

"Yes, with enemies as well as with friends. Men always seem to hold secrets within them. It is our job as Followers of the Secret Heart to draw those secrets from them to use to our advantage."

"Followers of the Secret Heart?" asked Fia. "Is that what the queen called her secret group of strong women?"

"Yes, it is what she called it. I am continuing the tradition," Imanie told them proudly. "Will you girls do your late queen the honor of following the life she had planned for you?"

"I'm not sure," said Willow, being the leery one of the bunch.

"She did save our fathers," Maira pointed out, always searching for adventure.

"We wouldna be here today if it wasna for the queen," Fia agreed.

"I'll do it," said Maira in a snap decision. She sprang to her feet, resting her hand on the hilt of her new dagger.

"Me, too," added Morag, copying Maira by jumping up.

"Nay." Imanie shook her head. "I cannot train you, Morag, I'm sorry."

"Why no'?" Morag's bottom lip stuck out in a pout. Fia wasn't surprised. She always did this when she didn't get her way.

"I am only instructed to train those chosen by the late queen herself," Imanie explained. "She chose the eldest of your fathers' daughters only. And now, since the queen is gone, there will be no other members. After Fia, Maira, and Willow, I will train no more. The Followers of the Secret Heart will cease to exist."

"Who are the other women in this secret group?" asked Fia, always wanting to know more.

"I cannot divulge that information. We will keep your involvement a secret, too."

"Do ye hear that, Morag?" asked Fia. "Ye have to keep this a secret."

"I dinna like secrets." Morag's brows dipped in disappointment. "Fia, ye never want me around."

"That's no' true, Sister." Fia sighed, realizing she had excluded Morag through the years and it wasn't fair. She loved her sister and would do anything for her. She had to ask Imanie. "Are ye sure my sister canna join?"

"I am sorry, Fia, but I can't. The last time I trained someone of my choosing, someone ended up dying, so I feel it is a curse."

"Oh, that's terrible," said Willow. "We don't want anyone to be cursed or to die."

"I am tired of bein' excluded. I dinna want or need any of ye," cried Morag. "I can make a secret group of my own." She got up and ran to her horse.

"Morag, wait," Fia called out, but her sister mounted her horse and rode off. "It isna safe. I need to follow her through the woods to make certain she returns to the castle safely."

"You can't protect her. I'll come with you to ward off any enemy," offered Maira.

"Don't leave me here. I'm coming, too." Willow headed for her horse.

Imanie got up and followed them over to their mounts. "It is destiny that led you here today, girls. And it is your destiny to do what your late queen wanted."

"But how can I be strong?" asked Fia. "I dinna ken how to handle a blade. And I dinna like to use my looks the way Willow does."

"Mayhap not, but you have something very special that neither of your cousins possesses. You can observe, and see things that others miss. You might be quiet, but sometimes the silent ones are the most powerful in the end."

"How can I use that to my advantage or to help someone?"

"Well, let's see." The old woman put her hand to her chin in thought. "I think you would make a very good informant."

"A spy?" asked Fia, feeling her heart pick up a beat. Something inside her adored the idea.

"In a way, yes, I guess so," answered Imanie. "With your skills of observation and being silent, you will be able to find out secrets of the enemy and bring that knowledge back to help your people."

"But my people arena the English, they are the Scots."

"I don't know how or when things will happen," Imanie told her. "Only you three will know when to use your skills and how to use them at the right times. But like Philippa, even if you use your talents to help others, you will not be able to take credit for the action. You will need to find a way to make men believe the ideas or information came from them alone. Men will not accept strong women. I will teach you skills, but the way to use discretion is up to you. I want you to come back to the secret garden every week. If we get started now, in a few years all three of you will be ready to serve the crown in secret."

"King Richard is only our age," Maira pointed out. "He is not more than a boy and doesn't even know how to be a king yet. Why should we want to serve him?"

"Aye, he is not Edward," Imanie agreed. "However, he is head-strong. I am not sure he will even listen to his uncles serving as his council. He knows nothing about the Followers of the Secret Heart. And just like his grandfather before him, he will never know. What we do, we do for our country."

"Countries," said Fia, not wanting to stay in England forever. She missed her homeland and someday hoped to marry a Scot and settle down near her parents to raise a family of her own. "What about Morag?" she asked. "She will probably give us trouble."

"Morag has her lessons to learn, but they do not involve us. The road ahead of her is rocky, but she will learn to be just as strong as the three of you in time."

"You sound verra wise, in more than a learned way," Fia told her.

"My, you are the observant one." The old woman winked and nodded her head. "I have insight, my dear. But even without insight, I can see that Philippa made a wise choice. The three of you will in some ways be even stronger than your fathers."

"Stronger than our fathers? That is impossible," Maira objected. "Our fathers are powerful. They were once the Demon Thief, and raided the king," she bragged.

"Aye, they were strong in physical ways, but you three are women. Your strengths come mainly from in here." Imanie put her hand over her heart. Fia felt as if she knew exactly what Imanie meant. This must be what the heart brooch symbolized.

"I feel it in my heart that the three of us have missions," Fia announced. "Aye, I will honor Philippa, too. I can only hope to one day be as strong as she was when she went in secret behind the king's back to save our faithers' lives." Fia reached out and took Imanie's hand in hers.

"Me, too," said Maira, adding her hand to the pact.

"And me." Willow clasped her hand atop the others. That sealed the promise they made that day to follow in the footsteps of the noble queen, who had not been afraid to do what she felt was right.

\* \* \*

THE THREE GIRLS rode back toward the castle, seeing Morag just up ahead. Fia was at the rear and slowed down when she heard the snap of a twig from behind her. Looking over her shoulder, she noticed someone move from behind a tree. If she wasn't mistaken, it was a flash of plaid.

"Scots," she said aloud, stopping her horse and turning around to look. She missed Scotland dearly, longing to talk to people from her homeland. Even though she was half-English, Fia's mother was a full-fledged Scot.

The others didn't notice she had stopped and kept riding through the forest following Morag. Then someone jumped out from behind a tree, scaring her mount. Her horse reared up and threw her to the ground. A whoosh of air released from Fia's lungs as her back hit the ground hard.

"I've got the horse," growled a burly-looking Scot. "Kill the wench."

"Nay, dinna hurt me," she begged. "I am a Scot like ye. Canna ye tell?"

Another man joined the first, and then two more. Each of them was just as frightening as the first. They looked nothing like the Scots of the Lowlands, but somewhat more rugged and fierce and unkempt. Aye, they had to be Highlanders!

One man raised his dagger, meaning to plunge it into her heart. She froze in fear, not able to react. With a whizzing noise above her head, a dagger split the air and embedded itself into the man's shoulder.

"Och, God's eyes, that hurts!" cried the man, ripping the dagger from his shoulder and throwing it to the ground. Fia's eyes opened wide when she saw the handle of the bloody blade right next to her on the ground. It was Maira's dagger; there was no mistaking it.

"There are more of them," announced the first Scot, still holding the reins of her horse. "Kill them all."

"Fia!" cried Maira from atop her horse, riding to Fia's rescue. Willow and Morag were mounted on their horses, bravely following right behind her. This wasn't good. They would all be killed. Fia had to do something fast or they would all die at the hands of these murderous Highlanders.

Noticing the rest of the men being distracted in one way or another, she took the chance of reaching out for Maira's dagger. Once her fingers closed over the hilt, Fia rolled under the horse, coming up on the other side. She was just about to mount the steed when the first Scot grabbed her wrist. His iron fingers clenched her so hard that it felt like he was going to break her wrist. "Drop the blade," he ordered.

"Go! Ride! Get help," she cried out to her sister and cousins, hoping to at least save their lives, even if hers would be sacrificed to do it. Maira hesitated to go, but Willow and Morag rode off quickly. Finally, Maira turned and followed.

When Fia was sure the Scot would kill her, another hand shot out and pushed the man away. She looked up to find herself staring into the mesmerizing silver eyes of a handsome Scot with long, black hair tied back in a queue. The hilt of his sword peeked out over his shoulder from the scabbard attached to his back. He was younger than the rest of the men but older than her. He looked to be just over twenty summers.

"Dinna touch the lass," the man warned in a deep voice.

"Alastair, ye fool. She has to go," spat the burly Scot. "She's seen our faces and our plaids and can identify us."

Fia studied the brown and red colors of their plaids, not sure to which clan they belonged. However, by the way they spoke and the ruggedness of their composures, she was sure they were from the Highlands. Then her eyes focused on the badge pinned to her rescuer's plaid at his shoulder. It was that of a wildcat with its paw raised in the air. The clan's motto was written on it, but she had no time to read it. The man they'd called Alastair reached out and lifted her chin to bring her focus back to his face.

"Ye're a bonnie lass. Who are ye and why are ye here?"

"I'll no' tell ye anythin'," she snarled.

"Ye talk like a Scot but are dressed like a bluidy Sassenach so ye must be a traitor."

"I'm no' a traitor," she protested.

"Then tell me yer name, lass."

She was going to deny him but figured if she kept them talking, it would give the girls more time to escape and possibly find help.

"My name is Fia," she told him, staring directly into his eyes.

"Fia?" asked Alastair. "What clan are ye from, lass?"

"It doesna matter. My faither and uncles will hunt ye down like a dog if ye so much as harm a hair on my head."

Alastair chuckled. "Now, we wouldn't want to harm a single lock of yer bonnie reid hair, would we?" He reached out and caressed it slightly. She watched as his eyes suddenly became softer and he no longer seemed so frightening. Then his hand trailed lower, stopping atop the heart brooch pinned to her chest. He pulled away from her with a jerk. Clearing his throat, he took a step backward to make distance between them.

"Look what I found," said one of his men with a low whistle. The man pulled her crown out of the travel bag tied to her horse. "This will bring in a lot of coin."

"That's my crown given to me by Queen Philippa. Put it back," Fia cried.

"No queen, especially a dead one is goin' to give a Scot somethin' like this," said the man. "I think we'll hold on to this little trinket. It should prove to be verra valuable."

"Let me see that." Alastair reached out and took the crown from the man. He held it up in the sunlight, turning it slightly. His eyes fastened to the jewels that winked in the sun. Then a look that Fia didn't understand crossed his face. It was an expression somewhere between surprise and sadness.

"We've found a treasure," spat the first Scot, chuckling lowly. "It is our lucky day."

"Nay." Alastair shook his head and shoved the crown back into the other man's hand. "Put it back," he commanded with force to his words. "And give her back her horse."

"My laird, what do ye mean?"

"Ye heard me. Do it!"

"Ye are making a bad decision," complained more than one of the men.

Fia didn't need to hear the men call Alastair laird to know he was in charge. She'd seen the badge that depicted him as chieftain of the clan. It was odd that he was so young and already a chieftain.

"Let me worry about that," he said. In two strides, he was next to the man and pulling the crown out of his hand. He quickly shoved it back into the travel bag. "Now step aside, men, and let the girl go."

"Nay!" shouted Fia's attacker, reaching out for her once again. Alastair reached behind his back and drew his sword. In a flash, the tip of his sword rested against the man's throat.

"Dinna make me slit yer throat, Brohain. Because if I have to, I swear I will," growled Alastair through gritted teeth.

Brohain glared at his laird, then turned around and spat on the ground.

"Time to go, lass," Alastair told her. "Dinna say a word about this to anyone if ye ken what is guid for ye." Alastair slid his sword into the scabbard on his back. Before Fia knew what was happening, his hands were around her waist, helping her mount her horse.

An arrow came whizzing through the air next and lodged itself into a tree. Brohain was going for his sword but jumped in surprise when it landed just next to his head.

"Let the girl be." It was Imanie from atop her horse with a bow in her hand and a quiver of arrows on her back.

"First a bunch of wenches and now an old hag?" spat Brohain. "What the hell is this? No wench is any threat to me."

At that, another arrow released from Imanie's bow. This time it landed very close to Brohain's foot.

"Think again," said Imanie. "The next arrow is aimed right for your groin." The old woman nocked another arrow and pulled back the bowstring.

"Nay. Put the bow down. We are leavin'," Alastair called out.

"Leavin'?" spat Brohain. "Ye canna mean to tell me we are bein' scared off by a young wench and a crone?"

"We have no quarrel with them. This time," added Alastair, slapping his hand against the rump of Fia's steed and sending her away.

Fia rode hard through the woods, with Imanie at her side. They didn't stop until they met up with the rest of the girls who were frightened but waiting for them up ahead.

"Imanie, thank ye," said Fia. "Ye, too, Maira. Ye both saved my life." Fia handed Maira's dagger back to her.

"Are ye sure about that?" asked Imanie. "After all, it seems to me that the Scot was the one who saved ye from the rest of his clan."

"Who were they?" asked Maira, stretching her neck, looking back into the woods, but the Scots had vanished.

"They are Highlanders," said Imanie. "They sometimes come across the border. I think they are spies. They have been in the king's forest before."

"Why didn't they kill us?" asked Willow with a tremble in her voice.

"It was their young laird, Alastair who saved me," Fia explained. "Imanie is right. If it wasna for him, the rest of his clan would have done away with me in the blink of an eye as well as stole my horse and crown."

"They let ye keep the crown?" asked Morag in surprise.

"That's odd," said Maira.

"Aye," said Imanie, looking back over her shoulder. "And my intuition tells me this is not the last you've seen of them either."

Fia became excited to hear Imanie's prediction. Perhaps it was wrong of her but, after looking into Alastair's eyes, she felt as if she wanted to see him again. She noticed something in his gaze when he'd touched her hair. And the way he caressed her locks had been gentle and caring . . . almost like a lover. The man had stood up to his clan and, against all odds, he saved her life.

"Imanie, we need to train with ye more than ever now so we can be strong," Fia told her. "And the next time they return, we will be ready."

# CHAPTER 1

ENGLAND, CASTLE ROTHBURY, 1385

If birthday celebrations were going to continue to be as harrowing as this one, Fia Douglas swore she was going to hide away where no one could find her until her birthday was over. A long line of knights and lords waited to greet her, but not one of them interested her in the least. Some were old, and others were ugly or fat. Even the handsome ones didn't catch her fancy. Perhaps it was because they were all English, and she felt more attracted to Scots.

Fia didn't like the way Lord Walter Beaufort paraded men in front of her whenever he had the chance. She and two of her cousins were granted permission from the late King Edward III to be able to approve or disapprove of a man before their betrothal. Lord Beaufort seemed adamant that she choose one of these men to marry. By right, Fia's father, Reed, should be the one to suggest a man for her to wed – not Beaufort. But since her father lived in Scotland with her family and she resided in

England by the late queen's wishes, the earl decided to take that task upon himself.

When would this torture end? Being a ward of one of the most prominent men in all of England didn't seem to have many advantages. For over an hour now, since the meal had finished, she had to stand here and pretend to be interested, when all she wanted to do was run.

"Fia, this is Lord George Peydon of Devon." Lord Beaufort introduced her to the uptight man, making Fia want to cry out when she saw him. He might be rich and also a noble, but the man had a face like a donkey and the ears to match. He'd been eyeing her the entire evening, following her everywhere she went and acting like nothing more than an ass.

"How nice to meet ye, Lord Peydon." She curtsied slightly and smiled politely. Instead of holding out her hand for a kiss as was proper, she busied herself straightening the elaborate crown upon her head. It was her grandmother's crown. That is, the late Queen Philippa, and she didn't want these men to forget it.

Lord Peydon's body odor was so strong that it could probably be smelled by the servants all the way over in the scullery.

Her eyes shot back and forth as she frantically searched for her cousins, Maira and Willow, hoping they would save her. They said they had a special present for her. In all her eighteen years, she had never needed more of a reason to leave than she did right now.

"My dear, Lord Peydon is waiting to kiss your hand," said Walter's wife, Ernestine, from his side. Walter was a tall man with gray hair, but his wife was very short and probably as wide as she was tall. Still, they were both kind people. Fia didn't want to disappoint them. She was grateful for all they had done for her during her stay at Castle Rothbury.

Her eyes shot back over to Lord Peydon. His smile from ear to ear about turned her stomach. Spinach stuck out from between his crooked teeth and foam from his ale clung to his mustache. At times like this, she wished she wasn't so observant. Begrudgingly, she extended her arm and held her breath as the man slobbered his lips against the back of her hand.

From the corner of her eye, she spotted her sister, Morag, crossing the great hall. Pulling her hand away from the cur, she held it high in the air, pretending to wave back. "Morag, yes, I will be right there," she called out.

Morag looked up in surprise and flashed her a bewildered expression accompanied by the shrugging of her shoulders. Hopefully, Lord and Lady Beaufort hadn't noticed.

"I do beg yer forgiveness, my lords and ladies, but I must depart," Fia excused herself. "My sister and cousins have a special present planned for my birthday. I regret that I have already caused them to wait so long."

"But Lady Fia, there are still so many more lords and knights waiting to meet you," complained Lord Beaufort as she slipped away.

"Walter, let her go," mumbled the man's wife. Fia nodded her thanks and lifted her skirts, hurrying across the great hall to join her sister.

"Morag, get me outta here," whispered Fia.

"What for?" asked Morag. "Ye have an entire line of noblemen waitin' to meet ye."

"I dinna want any of them. I just want to get away from all this."

"Well, Maira and Willow are waitin' for ye in the stable. We have a present for ye, Fia."

"I canna wait. Let's go." She grabbed hold of her sister's hand, and they made their way through the stuffy crowd, not stopping until they were across the courtyard and had entered the stable.

"There you are," said Maira, looking over as her sword clashed with that of Branton's. Branton was a fourteen-year-old boy who was still a page, hoping to become a squire soon now that he was of age.

"Put down the sword," said Fia. "I'm here for my present."

"Not shy at all about asking for it, are you?" Willow sauntered over gracefully, having been standing far away from the sword practice. As usual, she wore one of her best gowns made of satin and silk for the party. She always dressed this way even when doing naught but sewing in the ladies solar. But this gown, Fia recognized as one of Willow's favorites. It had brass buttons all the way down the bodice. One of those buttons seemed to be missing today, showing off the girl's cleavage more than usual. Fia didn't doubt Willow had torn it off herself, trying to catch the eye of any lord there. Willow liked to be the center of attention, especially in a group of men.

"That's good for today, Branton, thank you." Maira lowered her sword, looking flushed in the cheeks. While Willow was all lady and didn't like to get her hands dirty, Maira was just the opposite of her cousin. Maira loved weapons and wanted to know how to use as many as she possibly could. It wasn't a lady-like trait at all, and neither did she care. A little dirt or a few scrapes never seemed to bother Maira.

"You are getting very skilled with the sword, Lady Maira." Branton lowered his sword and smiled.

"So are you," said Maira. "I'm sure any day now Lord Beaufort will make you a squire."

"I hope so." Branton lowered his head. "I'm not sure the earl will ever see me as anything but a page. That is why I've been practicing my skills so hard. Soon, he will choose pages to be trained as squires, and I want more than anything to be one."

"Keep trainin' with Maira and prove him wrong," Morag told him. "I heard Lord Beaufort talkin' about ye. He thinks ye are nothin' but a skinny, worthless whelp, so ye will need to change his mind."

"Morag! Haud yer wheesht," Fia exclaimed, throwing her sister a scolding look. The girl never knew when to keep her mouth closed.

"He said that?" A look of horror mixed with disappointment washed over Branton's face. He shook his head and let out a long, deep sigh.

"Morag, ye need to learn to close yer mouth and mind yer own business," Fia told her in a low voice. If anyone could cause trouble, even without doing it deliberately, it was Morag.

"Maira is very good with the blade," said Willow, picking a piece of straw off her gown and flicking it to the ground. "But so are you, Branton. You are very skilled with that sword, so I wouldn't worry about whatever Morag tells you." Willow smiled sweetly, looking fondly at Branton. Fia swore the girl would flirt with any boy whenever she got the chance. "You are the only page I know who can even handle a sword without dropping it. Believe me; you have a wonderful chance of making it to the position of a squire."

"Really? Yes, I suppose you are right," said Branton with a satisfied nod of his head, standing a little taller. Once again, Willow was able to make a man believe anything she wanted, even if it wasn't true. She had a way of manipulating people that Fia would never even dream of trying.

"Although, I must say, I have no idea why my cousin insists on acting like a man when she is a woman," continued Willow.

"Nay, you wouldn't understand," grumbled Maira. "My father sent me this sword for my birthday two years ago. He understands me, and that is all that matters."

"Thank you and good day, m'ladies," said Branton with a bow, heading out of the stables.

"Fia, did ye come out to the stables for yer birthday present or was it just to get away from that long line of men waitin' to meet ye?" asked Morag, leaning lazily on the gate of the stall.

"You know it was the latter of the two," said Willow. "Fia, I can't understand why any woman would run from men the way you do. All three of you do it, for that matter." Willow fluffed out her gown and fussed with her long, dark hair that was loose and cascaded like a waterfall over her shoulders.

"I dinna do that!" Morag stood upright so quickly she lost her balance and had to hold on to the gate to right herself.

"Willow, that's no' the problem," said Fia. "The problem is that ye like men a little too much. Ye and Morag are goin' to have to start actin' more like ladies and less like strumpets when ye are around the laddies."

"I dinna do that, either," spat Morag.

Willow's eyes narrowed. Her hands went to her hips. "Mayhap you don't deserve the present we made for you, after all, dear cousin."

"Ye made me a present? What is it?" asked Fia curiously. "Let me see it." She eagerly held out her hands.

"It's not here." Maira polished her sword with the end of her skirt as she spoke.

"Really?" Fia looked at each of them and nodded. "I ken where it is, then."

"No, ye dinna," Morag challenged her.

"Aye, I do." Fia smiled and crossed her arms over her chest. "By the way ye were all actin' last time we visited Imanie, I'd say ye stashed it with her, didna ye?"

"Ye're right," Morag agreed with a sigh. "It's with Imanie because we kent ye would find it if we left it here at the castle."

"Do you want to go get it now?" Maira raised a mischievous brow.

"Now?" Morag looked up in surprise. "But it's right in the middle of Fia's birthday celebration."

"All the more reason to leave," mumbled Fia.

"What about all the men?" asked Willow. "They will be disappointed if they don't get the chance to dance with you."

Fia hurried over to her horse and started to saddle it. "Then ye go take my place dancin' with those men, Willow. But I am goin' to see Imanie."

"Me, too!" Maira headed for her horse as well. "Mayhap Imanie will show me a few more fighting skills while we're there."

"The guards are goin' to see ye leave," protested Morag.

"No' if we hurry," said Fia. "I noticed the servants bringin' food and ale to the guards on the battlements as we came out to the stables. I'm sure we can sneak out while they are occupied."

"I could go for a breath of fresh air. This stable is getting stuffy." Willow headed over to her horse.

"Then, I'm comin', too," said Morag.

"Morag, ye dinna have a horse of yer own," Fia reminded her.

"It's no' my fault Lord Beaufort favors ye three. I'll borrow someone else's horse." She stretched her neck to see the horses in the stalls that belonged to Lord Beaufort's visitors.

"Nay, dinna cause trouble, Morag. Just ride with me." Fia helped her sister mount the horse and then pulled herself up into the saddle. "If we're quick, we can sneak out and still make it back to the castle before the end of the celebration. Lord Beaufort will never ken we left."

"Do ye think Lord Beaufort doesna ken ye sneak out?" asked Morag.

"He probably does, but he looks the other way," said Fia, heading for the door. "He also kens that he canna control us, and we will go anyway. If he pretends no' to see us, then he willna have to tell our faithers and have their wraths upon his head."

"That's right," said Maira. "And if he doesn't see us leave, he won't have the chance to stop us either. Now, let's go."

* * *

A SHORT TIME LATER, Fia led the girls into the secret garden where she expected to see Imanie waiting for them. Instead, the garden was empty.

"Imanie," called out Maira. "Are you here?"

"Somethin's wrong," said Fia, scanning the grounds. Everything seemed too quiet. The birds were not even singing.

"Her horse is gone, so she has probably left to collect herbs or to fetch water from the stream," said Willow nonchalantly.

"Mayhap we should wait and give Fia her present after Imanie returns." Maira tied the reins of her horse to a tree. "After all, the gift was Imanie's idea."

"We canna stay long." Morag followed after Maira. "Lord Beaufort is bound to ken we're no' there and send someone to find us."

"She's right," agreed Fia. "As much as I dinna want to be at the castle, it is disrespectful to stay away long since the celebration is in my honor."

"Then I suppose Imanie won't mind if we give you your gift." Maira walked over to the shed and disappeared inside.

"I'll bet ye'll never guess what it is," said Morag excitedly.

"She probably won't have to since you usually spill all the secrets," sniffed Willow.

"Stop arguin'." Fia acted as mediator between the cousins. "Did ye want me to guess what it is, or no'?"

"No need." Maira handed Fia a small package wrapped in the broad leaves of the black poplar tree. It was tied closed with vines. The package looked very earthy.

Fia smiled. "This looks like somethin' that Imanie wrapped."

"Open it, open it," Morag coaxed her. She was so excited that Fia expected her to start jumping up and down next.

Sitting down on the ground, Fia put the package on her lap and adjusted the crown on her head. All the three cousins wore their crowns today since Lord Beaufort had invited many rich and powerful lords to the castle. He tended to use the girls in his favor to gain respect from the other nobles.

Carefully removing the vines, Fia opened the leaves to see a handmade bracelet. Leather strips made an intricate design. Woven right into the bracelet were several personal items.

"We each put something into the bracelet for you," said Willow. "I gave you a brass button off my favorite gown." Willow's hand went to her bodice.

Fia smiled. "I thought ye told me ye lost that button the last time ye went ridin'."

"I did," stated Willow with a sly smile. "I lost it right here when I added it to your present."

"Thank ye, Willow. I know how much ye like yer brass buttons."

Morag was next. "I added a piece of dried heather to yer bracelet. It is from our bonnie homeland of Scotland." She got on her knees and leaned forward, pointing it out to Fia. "I thought ye might like it. Da gave me that sprig of heather the day he brought me to live at Castle Rothbury." Tears formed in her eyes. "I used to hold it every night in bed as I went to sleep. It made me feel as if Da was with me."

"Oh, Morag, I ken how much this means to ye. Thank ye." Fia leaned over and gave her younger sister a hug and a kiss on the cheek. Morag was a pest most of the time, but she did have a big heart. This proved it.

"I added the shell we found when we used to play on the beach when you'd come to visit me in Whitehaven during the summer," explained Maira.

Fia ran her fingers along the white, smooth shell with the hole in the center. "I remember this. We were only about four or five when I found it and gave it to ye."

Maira laughed. "Remember, we both wanted it, but my father convinced yours to let me have it since I cried so much louder than you?"

All the girls laughed at that. The bracelet was filled with fond memories of the people Fia loved.

"Did ye see what Imanie put in the bracelet?" asked Morag, pointing it out before Fia could even answer.

"It's a wooden heart," she said, noticing the beautiful grain of the wood. There were small holes on either side of it where the leather bands held it in place. On the wooden heart was carved Fia's name.

"Imanie said she wanted to give you a heart since you were chosen by the queen to belong to the Followers of the Secret Heart group," Maira explained. "I have a feeling we will all get one at some time or another."

"No' me." Morag let out a frustrated breath, fretting once again.

"Morag, ye are just lucky that Imanie let ye stay and watch our trainin' these past few years," Fia reminded her.

"Girls! What are you doing here?" Imanie rode through the back entrance, sliding off her horse and making her way to them in a quick pace. Fia didn't miss the disturbed look upon her face.

"We came to give Fia her present," said Maira. "I hope you don't mind that we didn't wait for you, Imanie."

"She was tryin' to escape the men at the party," tattled Morag.

"Thank ye all for the beautiful bracelet." Fia admired it fondly and was about to try it on when Imanie took her arm and dragged her to her feet.

"You all have to leave. Right now."

"But we just got here," said Morag.

"It is my birthday, and I had hoped to spend some time with ye," Fia told her.

"I brought my sword." Maira held it up. "Can you teach me a few more moves before we leave?"

"Nay. You don't understand." Imanie's brows dipped in concern. "You must get back to the castle anon."

"What is it, Imanie?" asked Fia. Something was wrong. She could feel it in the signs all around her from the quietness of the forest to the look of disturbance on Imanie's face. "What's wrong?"

Imanie rubbed her chest and closed her eyes slightly as she struggled to catch her breath.

"You're sick, aren't you?" asked Willow.

"Nay. It's just my heart. The pain will pass," said the old woman, holding a hand in the air. "It has been happening lately when I ride too fast."

This concerned Fia. She had never seen Imanie's face look so pale. Her breathing was sporadic and not at all like that of a person who had ridden her horse too fast.

"You speak as if we are in danger," Maira observed.

"You are." Imanie rubbed her chest again, letting out a deep breath before she explained. "I spotted Highlanders in the woods not far from here."

"Highlanders?" Willow's head snapped up in alarm. "What would they be doing on this side of the border?"

"Mayhap they are here to hunt," suggested Morag.

"I don't think they are here to hunt." Imanie made her way over to a wooden bench and sat down. The girls followed.

"Why are they here?" asked Willow.

"They're spies," Imanie told them.

"Does this have something to do with those raids on the south coast lately?" Willow questioned.

"I thought King Richard's army already chased the Scots and the French that were helping them back over the border," said Maira.

"Aye, but I've just had word that Richard has troops of fourteen thousand men and he is moving up the coast of Scotland, headed for Edinburgh," Imanie told them.

"He is?" This news was alarming to Fia. Her family's home was in the Lowlands but directly in the path.

"Please, go back to the castle," begged Imanie. "You will be safe there."

"What about ye?" asked Fia, concerned for the old woman who didn't look well at all.

"I'll be fine. Don't worry about me."

"But the Scots might find you here," warned Willow.

"I'll stay and help protect you." Maira pulled her sword from the scabbard.

Imanie chuckled lowly and continued to rub her chest. She tried hard to steady her breathing. "Lady Maira, you might be good with a sword, but that is no good against an entire clan of Highlanders. Now go before it is too late." Imanie got to her feet and ushered the girls back to their horses.

"Who told ye this news?" asked Fia.

"I have my sources," the old woman explained. "But I will not divulge their identities."

"Are they women from the secret group?" asked Morag, always needing to know more.

"There is no time for talk. You must leave anon." Imanie hurried them to the entrance of the secret garden.

"Come with us, Imanie," begged Fia. "I am worried about ye."

"You know I can't do that." Sadness showed in the old woman's eyes. "I want you all to be strong and use what I've taught you to better your lives."

Fia's heart jumped at hearing the old woman's words. "Imanie, ye sound as if ye are sayin' guidbye."

Imanie's eyes became glassy, and a thin smile turned her lips upward. "I have been blessed to know each and every one of you. I have enjoyed training you these past three years, and you are fast learners. Each of you is a strong woman that Queen Philippa would have been proud of."

"Ye didna train me at all," Morag reminded her.

"Nay, and I am ashamed that I let old superstitions get in my way." Imanie unpinned the heart brooch from her cloak and held it out to Morag. "Take this, Morag. You are just as strong of a woman as your sister and cousins, and you deserve it."

"For me?" Morag's eyes lit up in excitement as she plucked the brooch from the old woman's hand. After examining it, she pinned it to her bodice.

"Nay, ye canna do that, Imanie," Fia protested. "Ye told us that the last time ye brought someone into the group without the queen's permission, someone died."

"The queen is dead, and I'm too old to be frightened by superstitions of what might happen," said Imanie with a fond smile. "Now go, and protect yourselves. If anything happens to any of you, I will feel as if I have failed in carrying out the wishes of our late queen."

Shouts could be heard coming from the forest. A flock of birds lifted from a tree in the distance.

"They're comin' closer," screamed Morag. "I'm frightened."

"Come on," said Maira, pulling Morag with her over to her horse. "I'll protect you. Now keep quiet before you alert them that we are here."

"Hurry, Fia," said Willow, already atop her horse.

Fia grasped the bracelet in her hand for strength. Something told her not to leave Imanie, and she didn't want to go.

"Go on, Fia," said Imanie with wisdom in her eyes. "Your journey starts today. I can honestly say that even I didn't expect it."

"My journey? What do ye mean?"

"This Highland clan is one we've seen before," explained Imanie. "It is led by the laird who saved your life three years ago."

"What does this have to do with anythin'? Have ye had an insight?"

"It's time you leave now, Fia." Imanie touched Fia's shoulder. When she did, a wave of grief passed between them. Fia's eyes shot up to meet Imanie's, confirming her suspicions. There was no doubt in Fia's mind Imanie was saying goodbye forever.

"I will never see ye again, will I?" asked Fia, trying to hold back the tears.

"I'm not long for this world, Fia." Imanie rubbed her heart again. "But either way, you must know that I will always be with you."

There was another shout from the forest, and it sounded much closer.

"Go!" said Imanie, pushing Fia toward her horse.

"Are ye sure ye willna come with me?"

"This is my home and where I will stay."

Fia mounted her horse, clutching the bracelet in her hand. Her emotions ran rampant, and confusion filled her head. Should she stay with Imanie or should she return to the castle with her sister and cousins? She felt torn because she wanted to do both but she couldn't. She needed to make a quick decision and hope it wasn't the wrong one.

"Come on, Fia. We need to go now!" Maira poked her head back inside the gate. Morag held on to Maira atop the horse, looking very frightened. Willow turned her horse in a full circle, as the animal was anxious to leave as well. Staying here was no longer an option. Fia had to stick with her cousins and sister and help them get back to the castle before the Scots found them in the woods.

"Let's go," said Fia, looking over her shoulder at Imanie. She nodded slightly. "Thank ye, Imanie. I will never forget ye." Why did this have to feel so much like a final goodbye? The idea tore her up inside. With a yank to the reins, Fia turned her horse and rode hard, trying to get back to the castle before the Highlanders attacked them in the woods.

# CHAPTER 2

"*H*old up!" called out Laird Alastair MacPherson raising his hand over his head, bringing his horse as well as his army to a halt. The clan gathered around him atop their horses, as well as on foot.

"Why are we stoppin'?" growled Brohain, the resident troublemaker of the MacPherson Clan. Ever since Alastair's father was taken prisoner by Clan Grant over three years ago, Alastair assumed the title of chieftain and laird. Some of the clan members didn't think he should take his father's place but, in the end, he walked away claiming the position.

Duncan MacPherson's wild nature was what put him behind bars to begin with. Alastair wasn't half as reckless as his father. While he was one of the clan's best warriors, Alastair didn't agree with his father's past decisions. Nay, he wasn't the cold-hearted bastard that his father turned out to be. Alastair also had a mixture of his mother's kind and loving nature running through his veins.

"I thought I heard somethin'," said Alastair in a low voice.

"Mayhap, it's Richard and his army movin' up the coast." Alastair's right-hand man, Niven rode to his side. Niven was three years younger than Alastair's age of five and twenty years. Half of the men in the clan were older than him, and some of them like Brohain and Rhodric were the age of his father. The older men resented Alastair and wanted to follow the aggressive ways of their last chieftain.

"I dinna believe so," said Alastair. He and his clan were sent out as scouts to find out King Richard's position and how many troops he was bringing to invade Scotland. One of the Scot's spies returned and told them days ago that Richard was already storming the border. Alastair needed to bring the news to the Highlanders who were gathering in Fife for an ambush. If the plan worked accordingly, the bloody English wouldn't know what hit them.

"There," said Rhodric, pointing at riders as they disappeared into the forest.

"It must be the English," said Niven.

"It is the English, but no' Richard's army." Alastair had been in these woods first as a child with his father and then again three years ago when they came over the border to spy. "Castle Rothbury is just beyond this section of the English king's forest."

"Let's get those bluidy Sassenachs," snarled Brohain, roiling up the men.

"Nay!" shouted Alastair, remembering the girl they had encountered in these woods three years ago. How could he ever forget her? As far as he knew, it could be her in the woods again. "We'll make camp here since nightfall is almost upon us."

"My laird, Brohain is right," said Rhodric. "The riders are just up ahead. If we dinna stop them, they might tell the others, and they might attack while we sleep."

"Then I'll stay up all night on watch if need be, but we are no' goin' after them. We are here on a mission. We willna be distracted by a few riders who may or may no' have even seen us. If they come for us, then we'll defend ourselves, but we are no' goin' to attack."

Brohain and Rhodric didn't like Alastair's decision but, then again, when did they ever?

Alastair looked up to the darkening sky, thinking about his father. For three years, he'd been a prisoner. The longer the man was gone the more Alastair's hopes were dashed that he would ever see him again.

"OH NO!" Fia followed behind her cousins on their way back to the castle. "Maira, Willow, stop."

The cousins stopped and rode back to her. "Fia, we need to keep going." Willow nervously scanned the forest.

"I must have dropped my bracelet." Fia checked her pockets, sure she was holding the bracelet when she left the secret garden. Not noticing it was gone wasn't like her. "I canna find it."

"Well, what did ye do with it?" asked Morag, holding on to Maira's waist on the back of her horse.

"I dinna ken."

"Fia, it's not like you to lose something," said Maira. "You are the observant one. You remember everything."

"I guess I was startled because of the Scots," she lied, not wanting to tell the girls she was worried about Imanie. Their parting had seemed so final that Fia now wished she had insisted that Imanie come with them to the castle. "I need to go back and find it." She started to turn her horse, but Willow brought her horse up behind her to block her.

"Fia, you can't! You heard Imanie. We are in danger. We need to get back to the castle anon."

"That's right," said Morag. "If we stay here any longer, we could be killed."

Fia's eyes swept the forest. She didn't see nor hear any Scots, so she didn't think they were in danger. Imanie's goodbye still haunted her. More than anything, she wanted to return to the garden. Plus, she wished she hadn't lost the bracelet. It meant so much to her with all the personal items put there by those she loved.

"I will just be a minute," she said, directing her horse around Willow. Maira rode in front of her next, pulling her sword from its sheath.

"I can't let you go, Cousin. Now, turn around and ride back to the castle with us before we're all killed."

Fia thought she heard voices in the distance, realizing she was careless, letting her emotions control her. If she went back now, the girls were sure to follow. By doing that, Fia was only putting all their lives in danger. While she cared deeply for Imanie, she didn't want to risk the lives of her cousins and her sister.

"Ye're right," she said, turning her horse. "I can come back to look for the bracelet after the threat of the Highlanders has passed. Now, let's get out of here before we're discovered."

As she rode toward the castle, she glanced over her shoulder, feeling as if she were being watched.

The girls made it back quickly and entered through the castle gate instead of sneaking in. They were passed up by soldiers armed for battle heading out of the castle.

"Girls! Where have you been?" Lord Beaufort rode up on his horse followed by some of the guests who were dressed for battle as well. Chaos broke out and women and children ran through the courtyard. Some of the women were saying goodbye to their husbands.

"We're sorry, Lord Beaufort," Maira said, taking the lead. She slipped out of the saddle and to the ground. "We went out for a ride."

"Egads, you girls are naught but trouble," said the earl. "When I return, I will send missives to all of your fathers telling them you have disobeyed my orders and have been sneaking out of the castle without an escort."

"We weren't in any danger," said Willow. "Not really."

"I had my sword to protect us," added Maira.

"Girls, there you are." Lady Ernestine ran up to greet them, wringing her hands in worry. "I was afraid the Highlanders found you and abducted you."

"Highlanders?" Fia asked, wondering what they knew.

"One of the guards said he saw a Highlander while out on patrol," said Lord Beaufort. "It seems the king's woods are crawling with them."

"Is that where ye're goin'?" asked Fia. "To fight them?"

"Yes, and more," was all the man said before directing his men out the gate. Ernestine ran after him.

"Fia, Maira, where have you been?" Branton approached with a sword at his waistbelt and carrying filled travel bags. He was on foot. "Lord Beaufort is leaving to fight the Scots. He got a missive from King Richard and has gone to be at the king's side."

"King Richard has called for knights and lords to join him?" asked Maira. "That means my father might be heading up the coast of Scotland with him."

"And mine, too," said Willow.

"They'll be fightin' our faither, Fia." Morag jumped down from the horse and headed over to join them.

"This isna guid," said Fia. "Our uncles and our faithers willna fight against each other."

"If your fathers pay homage to the king, then they don't have a choice," Branton told them. "If they are called to battle, they have to go, no matter what the circumstances." A knight summoned Branton. The boy hurried over to give him the travel bag since he didn't seem to be going along with the men.

"Do ye think our faither is goin' to have to fight against Uncle Rook and Uncle Rowen?" Morag asked Fia.

"For the sake of both Scotland and England, I hope no'," Fia answered. This was a situation no one would want to experience.

# CHAPTER 3

$\mathcal{A}$ lastair heard the English heading from the castle, coming down the road to most likely join up with the king and his army as they burned and pillaged the coast of Scotland. His men were settling in for the night, not expecting anyone to be traveling in the dark.

"They're comin'," shouted Rhodric, jumping up and grabbing his claymore.

"Kill the bluidy Sassenachs." Brohain rushed to mount his horse, not bothering with a saddle.

"Wait," called out Alastair. "They are no' comin' for us. They are on the road and headin' to meet with their king."

"So, we'll stop them from ever gettin' there." Brohain roiled up the others as usual, and Alastair tried to calm them.

"We were sent as a scoutin' party. If we're all dead, it will do the rest of Scotland no guid. Stay where ye are and dinna attack, I tell ye."

Brohain was not listening. Before Alastair knew it, half the clan was headed on horseback and foot to confront the English on the road.

"Damn ye," spat Alastair, heading for his horse as well.

"My laird, are we goin' to stop the English, too?" Niven was right on his heels.

"Nay. We are goin' to stop Brohain and the rest of the fools before they get us all killed."

With the rest of the clan who were loyal to him following, Alastair led the way.

* * *

THE SOUND of shouting woke Fia from a sound sleep. She sat upright in bed, listening intently. She was sure she heard Lord Beaufort's voice. What was he doing back so soon? She ran to the window and threw open the shutter, stretching her neck to see the gate being raised. Soldiers and wounded men heading into the courtyard.

The door to her chamber banged open and she turned abruptly, holding her hand to her heart. It was Maira and Willow who shared a bedchamber next to the one she shared with her sister.

"Something's wrong," said Maira, holding her sword in one hand even though she was only dressed in a nightrail.

"The Highlanders must be attacking the castle," cried Willow.

"I dinna think so," said Fia, rushing back to the window. This time, in the light of the torches, she saw Lord Beaufort and some of his guards leading Highland prisoners into the courtyard. There must have been half a dozen of them, and their hands were bound.

"Which of you is the chieftain of the clan?" shouted Lord Beaufort to the prisoners.

"I am," said an older man, spitting at Beaufort's feet. The earl swung at him, punching the man in the gut. Fia took a closer look at their plaids, remembering these men from the day in the woods when she was captured by them and then let go. Hadn't Imanie warned her that these were the same Highlanders in the king's woods again? Only, this man who stepped forward claiming he was their chieftain was not the man who saved her life. Instead, he was the one who had wanted to kill her!

"Morag, wake up," Fia called to her sister who could sleep through anything from a thunderstorm to an attack on the castle and never hear a thing. "These are the Highlanders we met in the woods three years ago."

"Fia?" Morag sat up in bed and rubbed her eyes. "What's goin' on?" She yawned. "Maira and Willow, why are ye here?"

"It's the Highlanders!" exclaimed Willow.

"We're bein' attacked? They entered the castle?" Morag sprang out of bed and ran to the window, pushing the others aside so she could see.

"I'm gettin' dressed and goin' down there to find out what I can," said Fia.

"Fia, nay. Please stay here where you're safe," Willow begged her.

"Aye, we should wait until morning," agreed Maira. "Now, everyone back to bed. I am sure Lord Beaufort will tell us all that has transpired as soon as it is light."

Fia laid in bed, tossing and turning, having had horrible dreams all night about Imanie. She worried for the old woman. If the Highlanders attacked the English soldiers, they might have attacked and killed her as well. She looked back at the open window, still hearing the sounds of the soldiers' voices. How could she sleep knowing Highlanders were inside the castle walls?

She sneaked out of bed and dressed quickly. First light would be here soon, but she couldn't wait. She had to know now what happened in the woods and if the Scots had been anywhere near the secret garden.

Her hand was on the door when she heard her sister's voice from the bed.

"Fia? Where are ye goin'? It's no' first light yet."

Damn. Wouldn't you know it? Morag could sleep through an earth tremor, but when Fia wanted to sneak out, the girl was awake.

"Go back to sleep, Morag."

"Ye're dressed!" Morag sat upright in bed. "Ye are goin' down to the courtyard, are ye no'?"

"Yes. I canna wait until first light to find out what is goin' on. I fear for Imanie and wish we had never left her in the secret garden all alone."

"Then I'm comin' with ye." Morag sprang out of bed. The last thing Fia wanted was a tag-along with a big mouth. She had hoped to go to the secret garden to check on Imanie and look for her bracelet at the same time. Now would be the only time to do it when there was still chaos in the courtyard. If she waited until sunup, Lord Beaufort would be sure to see her and make her stay within the castle walls.

"I'll be back, Morag. I ken how much ye like to sleep, so go back to bed. When I return, I will tell ye and the others everythin' I've learned."

"Ye are no' goin' to do anythin' stupid, are ye, Fia?" Morag yawned and sat back down on the bed.

"Ye dinna have to worry about me." She put her hand on the heart brooch, hoping her dangerous plan wouldn't be the end of her. Mayhap it was a mistake, but she couldn't tell the others. They would either keep her there or want to go with her as Morag had. And telling Maira to stay behind was not going to go over well. It was easier to sneak around in the shadows if she was by herself. "Get some sleep, Morag." She walked over and kissed her sister on the head and tucked in the blanket around her.

As she left the room, she looked back, hoping this wouldn't be the last time she ever saw Morag. It was dangerous, but Fia had to do it. She felt as if she'd already abandoned Imanie and it didn't sit right with her at all.

\* \* \*

ALASTAIR STUMBLED THROUGH THE WOODS, not sure how long he'd been passed out after being stabbed in the side by the English when he went to stop his clan from attacking last night.

The English were strong, and the battle fierce. The last he remembered, he ordered his clan to retreat to the border. Of course, Brohain, Rhodric and some of the others with bloodlust in their veins had not listened to his orders and continued to fight. Being the chieftain of the clan, Alastair couldn't leave them behind.

He'd been so intent on saving Brohain's ass that he hadn't even seen the young English boy dart out of the shadows. By then, it was too late. The boy scared his horse and Alastair fell to the ground, being stabbed by the lad before he knew what happened. Then to make matters worse, the boy stole his horse.

The last thing he remembered was seeing Brohain, Rhodric and some of the others being led away as prisoners. The damned fools! Why hadn't they listened to him?

Holding his plaid up against his gaping wound, Alastair searched for a horse. He came across several of his men dead on the ground, as well as some of the English. He still had his sword, thank goodness, since the fool boy was more interested in his steed than he was in his weapon.

Alastair felt fury flowing through his veins. He would never get the respect from the older members of the clan that his father once had. The past three years had been naught but a struggle since the clan was split. Hell, if he didn't care as much as he did, he would have left the older members to their fates and just concentrated on the ones who were loyal to him.

Now, because of a foolish move, some of his men were dead, others were captured, and part of his clan had left for the border without him. Could things possibly get any worse?

He didn't find a horse in the woods but, as he walked, he came across what looked like a hidden door in a knoll. His side bled profusely, and he couldn't go much further without tending to his wound.

Putting one bloodied hand on the wooden gate, he pushed it open. The first rays of sunlight illuminated the area inside, showing him a secret garden. With his vision blurred, he staggered forward, seeing a small cottage at the other side of the garden. He wasn't sure who lived here but hoped he could convince them to help him.

He made it to the cottage and was about to knock when the door swung open. An old woman stood there, looking as pale and weak as he felt right now.

"You!" she said, which made him take a closer look at her. She sounded as if she knew him.

"I'm sorry, but do ye ken me?"

"You're the Highlander that let Fia live when the others wanted to kill her."

"What?" he asked, taking a moment to clear his head. Then he remembered. This was the old woman who had come to the young lassie's aid three years ago in the forest. She was also the one who shot arrows at him and his men. "Och, I remember ye," he spat, not sure it was good luck to run across her. Still, it couldn't possibly get any worse. He needed to swallow his pride and try. "I need yer help, old woman. I have a sword wound in my side and require stitchin'. I've lost a lot of bluid."

"Why should I help you?" The woman curled her lip while she rubbed her chest as if she, too, were in pain. Her breathing was rather shallow.

"Ye said it yerself. I let the lassie live."

"Aye." She squinted an eye and cocked her head to peruse him. "Tell me. Why did you let her go?"

"I can tell ye, but I need yer help first." He nodded to the wound and removed his hand to show her the blood.

"Oh!" She swallowed forcefully at the sight. He couldn't help noticing the perplexed look on her face. Then she nodded slowly. "Let me help you."

He thought his worries were over, but the old woman took one step forward, clutched her chest and fell to the ground at his feet. He stepped backward, staring at her in disbelief and shaking his head. Her eyes and mouth were opened, but she wasn't blinking. He got down on his knees and laid a hand on her neck to feel for a pulse. When he couldn't find one, he leaned over to listen for her breath and nearly passed out.

"Damn it," he spat, struggling to get to his feet. Of all the rotten luck! The old woman was going to help him, and now she dropped down dead at his feet. He hadn't thought things could get any worse, but they just did.

# CHAPTER 4

*F*ia looked over her shoulder for the tenth time, watching for Highlanders to jump out of the bushes. Thankfully, she hadn't seen or heard any. However, she did see several dead Scots and also some dead English soldiers on her way to the secret garden.

Knowing Lord Beaufort would be scouting the woods as soon as the sun rose, she hurried, wanting to check on Imanie and get back before the men found her in the forest all alone.

As she approached the gate to the secret garden, something sparkled from the ground, catching her eye.

"My bracelet!" she said excitedly, jumping off the horse to see Willow's brass button reflecting in the early morning sun. She scooped up the bracelet, bringing it to her lips for a quick kiss. This had to be a good sign. Everything was going to be all right. "Imanie," she called out excitedly as she approached the gate. But the smile disappeared quickly from her face when she realized the gate was open and there was a bloody handprint upon it.

Holding the reins of her horse, she slipped the bracelet into her pocket and ventured forward. Was Imanie hurt? Seeing a bloody handprint could only mean one of two things. Either Imanie was injured, or possibly the blood came from someone else.

The handprint looked larger than a woman's hand. Her head told her to turn around and run, but her heart wouldn't let her leave until she knew Imanie was safe.

Cautiously and carefully, she entered the garden, ready to jump on her horse and ride away at the first sign of danger. She hadn't gone more than a few steps into the secret garden when she saw the red and brown plaid of a Highlander on Imanie's porch. She froze, wondering what a Highlander was doing inside the secret garden.

The man was down on his knees. When he got up, she saw Imanie lying on the ground, and she wasn't moving.

"Nay!" she shouted, not wanting to believe her mentor was dead. But by the look of fear in the old woman's open eyes, it told Fia that the Highlander had killed her. She started to mount her horse, but the man's words made her stop.

"Fia, wait! I need yer help," he called out.

With one foot in the stirrup, she looked up slowly, wondering how this rugged Highlander knew her name. From across the garden, she recognized his long, dark hair and his stance. His voice was familiar, too. Aye, she knew him. It was the chieftain of the clan of Highlanders she'd met in the woods three years ago. He was the man who stopped his men from killing her. It was because of him she was still alive today.

"Fia, come here. Please," he called out, collapsing atop a wooden bench on the porch. His head fell back, and she noticed the look of pain on his face. Then she saw the blood on his clothes and the way he held his hand against his side. He was wounded!

"I dinna trust ye," she called out. "Ye killed my friend."

"What?" He lifted his head and looked at her from across the garden. There was a slight pause before he answered. "I canna hear a word ye say. Come closer."

She'd learned from Imanie that when someone pauses before they answer, they are usually lying. She thought about turning and riding away, but she couldn't leave Imanie. What if she wasn't dead but only injured? Fia had to find out. She needed to help her.

Whether the Highlander was lying or not, Fia had to take the risk. Imanie would do the same for her. The woman had risked her life that day in the forest when she took on the entire clan of Highlanders with just a bow and arrows to try to save Fia's life. Fia owed it to her to do the same in return.

Tying the reins of her horse to a tree branch, she slowly walked toward the cottage, keeping her eye on the mysterious man.

"Why are ye here?" she asked, making her way closer to Imanie.

"It doesna matter," he mumbled. "I am sorry about yer friend, but I had nothin' to do with it."

Fia dropped to her knees, checking Imanie for any sign of life but couldn't find a one. Imanie was dead! Tears filled her eyes. She brushed them away with the back of her hand. Taking a closer look, she saw blood on Imanie, but it didn't seem to be from her. The woman's body was not cut or stabbed. The blood was on Imanie's clothes as well as bloody fingermarks around her neck.

"Ye killed her!" Startled and shocked by her discovery, Fia jumped to her feet.

"I dinna kill her, lass." The Scot got up off the bench. When he took a step toward her, she backed away. His body towered over her and his silver eyes bored into her, holding her in place. "I was wounded by the English and came here lookin' for help. The old woman was goin' to sew up my wound, but before she could, she dropped dead at my feet."

"How do ye expect me to believe that?" she spat. "I see yer bluidy fingerprints around her neck. Ye strangled her, didna ye?"

"Blethers, ye are a silly lass." He gripped his side again and let out a low moan. "Why would I kill the only person who could help me? Look at this, if ye dinna believe me."

He removed his hand from his wound, causing her to gasp when she saw the amount of blood leaking from his side.

"Y-ye're hurt," she stammered.

"I told ye that. Now help me by sewin' up my wound, and I will help ye by buryin' yer friend."

"I dinna ken," she said, still being very suspicious. "Mayhap ye have half yer clan hidin' inside the hut."

"Och, ye try my patience." He swiped his free hand through the air in a dismissing nature. "If I had anyone at all inside the cottage dinna ye think I'd have them sewin' up my side instead of me standin' here bleedin' to death while I argue with ye?"

"I suppose ye're right," she said, looking down at Imanie, feeling her heart break. She should never have left her here alone yesterday. "What happened to her?"

"I dinna ken. She clutched her chest and fell like a rock. It was all so sudden."

"It must have been her heart."

"Could be."

"Will ye really help me bury her body?"

"I promise," said the Highlander.

"All right," she agreed, bending down and using her hand to close Imanie's eyes. She leaned over and kissed her on the cheek. "I am sorry I wasna here to help ye when ye needed me," she whispered to the woman. Then she stepped around Imanie and made her way to the door of the hut. "The needle and thread are in her sewin' kit in the house. It will be better if ye come inside while I sew ye up."

He followed her into the cottage and collapsed atop Imanie's bed with a loud thump.

Fia filled a basin with water and found some old rags, bringing them over to the bed along with a needle and thread.

"Have ye ever done this before, lassie?" he asked as she threaded the needle.

"Nay," she admitted. "But I ken how to stitch, and I have tended to the wounded in other ways before."

"Then let's get this over with," he grumbled, removing his weapon belt and lying it on the bed. With his eyes fastened to her, he reached behind his back and drew his sword. Her heart about stopped until she saw him toss it on the bed and heard his next words. "Help me off with my tunic."

"What?" She wasn't sure she wanted to help the man undress.

"Well, did ye think ye could sew me up right through my clothes?"

"Of course no'," she said, feeling foolish. She put down the needle and thread and reached over to help him remove his tunic.

"Alastair," he said once his chest was bare.

"Pardon me?"

"My name is Alastair MacPherson." He feigned a half-smile. "I thought if I was goin' to be half-naked and on a bed with a bonnie lassie and all alone, ye should at least ken my name."

"Oh. Yes, I ken yer name. I remember it from the day ye saved me in the woods three years ago." She cleaned his wound while she spoke.

"One guid turn deserves another, right?"

"Somethin' like that." Fia inspected his wound, pushing the needle through his skin.

He bit back a curse and closed his eyes while she sewed him up. "What is this place and why are ye even here alone?"

"It's a secret garden," she told him. "My cousins, sister, and I would sneak out of the castle to meet here with Imanie."

"What for?"

She looked up, pulling the thread as she did so. She had started feeling comfortable around him and had already told him too much. She had to be careful. "Never mind. I shouldna have even told ye that." She put her head down and continued to sew. "What happened to ye?"

"I was stabbed with a sword," he told her, sounding as if he thought she was daft even to have to ask.

"I can see that. It looks as if ye were lucky since the wound is mainly in the skin. The man wasna a guid aim. Why didna the person who wounded ye, also run ye through again to make sure ye were dead?"

Her statement must have sounded cold and cruel to him because he made a face before he answered. "I suppose it was because he was too interested in stealin' my horse."

"Then ye have no way to get back to yer clan?"

"Half my clan has left without me by my orders, and the other half is either dead or have been taken prisoner by the English."

"Aye, I ken. Lord Beaufort brought the prisoners to the castle before sunup. There was one who was claimin' to be chieftain."

"Dinna tell me," he said, gritting his teeth and inspecting the job she did on his wound. "I am sure it was Brohain. Ye remember – the one who wanted to kill ye."

"Yes, he's the one."

"Help me wrap this wound, and I will make guid on my promise and bury yer friend."

"Ye are weak and need to rest," she told him, tearing a bed sheet and wrapping up his wound. "I will cover up Imanie with a blanket and be back with my cousins and my sister. We will bury her."

"Nay," he said, starting to get off the bed. He moved too fast and grimaced. Then he shook his head and sat back down. "Dinna bring any Sassenachs here. I will bury her myself."

"All right," she agreed so that he would stop fighting her. She had to get help and wouldn't be able to do it if he was keeping such a close eye on her. "I will dig the hole. Please, lay back and close yer eyes. I will tell ye when the hole is ready and ye can help me move her body."

"Nay, I am the man. I will do it." He reached out and gripped her wrist, causing her to struggle.

"Stop that," he commanded.

She panicked and fought him, raising her knee and hitting him right in his wound.

"Bid the devil!" he cried, letting loose of her hand and using both hands to hold his side. His eyes closed while he leaned back against the wall.

Through the open door, the sunlight streamed into the room. It was already daybreak. Fia had to get back to the castle quickly. If she didn't, Lord Beaufort would be sending out a search party for her. She couldn't take the chance they'd find the secret garden or Imanie. She also didn't want them to find Alastair because they would most likely kill him if they did.

Scooping up the blanket from the bed, Fia hurried out to the porch without bothering to close the door.

"I will be back, Imanie," she whispered, covering her mentor with a blanket. She wasn't sure what to do. Imanie was dead, and there was no evidence that the Highlander hadn't killed her. She needed to get help and back to the castle quickly. "I will miss ye, my guid friend," she said, kissing Imanie on the head for the last time. Then, getting to her feet, she ran for her horse.

ALASTAIR OPENED his eyes to find the girl gone. When he heard the sound of horse's hooves, he realized she had fooled him. She wasn't digging a hole to bury her friend at all. Nay, she was running right back to the castle to tell the English where he was.

He got off the bed and staggered to the door, holding on to the doorpost, watching the girl ride away.

For some reason, she stopped in the gateway and turned

around and looked right at him. No words were exchanged, but neither did they need to be. The girl might be Scottish, but she was also a traitor. Tugging on the reins, she turned and left the garden, leaving him alone with the old lady's dead body.

Alastair felt like hell and needed to rest, but he could no longer stay here. He noticed the old woman's horse in the single stable and decided to take it to find the rest of his clan. He went back into the house and donned his bloody tunic, fastening his weapon belt around his waist and replacing his sword into his scabbard.

As he left the cottage, he stepped over the body that was now covered with a blanket. "Well, Imanie," he said, using the name he'd heard Fia call the old woman. "I dinna suppose ye'll be needin' yer horse anymore. I hope ye dinna mind if I take it off yer hands."

He took a few steps but stopped in his tracks when he saw a bracelet on the ground. Scooping it up in one hand, he inspected it. In the center was a wooden heart and the name Fia carved into it. He thought about how the girl had helped him. They had made a deal, and now he was going back on his word – something he never did. His conscience got the best of him. Nay, he couldn't leave yet.

"Damn," he spat, not wanting to go before he buried the old woman's body as he'd promised. No other Highlander he knew would keep such a promise in such a dire situation. Then again, he wasn't like most Highlanders. That was his downfall. He cared too much about others than to turn his back on a woman in need.

Fingering the bracelet in his hand, he couldn't stop thinking of the red-haired beauty named Fia. Fate brought them together. This was the second time he'd seen her now. And the part that intrigued him the most was that, just like three years ago, she was still wearing the heart brooch. Curiosity ate away at him, and he needed to find the answers he'd been searching for. Perhaps she was the one who could do it. He slipped the bracelet into his pouch, shaking his head.

Seeing a shed at the opposite side of the garden, he headed toward it to find a spade, wondering if he would regret keeping his word in the end.

# CHAPTER 5

Fia burst into Willow and Maira's bedchamber, letting the door hit the wall. She had run all the way up there, having avoided Lord Beaufort in the courtyard. Morag was in the room, too. They all looked up when she entered.

"Fia, ye're back," said Morag. "We were worried about ye."

"Morag told us where you went," said Maira. "It wasn't smart of you to go out alone, Fia. Especially after the battle that just took place."

"Of course, Morag told ye," she grumbled, knowing her sister could not keep a secret if her life depended on it. "I had to go. I was so worried about Imanie."

"How is she?" asked Willow, lazily running a boar's bristle brush through her long hair.

"She's dead," said Fia, holding back her tears.

"Dead?" Maira rushed over. "Are you sure?"

"I saw her layin' there lifeless with my own eyes."

"What happened?" asked Willow, putting down the brush and coming to join them.

"I am no' sure. But when I entered the garden, I saw a bluidy handprint on the gate and then the plaid of a Scot on her porch."

"Highlanders!" squeaked Morag "They killed her."

"That's what I thought," said Fia. "But he said he didn't kill her."

"He? Who is he?" Maira demanded to know.

"It was the real chieftain of the clan, no' the liar in the dungeon. He was the man who saved my life three years ago."

"Fia! I canna believe ye escaped from him alive," said Morag.

"I didn't escape. I helped sew up his wound." Fia sat down on the bed, and the girls gathered around her.

"Don't tell me you helped the man who killed Imanie? How could you?" asked Maira in disgust.

"He said he didna kill her. He told me she dropped dead at his feet after agreein' to help him."

"I don't believe it." Willow crossed her arms over her chest and shook her head.

"She dropped dead?" Morag's hand went to the heart brooch pinned on her bodice. A look of horror washed over her face. "Oh, Fia, I killed her."

"Morag, quit talkin' like a fool," Fia scolded. Her sister tended to have crazy thoughts at times, and this was one of them. "Ye werena even there so how can ye say that?"

"Dinna ye see?" Tears formed in Morag's eyes. "Imanie gave me this heart brooch because she kent how much I wanted it. But she also told us the last time she did somethin' like this, someone died. Now she was the one to die, and it is all because of me."

"Morag, why couldn't you be happy just watching?" asked Willow. "You always cause trouble."

"Stop it. All of ye." Fia held her hands up, palms facing out. "No one killed Imanie." She said the words to calm her sister and cousins but, down deep, she couldn't be sure the Scot hadn't really killed her after all. "Imanie was rubbin' her chest which tells me she had heart problems. I saw her do it before she sent us away. My guess is that she kent she was goin' to die. That is why she gave the brooch to Morag."

"Oh, Fia, do ye think so?" asked Morag, tears dripping down her cheeks.

"Come here – all of ye." Fia gathered the girls in a circle and gave them one big hug. They all cried together for the death of Imanie. "We need to be strong," stated Fia. "After all, isna that what Imanie has been teachin' us to do for years now?"

"But what about Imanie?" asked Maira. "What did you do with her body?"

"Alastair was goin' to bury her for me in a deal we made. I sewed up his wound, and he was goin to help me in return."

"Alastair?" Maira raised a brow. "You are calling him by his first name now as if you know him."

"I do ken him. Now," added Fia.

"So, is she buried or still lying there for the ravens to peck out her eyes?" asked Willow.

Morag sobbed bitterly when she heard this. Fia pulled her sister to her in a protective hug.

"Willow, ye are so insensitive sometimes," snapped Fia.

"Well, what's the answer?" asked Willow.

"I dinna ken."

"What do you mean?" Maira picked up her sword and started polishing it.

"I didna want to stay there because I wasna sure if I was safe, so I left."

"You should never have gone there in the first place," scolded Willow.

"I had to do it." Fia shook her head. "I wanted to find out if Imanie was all right and I also went back to find this." She reached into her pocket for her bracelet but once again, found it missing. She frantically checked her other pocket, but her hand came up empty. "My bracelet! I must have dropped it again when I ran from the garden when the Highlander closed his eyes."

"Fia, what is the matter with you lately?" asked Maira. "You are the one who never misses anything. How can you have lost a bracelet twice now and not even realize you dropped it?"

"I dinna ken," said Fia, feeling so rattled every time she heard about the Highland clan. And now, after meeting Alastair and being alone with him in the cottage, she felt confused. Seeing his bare chest put ideas in her head and she couldn't get him off of her mind.

"We should tell Lord Beaufort," suggested Willow. "It is the right thing to do."

"Nay!" Fia released her sister and put her hands on her hips. "No one will mention a word of this to anyone. Alastair is hidin' in the secret garden and is wounded. We will tell no one. Do ye all understand?"

"Fia, have you lost your mind?" Maira raised her sword in the air and waved it around. "He is the enemy, or did you forget that?"

"I dinna believe he is like the rest of his clan," said Fia. "After all, he saved my life three years ago. He didna hurt me today either."

"What do ye plan on doin' about it?" asked Morag.

"There is nothing we can do," said Willow. "Lord Beaufort will be scouring the woods now looking for the dead. He might even find the secret garden."

"Nay. I canna let him find the garden or Alastair." Fia paced the room.

"You can't stop him," said Maira. "Face it, Fia, our days of sneaking off and meeting Imanie in the secret garden are over. Now that she is dead, there is nothing there for us anymore."

"I guess no'," said Fia, fingering the heart brooch, wondering how to be strong in this situation. "But we have to make sure Imanie's body is buried. We at least owe her that for all she's done for us. I willna let her rot in the sun and be eaten by the animals of the forest."

"How are ye goin' to find out if she is buried or no' if ye are no' goin' to tell Lord Beaufort?" asked Morag.

"There's only one way to ken."

"Fia, I hope you are not thinking of doing anything foolish." Maira slid her sword into her scabbard.

"Foolish, nay. Brave, yes." Fia held her hand over the heart brooch. "Ye are all members of the Followers of the Secret Heart. I am ashamed ye are goin' to just turn yer heads and look the other way when Imanie needs us now more than ever. We have to do this for her, no matter how frightenin' it may seem."

The girls were silent, all holding their hands atop their heart brooches as well.

"What should we do?" asked Willow.

"There is only one thing we can do, but we are goin' to have to work together to do it without bein' caught." Fia walked over to look out the window, devising her plan.

"Please don't say what I think you're going to say," whined Willow.

"We have to go back to the secret garden to make sure Imanie has been buried, and to pay our last respects," Fia told them. "Now, are ye all in or am I goin' to do this by myself? And please remember that there is nothin' ye can do or say to stop me."

"I'm going with you," said Maira, standing and strapping on her sword. "If anyone gives you trouble, I'll have my blade to protect us."

"Perhaps we should take a man with us," said Willow, always thinking about men.

"Nay," protested Fia. "Alastair didna even want ye three to come to the garden."

"Then let's ask Branton," suggested Maira. "We can trust that he won't say anything. Plus, he can help us get away from the castle without being questioned. And if we get into trouble, he knows how to use a sword."

"Fine," agreed Fia. "But ye will all wait outside the garden. I will enter alone to see how Alastair will react."

\* \* \*

ALASTAIR THREW the last shovel of dirt atop Imanie's grave, glad this chore was finished. It was a lot harder than he thought, trying to dig a grave and move a body when his side hurt like the devil and burned like the fires of hell. The sun was high and the day was hot. He felt as if he needed a drink of ale and some shade.

With his plaid covering his waist, he left his chest bare. The sun beating down atop his head was starting to make him feel faint. He needed water and had to get to the creek as soon as possible. Turning to make his way back to the cottage, a sharp pain shot through his side and his vision became blurred. With another step, he stumbled. Then the world went dark all around him.

\* \* \*

FIA SLID OFF HER HORSE, placing her hand on the old wooden gate. Her sister, cousins, and Branton were mounted on horses behind her. They had waited until the afternoon to come here since Lord Beaufort and his men had been in the woods collecting the dead bodies most of the day. The sun was hot, and Fia couldn't help thinking that if Imanie's body was still lying on the porch, it wasn't going to be pleasant.

"Stay here," she whispered. "I will let ye ken if it is all right to enter."

"Enter? What are you talking about?" asked Branton. "All I see is a lot of vines covering the hill."

"It's a secret," said Morag, holding her finger to her mouth. "Ye canna tell anyone, Branton."

"That's right," Maira answered with force. "If you do, you will have to deal with me." To add to her warning, she rested her hand on the hilt of her sword.

"Lady Maira, you don't scare me," said the boy with a grin. "I've been in the midst of a battle now. I'll have you know I killed a Scot and stole this horse from him as well." He reached forward from his mounted position, rubbing his hand over the horse's neck.

"Quiet," Fia said again, feeling a knot forming in her stomach. She gingerly pushed open the gate and took a step inside. Her focus was only on the cottage, trying to see if Imanie's body was still there. When she couldn't find it, she scanned the rest of the garden. Then she saw a fresh grave as well as Alastair's body lying prone on the ground. "Alastair," she called out, rushing forward, falling to her knees. She flipped him over and breathed a sigh of relief when she heard him moan.

"Fia? Are you all right?" Maira shouted from the gate.

"Get in here, all of ye," Fia commanded. "We have to get him out of the sun and into the house."

The rest of the girls and Branton rushed up to help her.

"I'm the strongest, let me carry him," said Branton. Just as he bent over to help, Alastair's eyes opened. The Scot's hands shot up in the air and grabbed Branton around the throat.

"Ye bastard, ye are the one who did this to me," shouted Alastair, tightening his hands around Branton's neck. "What did ye do with my horse?"

"Let him go," shouted Fia, trying to pull his hands off of Branton.

"Out of the way," said Maira, holding out the tip of her sword, just under Alastair's throat. "Put him down, or I'll run you through with my blade."

"Och, ye are naught but a bunch of lassies and a scrawny lad." Alastair released Branton, throwing him down on the ground. The boy gasped for air and jumped to his feet, drawing his sword and holding it up to Alastair as well. "I dinna have time for this," spat Alastair. In one motion, he'd not only drawn his sword but also knocked the swords out of both Maira's and Branton's hands. "Now, bring me my horse, lad, and dinna tarry."

Branton ran for the Scot's horse while the girls stood at the end of his blade, not sure what to do.

"Here's your steed," said Branton, handing it over. Alastair turned his back to Fia as he started to mount his horse. Fia took advantage of the situation by bending down and picking up Branton's sword. She didn't want to hurt Alastair, but neither did she want him to leave. Swinging the hilt of the sword at him, she walloped him in the back of the head, knocking him out.

* * *

"Bluidy hell," grumbled Alastair feeling like he'd been run over by a horse that stomped on his head. He opened his eyes to find his hands and legs tied with rope as he sat on a chair in the cottage. In front of him, the four girls and the lad who stabbed him stood watching with wide eyes. Both the boy and the girl with the strawberry-blond hair held their swords pointed right at him. His sword and weapon belt had been removed and were on the table on the other side of the room. "What did ye do that for, Fia?" He wanted to touch the back of his throbbing head but wasn't able to move his arms.

"I didna want ye to leave before I had the chance to thank ye for buryin' Imanie," Fia told him.

"If that's the way ye thank someone, I will never do a favor for ye again. There was no need to knock me over the head and tie me up."

"You just about strangled poor Branton," Maira snapped. "That is reason enough."

"Reason enough?" Alastair's eyes opened wide in disbelief. "The lad tried to kill me and stole my horse."

"Aye, I did do that," said Branton sheepishly. "But his clan was trying to kill us, so it was done in self-defense."

"Next time ye stab a man in the side and steal his horse, be sure to finish him off," growled Alastair. "If no', ye are always goin' to be lookin' over yer shoulder because he is goin' to come for ye, I promise. Ye'd be wise to remember that."

The tip of Branton's sword lowered. He swallowed forcefully. "I – I have never killed a man before," he admitted.

"And ye still havena," Alastair pointed out. "Now untie me, anon."

"No' until ye promise no' to hurt Branton," said Fia.

"Or us," added Willow.

"Fine, I promise. Now, untie me."

"Dinna do it," warned Morag shaking her head furiously. "He is no' to be trusted."

"He did bury Imanie, just like he promised," Fia reminded her. The girls seemed to consider the situation. "What do ye all think?"

"Don't untie him, or he'll come for me," said Branton, sounding very scared.

"I said I wouldna, so ye have no reason to fear me," Alastair told the boy.

"How can we trust you?" asked Willow, giving him the evil eye.

Alastair looked at one girl after another, and his gaze stopped on the young lad they called Branton. He wanted to kill him for what he'd done, that wasn't a lie. Usually, he wouldn't hesitate to kill any man who wounded him and stole his horse. But this boy was a lad no older than about four and ten years of age. He wasn't even old enough yet to know how to handle a sword, let alone hold it correctly with one hand. Alastair remembered when he was that age. It was the first time he'd killed a man, going to battle with his father and his clan. He was as frightened as Branton looked right now. It wasn't a good feeling at all, but he got numb to it over time.

"I gave ye my word, and I willna break it."

"I believe him," said Fia with a satisfied nod. "He promised to bury Imanie, and he did just that when he could have verra well left on her horse."

He almost did leave, but they didn't need to know that. Part of him was glad he had honored their agreement, but now he started to wonder if he should have left and never even looked back. If so, he wouldn't be in this position right now.

After much deliberation, Fia talked the group into agreeing with her. "We'll untie ye, but first we will pay our last respects to Imanie," she announced.

THE SMALL GROUP made their way to the old woman's gravesite, talking amongst themselves.

"I still don't like the idea of setting a Highlander free," complained Branton. "Especially since I was the one who wounded him and stole his horse. We need to tell Lord Beaufort he's hiding here."

"Nay!" Fia didn't want that to happen. "Alastair kept his word. Now we must keep ours."

"Fia, he's the *enemy*," Willow said, stressing the word enemy.

"Aye. A wounded enemy who moments ago wanted to take off my head," Branton added. "What is this secret garden anyway and how come no one knows about it?"

"Ye canna tell anyone," said Morag. "It is where Imanie trained my sister and cousins and where she met in secret with other members of the group."

"What group?" asked Branton in confusion.

"Morag!" Fia scolded. "Ye werena supposed to tell him that. Now, no more."

"What difference does it make now that Imanie is dead?"

asked Willow. "We'll probably never come to this garden again after today, anyway."

"I'll miss comin' here, and I am goin' to miss Imanie." Fia knelt down, paying her respects to their departed friend.

"So will I," said Maira. "I had so much more to learn."

After a few moments of silence, the group headed back to the cottage. When they walked in, Fia stopped dead in her tracks. The chair was empty, and the ropes that had bound Alastair were lying in a pile on the floor. Her eyes shot over to the table. His weapon belt and sword were gone as well. They had been careless and because of it, he had escaped.

"He's gone!" shouted Maira, pulling her sword from the scabbard at her side, holding it with two hands and turning to look around the room.

"I knew we shouldn't have trusted him." Branton's sword was at the ready as well.

"Where is he?" asked Willow.

A horse neighed loudly from outside. They all ran to the door to see Alastair atop his steed, leaving the secret garden without looking back.

"Well, I guess that's the end of that," said Maira, sliding her sword into the sheath on her back. "He's probably on his way back to Scotland right now."

"I dinna think so." Fia noticed that Alastair didn't turn right when he left the garden, but instead went left, heading down the road that led back to the castle. The only reason he would go that way was to try to help his clansmen escape from the dungeon of Rothbury. She should probably tell the others or at least let the earl know, but something made her keep it a secret instead.

"Where do ye think he went?" asked Morag.

"It doesna matter." Fia didn't want them to alert Lord Beaufort that Alastair was heading to the castle. If Beaufort knew, he would watch for Alastair and kill him when he arrived. "Imanie is gone now and so is Alastair. We need to keep this to ourselves and put it all behind us."

As they exited the secret garden, Fia left behind a good friend in Imanie, and a man who she found very intriguing in Alastair. Imanie was gone forever. But something deep down made her feel as if this wasn't the last she'd seen of Laird Alastair MacPherson.

# CHAPTER 6

*A*lastair rode toward the castle, meaning to free the other clan members. Then he realized that in his condition, he would never be able to do it alone. Instead, he turned and headed through the woods in a hurry, making his way toward the border. After a short while, he heard a twig snap from up ahead and slowed his horse. This was the spot where he'd instructed the rest of his clan to go. He only hoped they were still in the woods and not already heading back to the Highlands without him.

"Clan MacPherson, it is yer chieftain, Alastair," he called out, taking the chance that they were hiding nearby. As he suspected, one by one, his clan emerged from the thicket.

"My laird, ye are alive," shouted Niven, running toward him, followed by more men on foot and others on horseback. "We thought we'd lost ye in the battle, but couldna find yer body."

"Nay, I'm alive but a little worse for wear. What is the death toll of our clan?" he asked.

"We lost six men," announced Earc, one of the members who had never wavered from following Alastair's instructions.

"Aye," added Fearchar, another of his most loyal warriors. "We buried them in the woods and kept lookin' for ye. One of the men said he saw ye struck down, but that ye werena taken prisoner."

"How many do we figure have been captured?" asked Alastair from atop his horse.

"Five men were captured," Niven told him. "But it was only Brohain, Rhodric, and their friends."

"Shall we head back to Scotland now?" asked Earc. "We've heard that King Richard's army is already headin' up the border toward Edinburgh, ransackin' everythin' along the way."

"Nay. We need every man we can get," said Alastair. "We will no' leave before we've rescued the rest of our clan from the dungeon of Castle Rothbury."

"But it was Brohain's fault we are in this position to begin with," complained Fearchar. "I say we leave them there to rot where they belong."

"Enough!" Alastair held his side. The stitches had loosened, and his wound was bleeding again. "We will rescue them just as I would instruct them to do if any of ye were prisoners."

"But my laird, our liaison has told us the English are already pillagin' and burnin' our homeland," Earc explained.

"Then we'll have to move faster." Alastair turned his horse. It felt good to have his steed beneath him once again. "Hopefully, the castle willna be as well guarded if Lord Rothbury and his men have left to fight at their king's side."

"Even still, how are we goin' to get into the castle to set them free?" asked Niven.

Alastair opened his pouch, taking out Fia's bracelet, running his fingers over it in thought. "I have an idea." Fia had told him that she and the other girls would sneak out of the castle to meet Imanie in the secret garden. If there was a secret way out of the castle, then there was a way in as well. "If all goes as planned, we'll be able to walk right in, save the others, and leave before anyone even kens we are there."

* * *

FIA, her sister, and her cousins watched as Lord Beaufort and his men once again prepared to leave the next morning to fight for the king. Now that the Scots were their prisoners, the soldiers and knights planned to join the other English troops in following King Richard into Scotland. Fia guessed they were keeping the Highland prisoners to use in a trade should any of the English be captured during the battle.

"I dinna like it." Fia crossed her arms over her chest and frowned. "They are goin' to fight against my homeland. My family could be in danger."

"Fia, don't worry," Maira told her. "Your father won't let anything happen to your mother and siblings."

"I miss bonnie Scotland, mathair, faither, and our brathairs," Morag told Fia. "I am worried about them, too."

Fia reached out and took Morag's hand. "So am I, Morag. So am I."

As soon as the troops left, a peasant boy came through the gates. He was young and bedraggled. He stopped some of the guards that had been left back to watch the castle, but they only growled and pushed him aside.

"I wonder who that is and what he wants," said Willow.

"I'm goin' to find out." Fia hurried across the courtyard to meet the boy.

"My lady," said the boy. "I am lookin' for someone named Lady Fia."

"That's me," she said in surprise. "Why are ye lookin' for me?"

"I was told to give this to ye and that ye shouldna tell anyone about it. It is a secret." He handed an item wrapped up in a piece of plaid that looked just like that of the MacPherson Clan.

"Who gave this to ye?" She noticed a drop of blood on the plaid as well.

"It was given to me by a Highlander on the road. He said to tell you to meet him in the secret garden and to come alone."

Fia's eyes darted upward. Her heart skipped a beat. Besides the girls and Branton, no but Alastair knew about the secret garden. "Thank ye," said Fia, handing the boy a coin from her pouch. He scooped it up eagerly and then turned and hurried out the gate. Quickly, she unwrapped the parcel, delighted to find her bracelet inside.

Knowing for sure this came from Alastair, she felt leery but excited to possibly see him once again. He must have found her bracelet when she dropped it in the garden. But why did he want to see her and why did he say to come alone? Perhaps his stitches broke open, and he needed her to sew him up again. Her head told her not to go, but her heart made her trust the man. She wanted to be with him again. He was a Scot like her and, right now, she wasn't happy being on this side of the border. Perhaps, if she went to meet Alastair, she could convince him to help protect her family and clan when he headed back to Scotland.

"Fia, who was that?" asked Maira as the girls walked up to join her.

Fia quickly hid the piece of plaid in her pocket, turning around to show them the bracelet.

"Yer bracelet!" exclaimed Morag. "Where did ye find it?"

"That peasant boy gave it to me," she explained.

"Where did he find it and why would he bring it here?" asked Willow suspiciously.

"I gave him a coin, and he was happy," was all she said, turning and walking away.

"Fia, you are up to something." Maira rushed up behind her. "What is going on?"

"Nothin'," she told her cousin, hating to lie, but knowing if she told the girls the truth they would not let her go. "I feel like wearin' my crown today," she told the others. "I am goin' to go back to my chamber to get it."

Fia hurried back to her chamber, getting her crown and placing it on her head. She wanted to look her best when she met with Alastair since he was a laird. She waited until she saw her sister and cousins head to the mews. Then she hurried down to the courtyard and took a horse, bringing it to the postern gate that was well hidden behind the gong pit. No one used this gate anymore, and most people had even forgotten it existed at all. It was covered in vines and hidden in the wall. It was directly behind the gong pit that contained the feces from the garderobes. The area stank horrendously. A new postern gate was built years ago at the east end of the castle.

Fia looked over her shoulder and then found the hidden key and opened the gate. After she went through, she replaced the key behind a loose brick, got on her horse, and headed into the woods to meet Alastair in the secret garden.

* * *

"OVER THERE," said Alastair, pointing to the castle from his hiding position on the ground. Niven and Earc were at his side, while the rest of his men were spread out. They were waiting and watching the outer castle walls. Alastair knew Fia was sneaking out somehow without the guards seeing her. He had to know how she was doing it, and how his men could enter the castle without being seen.

"It's a secret door," said Earc.

"She hid the key behind that brick at the top," added Niven.

"Take the others, get to the dungeon and set the men free," Alastair instructed.

"Do ye really think it's goin' to be that easy?" asked Niven.

"We saw Lord Beaufort and most of the soldiers leave, so the castle willna be well protected," Alastair told them. "Get Brohain and the others and meet me at the border at our designated spot."

"What about ye?" asked Earc. "Where are ye goin' that ye're no' comin' with us?"

"I'm goin' to see Lady Fia once more before we leave."

"Och, ye're no'," said Earc, shaking his head in disagreement. "Why would ye do that? We ken how to sneak in now; ye dinna have to meet with her."

"Nay, I dinna, but I want to. I am a man of my word. If I say I'll do somethin', then I do it."

"Nothin' guid can come from it," said Niven. "My laird, I beg ye no' to go. Let's rescue the others and head over the border to meet with the rest of the clans in our designated spot."

"Aye," agreed Earc. "Richard's army is strong and large. Scotland needs us to join with the others to defeat those stinkin' Sassenachs."

"Just go and do what I told ye," said Alastair, wanting to thank Fia for sewing him up before he left and never saw her again. "I'll only be a moment. Then, I will meet ye there."

With that, Alastair turned and rode toward the secret garden to say thank you and goodbye to the bonnie Scottish lassie. It was the least he could do after she went against the English to help him in the first place.

# CHAPTER 7

$\mathcal{F}$ia rode as fast as she could to the secret garden, hoping to get there and back before her cousins or sister realized she had left. If they found her missing, they were sure to come after her.

They wouldn't agree with her about meeting with the Highlander who had escaped. Fia didn't care. She had to do this. Alastair must need her if he sent the message. Instead of having returned to Scotland, for some reason he was still here.

Fia only hoped she could convince him to stop by the Gordon Clan and help protect her family. She had a bad feeling about the attack by the English and needed all the comfort she could get to know her loved ones and clan would not be in harm's way. But would he do it? She wondered. She could only hope he was thankful enough that he would agree to help her in return.

She entered the secret garden, feeling the dense air all around her. The place was no longer inviting and magical like it was when Imanie was alive. Now, it was gloomy and a little scary as well. The day was dreary. It looked as if it were about to rain. She didn't see Alastair or a horse anywhere. Eyeing the gray clouds overhead, she decided to go back to the castle.

As she turned around, she stopped short, seeing Alastair entering the garden on his horse.

"Alastair," she called out, making her way toward him. "I got the bracelet and the message. Thank ye." She held up her wrist to show him the bracelet that she proudly wore. "How are ye feelin'?"

"My side is sore and some of the stitches need replacin'." So he did need help, just like she thought.

"I can help ye," she said, eagerly hopping off her horse. "Is that why ye sent me the message with the peasant boy?"

ALASTAIR WASN'T PLANNING on telling Fia the real reason he sent the message. Something in her bright green eyes drew him in, making him want to not only see her again, but also kiss her. He had been attracted to the lass since he first saw her in the woods years ago. She wasn't like anyone he'd ever met before. She was brave, yet meek at the same time. And her demeanor told him she wasn't as afraid of him as were her cousins or sister.

"Nay, that's no' why I sent ye the message," he ended up saying. "It's because . . . because I never properly thanked ye for helpin' me."

"Oh. I see. Well, it was the least I could do." She straightened the crown on her head as if she wanted to make sure he saw it. Not that he could miss that big, ornate thing. "After all, ye saved my life as well as returned my crown. Why was that?"

The reason he saved her life years ago, besides not wanting to kill a woman, was because her heart brooch intrigued him. It brought back memories of something that happened to him that raised questions he'd been desperately trying to find the answers to for many years. Nay, he couldn't allow her to be hurt, and he couldn't steal from her either. After his experience, it just wouldn't feel right. "I suppose I was too mesmerized by yer bonnie reid tresses to think straight. My clan dinna agree that I gave back to ye such an expensive item. The amount of coin from the crown alone could have fed our clan for several winters."

Her cheeks looked rosy, and she seemed full of life. "Come. Let me sew up yer wound again. The needle and thread are in the cottage."

Alastair looked over his shoulder toward the gate. His men would be done soon, so he couldn't tarry. There was no telling if Brohain would want to kill Fia again and steal her crown once he saw her here unprotected. Then again, his side did need stitching. Not to mention, he wanted to spend a few more minutes with Fia.

"Aye, but we need to make it fast."

"Why?" asked Fia as they headed for the cottage. "Lord Beaufort and most of his best warriors have already left to help King Richard. They willna bother ye."

"Aye," he said with a nod, not wanting to tell her that at this very minute his men were rescuing the prisoners from her half-guarded dungeon.

"Sit on the bed," she instructed, fetching the needle and thread. She looked around and frowned. "I will need to go to the creek to get water to cleanse yer wound." She started to turn toward the door, but he reached out and took her wrist to stop her.

Bright green eyes stared up at him, her smile disappearing quickly. Perhaps, she still held a little fear toward him after all.

"Dinna worry, I willna hurt ye," he promised. "Just sew me up. We dinna need water."

"If ye're sure," she said, sitting on a chair opposite him to thread the needle. She took the thread between her lush lips and sucked on the end, about driving him out of his mind. He imagined her doing that to him instead. Instantly, he felt his body stir beneath his plaid.

"Where did ye get that crown?" he asked, staring at the top of her head as she bent over and stuck the needle through his skin.

He winced, but held back the pain, not wanting to look weak in her eyes.

"It was once Queen Philippa's. Before she died, she left crowns for me as well as for two of my cousins."

"An English queen left a Scot a crown? I dinna understand."

"There is a little more to it than that," she said, tying a knot and leaning over to break the thread with her teeth.

The smell of lilacs and fresh air wafted from her body, making him want to touch her. Slowly, he reached out and caressed a lock of her long, red hair between his fingers. It felt silky. Desire coursed through him, making him want to smell it too.

She sat up and blinked twice. Her eyes sought out his, holding curiosity as well as a little excitement mixed with fear. Mesmerized by her beauty, his mouth went dry. It was a chore to speak. All he could think of was pulling her into his arms and brushing his lips up against hers.

"Thank ye," he finally managed to spit out.

He noticed her staring at his mouth now, and her reply wasn't above a whisper. "Ye dinna have to thank me. I feel as if I owe it to ye."

She probably could have said anything, and it wouldn't have mattered. He was so taken by this girl that nothing else seemed important than the moment he was spending with her. Then, before he could talk himself out of it, he leaned over and gently pressed his lips against hers.

Like honeyed mead, her mouth tasted sweet. Her lips were as soft as the gossamer wings of a butterfly. Alastair cradled her chin in his hand, not wanting to do anything to hurt her. His thumb brushed against her flushed cheek, her skin feeling hotter than he expected. It was odd, but he swore he felt a connection to this woman, just like he had when he'd saved her life three years ago. It was as if, somehow, they belonged together. Fia was fragile like a child, yet in some ways as strong as a warrior. She seemed to take in every aspect of life, finding the joy in every little thing. Everything about her from the way she talked to the way she blinked held his interest. And she wore that damned heart pin that had haunted his dreams since he'd almost died on the battlefield.

He would have dared to kiss her again if she hadn't lowered her head and turned away.

"What's the matter?" he asked. "Didna ye like that?"

"I did," she said with a shy smile, holding her hand to her mouth. "It was verra nice."

"Fia, I have to say guidbye," he told her, putting his hand on her shoulder. Her back was toward him. She reached up and covered his hand with hers.

"I understand," she said in a breathy whisper. "Ye need to get back to the Highlands where ye belong."

"Ye never told me where yer family resides in Scotland," he said, wondering about her background.

"I am Fia Douglas," she said, turning around.

"Aye. Ye are the daughter of the English king's bastard. I ken."

"My faither was raised as a Douglas, no' knowin' he was spawned by the English king until he was twelve years old. After Burnt Candlemas, he lived with Ross Douglas in the Highlands with the MacKeefes."

"Aye, I ken the MacKeefes. Their chieftain, Storm MacKeefe is well honored throughout the Highlands as well as the Lowlands. So, ye grew up there as well?"

"Nay, I didna. My faither married a Scot. Her name is Maggie Gordon. That is where my family resides now."

"Did ye say Gordon?" he asked, feeling his blood boil just at the mention of the clan's name.

"Aye," she said with a slight smile. Do ye ken the Gordon Clan?"

"Och, I ken them," he said, wanting to spit at hearing the

name. His hands balled into fists. "They are strong allies of Clan Grant."

"Aye, that's right. The Gordons and the Grants are guid friends."

Clan Grant was the clan that the MacPhersons had been feuding with for years. They also held his father, Duncan, in their dungeon in the Highlands right now. Alastair had been trying to rescue him but had been unsuccessful. Everything he ever tried had turned out badly. They had never been able to penetrate the walls of the Grant keep.

"Fia? Fia, are ye here?" came shouting from in the secret garden.

"Losh me, it's Morag," mumbled Fia, running for the door. "I should have kent she'd follow me here."

Fia ran out into the garden with Alastair right behind her. She wasn't happy to see Morag, Willow and Maira, and furious when she realized they brought with them two of the castle guards.

"Morag, what did ye do?" She ran over to meet them as they rode into the garden.

"Fia, we thought ye were in trouble when we found ye missin'," said her sister.

"Nay, ye fool. Why did ye bring the guards to the garden?"

"Don't be angry with her," said Maira. "When the Highlanders snuck into the castle and released the prisoners, a battle broke out."

"What? The prisoners escaped?"

Willow relayed what happened. "Aye, they were rescued by members of their clan that snuck in through the old postern gate. When they left and we couldn't find you, we figured you might have come here."

"The guards wouldna let us leave without them. We had no

choice, Fia." Morag had tears in her eyes. "I'm sorry, but we were worried about ye and had to do it."

"Get him," said one of the guards to the other.

"Nay! Leave Alastair alone." Fia turned around to find Alastair atop his horse and leaving through the garden gate.

"Follow him and kill him," commanded one of the guards.

"Nay!" Fia shouted again. She ran to her horse and mounted and rode out of the garden in front of the soldiers. Alastair was just up ahead. As she caught up, more guards led by Branton appeared in the woods, blocking his escape.

"There he is. Just like I told you." Branton, the traitor, led the way toward the secret garden.

"You should never have left the savage before you were sure he was dead," snapped George, one of the sentries that had been left to guard the castle while Lord Beaufort and his men went to fight for the king. "Men, finish the job and kill him now."

"Wait! Dinna hurt him." Fia rode to Alastair's side. Alastair was trapped with men all around him and no way to escape. Just as the guards moved toward him, Alastair drew his sword with one hand and reached over and grabbed Fia with the other. He pulled her in front of him atop his horse and held the cold steel to her throat.

"Move aside, or I'll slit her throat," spat Alastair.

In too much shock to speak, Fia kept silent. How could Alastair act this way after she'd helped him and trusted him? This couldn't be happening.

"Lower your blade, Highlander," commanded another of the guards named Roger.

"Move aside, or I'll kill her, I swear I will," shouted Alastair.

"Please dinna let him hurt my sister," shouted Morag from behind her.

"You aren't going to hurt her, and we're not letting you go," answered George. "It is my job to protect Lord Beaufort's wards while he is away."

"If I kill her, ye'll have the bastard triplets huntin' ye down like dogs for lettin' anythin' happen to her," said Alastair.

The guard hesitated for a moment and then mumbled something to Roger. He raised his hand in the air. "Let him pass," commanded George, not wanting to risk it.

With the blade still pressed up against her throat, Alastair directed his horse around the Englishmen and took off at a full gallop.

Fia held on to her crown as they rode away. Glancing over her shoulder, tears formed in her eyes as she saw her sister and cousins crying. Why was Alastair acting this way? She realized he was doing it to save his life. But when the English could no longer be seen behind him, she didn't understand why he didn't let her go.

"Release me," she commanded, struggling against him.

He lowered his blade but held her tightly around her waist. "I canna do that, lass."

"The guards are no longer followin' us. Let me down."

"Nay. Now that I ken who ye are, ye are much too valuable to leave behind."

"What do ye mean?" she asked. "Is it because my faither is the bastard of the late king?"

"Nay. It is because ye are a stinkin' Gordon, the clan who was once aligned with the MacPhersons but left to team up with the traitorous Clan Grant instead! The Grants are the ones holdin' my faither prisoner."

"I dinna understand."

"Ye are my assurance that my faither will be set free. A little trade is just what I need." He slowed the horse and replaced his sword into the sheath strapped to his back. Then he plucked the crown from her head.

"Give me that," she spat, reaching for the crown, but he wouldn't release it.

"I think this would be safer off yer head for the trip." He

reached down and shoved the crown into the travel bag. Then his arm closed around her, holding her tightly up against him.

"I'm to be a hostage then?" This thought surprised and appalled her at the same time. Never had she thought she'd be in this position.

"Ye are more than a hostage. Ye are my answer to all my troubles. I'll no' only get my faither returned now, but will earn the respect of the rest of my clan."

"Yer clan doesna care about ye, or they would never have left ye behind."

"Dinna be so sure about that." Alastair stopped his horse, looked around, and put his fingers in his mouth and whistled. Out of nowhere, a clan of Highlanders appeared, surrounding him. To her dismay, Brohain and the rest of the escaped prisoners led the way.

## CHAPTER 8

"What is she doin' here?" snarled Brohain. "We should have killed her three years ago when I wanted to the first time."

"No one is harmin' a hair on this lass's head," warned Alastair. "She is under my protection until we get back to the Highlands."

"The Highlands?" asked Earc. "We need to fight against Richard and his troops. I've heard from a traveler on the road that Richard's army passed through this area days ago and are movin' up the coast at a good clip. They even have ships with more troops at every port."

"We'll head north, but I'm no' stoppin' until we reach the Highlands. This lass is goin' to be a trade to the Grants for the release of my faither."

"Why would they want her? She's a stinkin' Sassenach," spat Rhodric.

"I am no'," protested Fia, raising her chin proudly. "I am a Scot."

"Half-Scot, or did ye forget?" Alastair reminded her. "Yer faither might think he's a Scot, but he is nothin' more than the bastard of the late English king and the king's English mistress."

"Ye willna get away with this," cried Fia.

"On the contrary, ye have nothin' to say about it," Alastair told her. "And it will work like a charm. I do believe my luck is changin'."

"I trusted ye, Alastair MacPherson! I helped ye, and now ye are treatin' me like a prisoner? How could ye? I thought our kiss meant somethin'."

"Ye kissed her?" Earc asked in disgust.

"Never mind," growled Alastair. "Now, let's get goin' before the English decide to follow us. I am in no condition for a fight." His hand went to his wounded side again before he took off toward the border holding tightly to Fia to make sure she wouldn't fall . . . or try to escape.

\* \* \*

THEY RODE ALL DAY, making it over the border, stopping for the night on the banks of the River Tweed.

"We'll camp here," Alastair called out, halting his men. In the distance toward the coast, smoke could be seen billowing up into the air. Fia listened closely. She was sure she could hear the sounds of shouting and fighting way off in the distance.

"Somethin's burnin'," said Fia. Alastair reached out for her and lifted her from the horse.

"That is the land burnin'," he told her.

"Richard must be pillagin' and burnin' his way up the coast."

"Nay, lass. The Scots set those fires."

"Why would the Scots burn their own land? That makes no sense." Fia studied the smoke in the distance, thinking about the safety of her family.

"They are burnin' the land to starve out the English to make them leave Scotland," Niven explained.

"That's right," added Alastair. "If our enemy canna find food, the troops willna stay and fight."

"How close are we to West Lothian?" asked Fia.

Alastair studied her face as he answered. "Not far. Why?"

"That's where my family lives. I want to see them."

"Ye said ye are a Gordon. Clan Gordon is in the Highlands."

"Yes, but no' all of them. There is a small sept of the Gordon Clan in the Lowlands. That is where my family resides. Can we pass through to make sure they are safe?"

"Nay, we canna do such a daft thing. I dinna trust ye willna try to escape. Dinna ye understand?" spat Alastair. "My clan has been feudin' with the Grants for years. Yer clan has betrayed us by makin' an alliance with the enemy. The Grants captured my faither and have taken him prisoner in their dungeon."

"I'm sorry about that, but I assure ye my family has nothin' to do with it," Fia protested. "Ye canna hold it against them."

"Either way, we are no' goin' anywhere near yer home. Now stay close because I dinna want to have to chase ye in the dark. And dinna even think about escapin', because it is no' safe out there with the English army so close."

"What are ye goin' to do to me?" she asked, eyeing up the rest of the clan. She didn't trust any of them. Not even Alastair since he'd abducted her.

"I'm no' goin' to do anythin' to ye. Just the same, I'd stay close if I were ye. I canna guarantee the rest of my men are as honorable as me."

"Honorable?" she snorted. "If ye were honorable, ye wouldna have taken me captive. Or ye would have at least set me free once ye realized the English were no longer followin' us."

"Fia, please. It is better if ye keep quiet. I need to think."

Fia stayed close to Alastair as nightfall covered the land. She wasn't exactly sure where they were and couldn't risk sneaking off, hoping to find her home. As Alastair said, there was a war going on. Plus, it sounded as if he didn't even trust his own men, so why should she?

The Scots eyed her up and down. Several of them made some

crude remarks about what they'd like to do with her, and she tried to ignore it. Later, as they sat around the fire consuming the last of the hare and pheasant, she decided she needed to push her fear aside, just like Imanie would have told her to do.

Fia's heart ached for Imanie. Every time she closed her eyes, all she could see was Imanie's dead body crumpled up on the ground. Her thoughts drifted back to her lessons over the years. The old woman helped her sharpen her skill of observation to find out anything she wanted to know about anyone. It was easy now that she knew how.

*"Try it again, Fia," Imanie told her, sitting back in her chair, looking up to the sky. "I will say something, and you tell me if it is a lie or not."*

*"All right, I'm ready."*

*"I like . . . beets," Imanie said, touching her nose as she spoke.*

*"Nay," Fia said with a smile. "Ye touched yer nose when ye said it, so it is a lie."*

*"Very good. And what does it mean when someone stands with their arms crossed over their chest like this?" She folded her arms in front of her.*

*"It means they are disagreeable or defensive."*

*"That's right." Imanie, got out of the chair. "And what about this stance?" She stood up straight with her shoulders back.*

*"That means ye are confident," Fia answered.*

*"And this?" Imanie opened her hands at her sides with her palms facing forward.*

*"Besides showin' ye dinna have a weapon, it depicts honesty and sincerity."*

*Imanie smiled. "You are a fast learner, Fia. Plus, you notice things that others don't even see. Someday you will be able to use this skill to benefit you. But remember not to get distracted. If you do, you might miss something of importance that could cost you your life."*

# CHAPTER 9

*A*lastair awoke early the next morning, wanting to meet with his men before Fia noticed. He'd barely slept a wink, trying to keep an eye on her. His men were looking at her in lust. He didn't like that.

"Alastair, why in God's name did ye wake us so early?" complained Brohain, coming to join the rest of them quite far from the fire. "The sun hasna even risen yet."

"Aye," added Rhodric. "I'd rather be curled up on a blanket by the fire with the wench."

Alastair looked over his shoulder at Fia. She was sleeping with the blanket wrapped around her and had one leg sticking out. Her gown rode up, showing off her long, lean leg covered by her hose. "Concentrate on our mission," Alastair commanded. "Is everyone here? I need to go over our plan."

FIA'S EYES fluttered open at the sound of Alastair's deep voice. Quickly scanning the area, she realized it was not yet daybreak. All the men were gathered at the edge of camp talking softly.

103

Straining her ears trying to hear them, she could only make out bits and pieces of what they said.

Then the wind shifted, and she was able to hear every word. Through partially closed eyes she watched as well as listened. They'd moved far from the fire for their meeting, and that told her they were discussing plans that they didn't want her to hear.

"Earc rode out durin' the night to meet with one of our informants," Alastair told the men in a low voice. "We have the update on the battle."

"What did ye find out?" asked Fearchar.

"The English are pushin' the Scots up the coast and gettin' closer to Edinburgh," Niven relayed the information.

"But we've got the French helpin' us," said one of the men in the clan. "We dinna need to worry."

"No' true," said Alastair. "The French only give us an extra thousand soldiers. Our sources say Richard has over nine thousand archers and nearly forty-six hundred men-at-arms. Our own king, Robert, is planning an ambush, but he kens as well as us that we are no match for those stinkin' Sassenachs, even with our French alliance."

"That's right," agreed Fearchar. "They moved faster than we thought. Our only hope is the ambush with the Highlanders waitin' for the English in Fife."

"How do we ken the English will go to Fife?" asked Niven.

Earc answered. "Richard is a boy. He doesna have half the bloodlust of his grandfaither. But his uncle, John of Gaunt, will push him to move toward Fife. I have received word from our contact that John has already suggested it."

"Then we need to move north quickly," Alastair told them.

"We're no' goin' to stay and fight?" asked Brohain, crossing his arms over his chest. Fia recognized the man's position as an act of defiance.

"Brohain, ye ken the plan," Alastair reminded him. "We canna go against our king's wishes. We are to spy and find out all we can and bring back word to the Highland clans waitin' in Fife. Are ye goin' to give me trouble?"

Brohain scratched his nose as he answered. "Nay, of course no', my laird."

Fia's heart beat faster. He touched his nose when he answered! That meant he lied and was going to cause trouble for Alastair after all. Then she spied Brohain and his sidekick, Rhodric, with their fists clenched at their sides. That told her they weren't going to be open to Alastair's ideas. She didn't need to hear their words because their body actions said it all.

"Guid," answered Alastair, sounding as if he believed him. "Pack up quickly. We need to move out and head to the Highlands."

"We havena eaten yet," complained one of the men.

"We'll stop along the way and eat later." Alastair ran a weary hand through his hair. "I need to get back to the Highlands quickly." Worry showed on his wrinkled brow.

"Ye said I, no' we," Brohain pointed out. "This all has to do with that wretched wench, doesna it?"

Alastair turned to look at Fia. She quickly squeezed her eyes closed hoping he hadn't seen her watching them.

"Fia is a bonnie cailin, no' a wretched wench," Alastair told his men.

She smiled inwardly at hearing him say this.

"Ye said she was a hostage to exchange for yer faither," said Rhodric. "Now ye sound as if ye are smitten with the lass."

Fia's eyes opened slightly as she waited for Alastair's response. "Nay, I'm no' smitten, just concerned. We can use her to bargain so the Grants will release my faither. She means naught else to me but the answer to all my problems."

Fia's heart sank in her chest. This wasn't what she wanted to hear. But then Alastair pinched the bridge of his nose and pushed back his hair with one hand. He lied! His body actions just made it clear to her that she meant something to him after all and he didn't want his men to know it.

She rolled over and smiled. So, the laird of Clan MacPherson was attracted to his prisoner. That kiss they'd shared in the secret garden meant something to him even if he denied it. Perhaps she wasn't the only prisoner here. If he was a prisoner of his emotions, she could use that to her advantage.

That pleased her. The part that bothered her was the battle going on between the English and the Scots. She had the blood of both sides flowing through her veins. Fia didn't want her family or her friends killed. Richard was her half-cousin so, by right, he was family, too. He was young like her and didn't deserve to die either. She was fond of her cousin, though she didn't know him well. Once a year while being fostered by Lord Beaufort, she and her cousins would visit with the young king. Richard had always been pleasant to them although he didn't care for Fia's father or uncles.

"Get up," she heard, turning over to see Alastair's tall body looming over her. The early morning rays of sun coming up on the horizon shone from behind him, casting a sheen around his body and illuminating his dark hair. He looked tired. Stubble peppered his jaw. Seeing his mussed hair made her want to run her hands through it to fix it. "We need to go."

"Where are we goin'?" she asked, pretending not to know. She sat up, stretched and yawned.

"Dinna play games with me, lass. I ken ye heard us talkin'. I saw ye watchin' us through yer half-closed eyes."

"Blethers! Then why dinna ye have yer secret meetin's in front of me from now on instead of tryin' to keep things from me?"

"Fine. I will." He grabbed her arm and pulled her to her feet. "Ye are my prisoner, and I am goin' to exchange ye for my faither who is bein' held by the Grants."

"I ken that. But it isna goin' to work."

"What do ye mean?" He walked over and dumped water over the fire to douse it, and then started kicking dirt atop it.

"Clan Grant barely even kens me," she told him, hoping he would believe it. "They willna want me, so yer plan willna work." The Grants knew her well, but she didn't want Alastair to find out. Also, the MacKeefes and the Douglas Clans were close friends of her father since they had been a big part of his life. Most of the Lowland clans of Scotland knew her, too, since she was a daughter of one of the Legendary Bastards of the Crown. They admired and respected Reed Douglas for being the only one of the three brothers who refused to pay homage to the late King Edward, staying loyal to Scotland instead.

"We'll see about that." He released her and took a step backward, moving away from her. That told Fia he didn't believe her story. Perhaps she wasn't going to be able to fool him the way some of his clan members were. She wanted to tell him that some of his men were lying, but didn't think this was the place or time since his men were watching her every move. "Get on the horse," he commanded.

Before she had a chance to move, his hands were around her waist, and he hoisted her up into the saddle. She landed with a plop, having to grab on to the horse's mane to keep from going over the other side. He was strong, and she was sure he could be quite forceful.

He swung his body up behind her, gripping her around the waist with one arm. With his other arm, he reached around her and took the reins.

Her body warmed being pushed up against him. Her cheeks tingled with blood flowing to her face, making it hard to breathe. He was her captor, so why did she like the feel of being held tightly in his embrace?

"Let's move on out," he commanded, turning his horse and speaking to his men.

"Wait!" cried Fia. Her hand flew to her head while her eyes

scanned the ground where she'd slept last night. "My crown. I need to find my crown."

"Relax," he whispered in her ear. His breath tickled the small hairs at the back of her neck. "Did ye forget I've got it in the travel bag attached to the horse?"

"I dinna want yer men to steal it."

"If anyone is takin' it as a token of war, I assure ye it'll be me."

"A token of war? But, I'm no' the enemy!"

"The crown is from English nobility, is it no'?"

"Ye ken it is. I told ye it was given to me by the late Queen Philippa."

"The Queen of England," he stated.

"Aye. Of course."

"I prove my point."

"I'm no' the enemy," she said once again.

"Ye're a Gordon and aligned with the Grants who are enemies of the MacPhersons. So that makes ye my enemy after all."

"Then why did ye kiss me?" she spat.

"I kissed ye because . . . because ye sewed up my wound," he said, though she didn't believe that was the only reason. "And it was before I kent who ye really were."

"I did nothin' to ye or yer clan. Do no' blame me for yer misfortune."

"Nay, that's no' true, lass," he said, directing his horse into a gallop, leading the way to the Highlands.

"What did I do?"

He didn't answer but only mumbled something under his breath. She would have to ask him about it later.

# CHAPTER 10

"Richard's troops are approachin' Edinburgh," Brohain announced as he rode back to camp with Rhodric later that day. They were the scouts that Alastair had sent on ahead to spy on the English troops pillaging the coast.

Alastair jumped up, meeting them halfway. "How close are they?" he asked anxiously. He glanced over his shoulder to see Fia watching them. Something told him not to let her hear them, but there wasn't much he could do to stop it. He didn't want her out of his sight. They were nearing West Lothian where her family lived, and he wouldn't put it past her to try to escape and go home.

"They're no' a half-hour's ride from here," said Rhodric. "I say we join the Lowlanders waitin' in the shadows and run those bastards through with our claymores now and no' wait for the ambush."

"Nay," said Alastair, pacing back and forth. His eyes wandered back to Fia. He had to get her far away from Richard and his troops. They were too close to the fighting, and he didn't want anything to happen to her. She was his only means of getting his father released. A half-hour's ride west and she would be home. A half-hour's ride east, and she'd be with the English. The king being her cousin had him worried. He questioned Fia's loyalties, since she had connections with both sides. He decided to head back home to Aberdeenshire as fast as possible because he didn't want to be around either place right now.

"We will leave for Cluny Castle anon. We'll make one stop at the Iron Eagle to pass on the information to our contact to take to our king. Then we're goin' home." He raised his hand in the air to get the rest of his clan's attention. "Move on out. We have no time to waste."

FIA OVERHEARD EVERYTHING ONCE AGAIN. Sitting on a log finishing off a piece of bannock, she studied Alastair's stance and disposition. He stroked his chin as he talked with his men. He was contemplating a decision. Something had him upset, and it was more than just the fact the English were attacking. She'd noticed the way he'd glanced sideways over his shoulder several times to make sure she was still there. Plus, he paced a lot today and dragged his hand through his hair more than usual. That told her he had a lot on his mind and wasn't sure of his decision. He was worried. It had something to do with her, she was sure of it.

He came back to his horse and tied the travel bag to the side. The bulge within the bag let her know her crown was still safe and secure.

"We're leavin', are we no'?"

"Aye." He hoisted her up into the saddle, not saying another word. It wasn't until he mounted behind her and wrapped one arm around her waist that she dared to speak.

"I want to go home. I ken we are close to my family. I demand ye drop me off where I belong."

His arm stiffened and he held her tighter. Aye, he was afraid she was going to escape.

"I told ye, that is no' goin' to happen. Now, I willna hear another word from ye about it."

All hope seemed lost as the clan headed north. In the distance, the sound of shouting was heard. Billowing tendrils of smoke filled the air. She was so close to freedom but yet so far away. There was no way Alastair was going to give her a chance to escape. Nay, she would have to find another way to get back home. Fia was only one woman but felt the weight of the world upon her shoulders right now. Having overheard the plan about the Highlanders waiting to ambush Richard and his troops in Fife, it worried her. If that happened, the Scots would have the advantage of surprise, and there was going to be a very deadly battle. Her gut twisted. She had to stop it somehow. No matter what happened, people she loved were going to be killed. Somehow, she had to get word to Richard to warn him before a bloody battle ended the lives of many English as well as Scots. Her only hope was that Richard would retreat and take his troops back to England before things went too far.

* * *

ALASTAIR FOUND it hard to think straight with Fia's long, soft, red hair blowing in the breeze and brushing against his cheek. Her feminine essence warmed him in ways that made him want to stop and bed her around every curve in the road. But he couldn't do that. If so, he wouldn't be any better than the rest of the lust-filled men of his clan.

He needed to concentrate on his mission and keep his mind from going astray. But if he didn't make a little distance between him and Fia soon, this was never going to work.

"There's the Iron Eagle," said Alastair, stopping his horse out front of the two-story tavern that had rooms upstairs and also served as an inn. "We'll stop here for the night," he told his men.

"For the night?" asked Niven in confusion. "We still have a few good hours of sunlight left. Shouldna we keep ridin'?"

"Nay," Alastair answered, slipping out of the saddle and helping Fia to dismount. Damn, her small waist and the curve of her hips under his hands were driving him mad. "I have set it up to meet our contact here who will take the message to the Highlanders waitin' in Fife. I'll pass on the information to the courier and first thing in the mornin' we will head home."

"I still think we should stay and fight," complained Brohain, always disagreeing with Alastair, and always wanting a battle.

"If it's fightin' ye want, ye'll get it when we rescue my faither from the Grants."

"Fight?" asked Fia. "I thought ye said I was to be a trade. Why would there be fightin' involved?"

"Ye are a means to the release of my faither." Alastair untied the travel bag from the horse. "However, I highly expect the Grants to stab us in the back."

"Ye dinna trust anyone, do ye?"

"Should I?" His eyes drilled deeply into big, round, green orbs. He wasn't sure he could trust her, and she knew it. The lass wasn't shy about staring him boldly in the eye. He had never met anyone like her. The way she met his perusal in challenge, not looking away, made him feel exposed and naked. It was almost as if she could see into his very soul, knowing all his secrets.

"I'm hungry," he said, looking the other way, wanting to break the connection. If she continued to look at him like that, it was going to make him vulnerable, and he couldn't allow that. He had never let a lassie get that close to him before. This one drew him in, as well as rattled his nerves. "We'll get food inside as well as a room for the night." Alastair slung the travel bag over his shoulder. With his hand at the small of Fia's back, he guided her into the tavern. Inside the doorway sat a burly man on a tall wooden stool. He held his open palm out, waiting for the charge required to enter the tavern. Alastair pulled several coins from the small pouch attached to his waist belt and handed them to the man.

"This is for my entire travelin' party, includin' the girl," he said. "And there is an extra coin for a room for the night." The man nodded, satisfied, and let them pass.

"Oh, guid, I wouldna mind sleepin' on a pallet tonight instead of the hard ground," said Niven, following at Alastair's heels. A broad smile spread across his face.

"The rest of ye will sleep outside," grumbled Alastair. "I'll be the only one stayin' with the lass to make sure she doesna escape."

Protests went up from the clan members as they entered the Iron Eagle behind them, having heard Alastair's announcement.

FIA WASN'T sure what to think about what she'd just heard. Sharing a room and, perhaps, a pallet for the night with Alastair had her mind soaring. Would he try to kiss her again? Or would he want to take her like a lover in the night? Either way, the thought excited and frightened her at the same time. The man was handsome. She felt attracted to him, but he was her captor. And according to him, they were enemies.

"Alastair, welcome back," called out an older woman, rushing over to greet them when she noticed Alastair walk into the room. Her long, graying hair was in a braid, over one shoulder. Dressed in a plain gown covered by a leather apron, she looked to perhaps be the proprietor's wife. She was tall for a woman. By the way she walked with her back straight and her gliding steps, it seemed to Fia she was someone with confidence and was to be respected.

"Lorraine." Alastair nodded, his eyes scanning the room as he spoke. He reminded Fia of a wild animal constantly scoping out the area with his perusal, always expecting trouble. "Have ye seen Fergus in here at all?"

"Aye, he just arrived," she told him. "He's out back tending to his horse and talking with my husband."

"Hello, I am Fia." If Alastair was going to be rude and not introduce her, Fia decided she would do it herself.

"Hello." The woman's eyes settled on Fia's heart pin attached to her bodice. Fia's eyes darted back to Lorraine. The woman brushed aside her braid, exposing the same pin attached to her gown.

Fia's jaw dropped. She started to comment on it when the woman replaced her braid over the pin and headed in the opposite direction.

"Niven!" Alastair called out. "Watch over the lass until I return. And get us some food." He set the travel bag down on a vacated table that wasn't even cleaned yet and started toward the back door.

"Aye, my laird." Niven hurried over, his eyes fastened to Fia. This was going to make any chance of escape impossible.

"And Niven," Alastair called over his shoulder. "Dinna take yer eyes off of her even for a minute."

"Aye, my laird."

Fia settled herself on the bench as Niven did the same on the opposite side of the table. He was an odd-looking boy, short but with a long neck. His blond hair was fair yet his brown eyes so dark that they seemed to contradict each other. He had a large, curved nose that reminded her of the beak of a raptor. When he smiled, she saw what looked like twice as many teeth than she expected him to have. He leaned forward on his elbows with his eyes fixated on her. It made her feel uncomfortable since it was more than evident that the boy liked her.

Fia surveyed the tavern area of the building, noticing the stairway that led to the upstairs rooms. The place wasn't nearly as dirty or stale-smelling as some of the places she'd visited through the years, traveling with her father and then the earl. Nay, the rushes on the floor looked as if they'd been changed recently, and they smelled faintly from rosemary and mint. The tables and benches, though old and rugged, were sturdy and in good shape. She noticed the woman named Lorraine watching her from the other side of the room. Needing to talk to her to find out why she had a heart pin, Fia had to find a way to get rid of Niven first. Perhaps this woman was one of the members of the late queen's secret group. If so, this would be a stroke of good luck.

"Niven, I see a servin' boy with tankards of ale over at the drink board on the other side of the room. Can ye get me some ale? I am verra thirsty."

"I am sure he will be here soon." Niven continued to stare at her. "Laird Alastair told me to keep my eyes on ye at all times."

Och, this wasn't going to be easy. The lad was taking his job to the extreme, not even looking away for a moment. "I am no' goin' anywhere," she said, flashing him a smile. "I just really need somethin' to drink."

When it didn't seem as if he were going to leave, she faked a cough and then another pretending as if she were choking. He jumped up. But instead of heading over to the drink board, he patted her on the back with short, sharp slaps. She groaned inwardly, making eye contact with Lorraine again. Alastair would return at any minute, and she was desperate. Not wanting to have to revert to this tactic, she decided she had no other choice. She batted her eyelids and flirted with the boy like her cousin would do.

"Can ye please get me some ale? I would be ever so grateful." She used a high, sing-song voice the way Willow did whenever she wanted something from a man.

"Oh." He sat up straighter, seeming surprised by her action. "Well, I suppose I can keep an eye on ye from across the room."

It worked! Niven left the table. It made her feel sick to her stomach to use this tactic, but it didn't matter right now since it bought her a little time. Now, with Niven out of the way, she would have a chance to talk to Lorraine. She motioned the woman over with a nod of her head.

Lorraine came to the table to clean it. There were still empty mugs and trenchers of half-eaten bread from the last occupants left there.

"Who are ye?" asked Fia. "I saw yer brooch and it is the same as mine."

"Shhh. Keep your voice low." Lorraine's eyes scanned the area as she picked up the dirty dishes and loaded them into a large wooden bucket. "I have worked for the late queen for many years."

"Ye're English," said Fia.

"I am, but I married a Scot. Scotland is my home now. I am surprised to see you. Since the queen died, I didn't think that Imanie was training anyone new."

"I am Fia, daughter of one of the Legendary Bastards of the Crown."

"You are?" The woman's eyebrows lifted. She stood up straight. "Ah, with that red hair I assume you are Reed's daughter."

"Yes, I am. I, as well as two of my cousins, have been trained by Imanie. It was the late queen's wish, but we didna find out until we heard it from King Edward on his deathbed. He is the one that gave us the brooches." Her hand covered her heart pin as she spoke.

"How is Imanie?" asked the woman, running a rag over the old, wooden table.

"She's dead."

Lorraine's hand stopped. She spoke without looking up. "Then it truly is the end of the Followers of the Secret Heart."

"Nay, I dinna think so. It will live on as long as there are members."

"I will always be here if you should need me," Lorraine promised.

"Well, I do need yer help. Do ye have a way to get a message to King Richard?"

The woman's eyes snapped upward and her brows squeezed together as she studied Fia's face. "What are you saying?"

After making sure Niven was still occupied, Fia leaned forward and whispered. "I have heard that the Scots are plannin' to ambush the English. They have an alliance with the French and are goin' to surprise Richard. The Highlanders along with Lowlanders have joined together to fight. They have burned their own land to take food from their attackers, and have been lyin' low, waitin' for Richard to cross over into Fife."

"Richard's men are already in Edinburgh," Lorraine told her with trepidation in her voice. "I have heard just this morning they started burning Holy Rood. John of Gaunt is power-hungry and loves a battle. I am sure they will head to Fife next."

"I want to stop them from goin' there," Fia explained.

The woman leaned in closer. Her eyes narrowed, and her words were stern. "Our job is to bring about changes by making men think they thought of the idea. This is out of our control. There is no way one woman can make a difference if a battle takes place or not. You are crazy if you think you can influence the outcome."

"I only need to get a message to my cousin, King Richard. He is no' the warrior his grandfaither was. If he kens his army is about to be slaughtered, there's a chance he might turn around and head back to England."

"Mayhap the boy doesn't have as much bloodlust in his veins as his father or grandfather, but don't forget John of Gaunt is his uncle and still advises him. He will want to raid the whole country if he can. I know him personally. He is as ruthless as he is unpopular even amongst his own people."

"But Richard is the king and gives the commands," Fia protested. "I am sure if we can get the message to him, he will reconsider. Do ye have a way to do this?"

The woman's eyes lowered to the table. She sighed and nodded slightly. "I do have the means, but I don't think it will work. How do we know he will believe it and not think it isn't just a trick?"

"Richard trusts me. He will ken if the message comes from me then it is true."

"There is no way to prove to him that the warning has come from you. It will not work, so forget it. It is too dangerous of a plan."

When Lorraine stood up and looked as if she were going to walk away, Fia reached out and locked her fingers around the woman's wrist.

"Wait! I ken how we can get him to believe the message came from me."

"How?"

Fia reached over and opened the travel bag, letting the woman see the crown within. "This is my proof."

Lorraine peered into the bag. "Is that the late Queen Philippa's crown?"

"Aye, it is. And Richard kens it well. He has wanted it ever since it was given to me as a child. If ye get the message to him along with this crown, he will ken it came from me. Then he will heed my warnin'."

Lorraine pulled back her hand and shook her head. "Nay. There is no way to sneak something like that out of here without Alastair knowing it is gone. You're his prisoner, aren't you?"

"I'm to be a trade for his imprisoned faither. Clan Grant has him locked in their dungeon. They have been feudin' for years."

"Then you'd better not anger Alastair. I have seen the temper he holds at bay, and it is not pretty."

"I have to do this," said Fia. "I owe it to Philippa. I canna let so many of the Scots or the English die needlessly. Ye are English and married to a Scot. Surely, ye can understand how I feel?"

The woman hesitated before she answered. "I do understand, Fia. You are right. I will do it." Her eyes darted back and forth. "Sneak the crown into my bucket with the dirty dishes. Fast. No one is looking."

Fia's hands shook as she quickly removed the crown and placed it into the bucket, covering it with scraps of food and empty drinking vessels. "We'll need to replace it with somethin' or Alastair is goin' to notice the bulge in the pack is gone."

"Use this." Lorraine handed her a round of half-eaten bread along with an empty tankard.

Fia shoved them into the travel bag and quickly closed them inside.

"Thank ye, Lorraine. Because of ye, we might have just saved the lives of those we love."

"There isn't much of a chance that this will work, but we have to try. Although, it is very risky."

"It is a risk I am willin' to take."

"Me too." Lorraine stood up straight and lifted her chin. Her stance told Fia she was confident now. "I can see why the late queen chose you. Philippa would have been very proud of you, Fia. But I am worried about your safety when Alastair finds out what you did."

"Dinna worry. I think I can keep him from noticin' the crown is missin' until we get to the Highlands. And by then, it will be too late to do anythin' about it."

"Good luck," said Lorraine.

"The same to ye." Fia smiled. "I am sure Philippa would be proud of both of us. I am happy to have met ye, Lorraine."

"Fia, here is yer ale." Niven squeezed around Lorraine and plunked three tankards of ale down on the table. "I brought one for Alastair and myself as well."

"Have ye been watchin' her?" asked Alastair, approaching the table at the same time.

"Aye my laird," answered Niven.

119

Alastair picked up a tankard of ale and downed it in three gulps. Lorraine turned away.

"Wait, Lorraine! Dinna go anywhere," Alastair commanded.

"My lord?" Lorraine stopped and looked back over her shoulder. Fia held her breath. Had he seen them talking and did he know what she did?

"Put this in yer bucket as well." He handed her the empty vessel. "Bring me a bottle of whisky instead."

"Of course." Lorraine took the cup and added it to the top of the bucket, using it to help hide the crown. Her eyes interlocked with Fia's.

Fia's heart lodged in her throat. Alastair slid onto the bench next to her. "And hurry up with that food. I am tired and have secured a room for the night. I am anxious to get some shut eye."

"Right away," Lorraine answered and nodded to Fia. Then she quickly left the table.

Fia let out a sigh of relief. The plan was working so far. Now, all she had to do was to keep Alastair from looking into the travel bag until they got to the Highlands. Hopefully, by then, the English will have turned around and the deadly battle would not take place after all.

## CHAPTER 11

"*N*iven, watch over the horses tonight and dinna bother me unless there is a problem." Alastair pushed the empty bowl from the pottage to the middle of the table. He stretched and yawned and stood up.

"Problem, my lord? Like what?" asked Niven.

"If Brohain and Rhodric do anythin' suspicious, tell me. I still canna trust those two."

"Aye, my laird. Should I alert ye for anythin' else?"

"Nay. Dinna be knockin' at the door unless the English are burnin' the place down." He reached over the table for the travel bag, but Fia snatched it up before he could grab it.

"I've got the bag," she said, standing up, clutching the thing to her chest.

"Why are ye actin' so odd?" he asked, thinking she seemed a little nervous.

"Odd? I'm no' actin' odd." She flashed a smile and yawned. "I am tired as well."

"This way," he said, guiding her to the stairs.

"I think I need to relieve myself outside first."

"Ye're no' goin' alone with all these men watchin' ye like bulls in heat. I'm comin' with ye."

"Nay." She put her hand on his chest. "I see Lorraine. I will have her keep watch. I'll be right back."

He noticed Brohain and Rhodric staring and talking behind their hands. Matter of fact, everyone in the place was looking at Fia. He didn't like it. The idea of letting her out of his sight bothered him, but it was probably better that another woman went with her. Lorraine was a tough lassie and had even hit him over the head with a pitcher once when she thought he was being fresh with her. She wouldn't let anything happen to Fia.

"All right, but if ye're gone longer than two minutes, I am comin' after ye. And dinna even think to try to escape because, if so, I will be right on yer tail."

"Well, I wouldna want that to happen, would I?"

"Wait! Give me the travel bag," he called out, but she kept going and didn't even turn around.

"Lorraine," said Fia, clutching the bag, looking over her shoulder to make sure Alastair wasn't watching. "Quickly, step outside with me."

Lorraine grabbed her cloak and a bag off the hook and walked out back with Fia.

"I'll set up the exchange and meet my contact, giving her the crown and the message for Richard," Lorraine explained, heading over to her horse.

"Her? Is it another lassie taught by Imanie?"

"It is better if you don't know too much." Lorraine tied the bag containing the crown to the side of her horse and then mounted. "This will have to go through several people before actually getting to King Richard, but I think we can do it."

"How will ye be able to make it through his army and to him directly?" asked Fia.

"Didn't Imanie teach you that we do nothing directly? I have connections; don't worry. I know someone with the means to get this crown directly into Richard's hands."

"How wonderful! If this works, it will be the most important thing I have ever done in my life."

Lorraine turned her horse. "Fia, there is no doubt in my mind now that this message will get to Richard. Whether he heeds your warning or not is yet to be determined. What I'm not so certain about is how you are going to get away from Alastair. Mayhap when I return, I can help you."

"Nay, Lorraine, but thank ye. I am no longer sure I want to escape."

"But you are his prisoner. What are you saying?"

"There is somethin' about him that is different from the rest of the men I've met. I dinna ken for sure yet, but somethin' draws me to him. I have to find out why."

"Good luck," said Lorraine. "I wish you the best." She kicked her heels into the horse, and it took off at a run.

When Fia turned to go back into the building, she thought she saw someone lurking in the shadows, so she called out.

"Who's there?" When there was no answer, she started wondering if she'd imagined it. Then from the door to the tavern came a voice.

"Yer two minutes are up. I'm comin' out there to get ye." Alastair walked out the door, quickly scanning the area as usual. "Where is Lorraine? I thought she was out here with ye."

"She was . . . but she had to leave."

"Hrmph," he said with a puff of air from his mouth. "It seems I canna count on anyone lately. Come on; we're goin' up to our room." With his hand on her elbow, he guided her back inside. "And give me that already." He snatched the travel bag from her hands so quickly that she didn't have time to hold on tightly.

"Nay." She grabbed for it, but he moved it to his side. "Dinna worry, I am no' goin' to pilfer yer precious crown while ye sleep.

Although, mayhap I should. Then ye wouldna have to worry about it so much."

They headed up to the room, climbing the tall, creaky staircase. Following the long corridor, they made their way down to the end. Once inside the room, Alastair closed the door. It was dark and cold inside. Fia heard him put down the bag and go to the hearth to light a fire. The room lit up in a soft, orange glow. In the dim firelight, she took a look at her surroundings.

There was one pallet held up by ropes and positioned atop a wooden frame. Two chairs with a small table made from a barrel were in the center of the floor. The room had a small window with a shutter that hung by one hinge. The shutter swayed in the breeze making a squeaky sound like a mouse.

"It's cold in here," she remarked, wrapping her arms around her.

"The fire should help, but what did ye expect? This is a room above a tavern, not a bedchamber in a castle like ye're used to."

He walked over and closed the shutter. Since it was broken, they were still exposed to the cool night air.

"Not much we can do about this," he said, playing with the hinge. "Mayhap I have somethin' in my bag to fix this." He headed over to the table where he'd deposited the bag. Her heart picked up in pace.

"Nay, that's fine. I'm no' that cold anymore," she said, trying to stop him.

"What?" He squinted one eye. "Make up yer mind, Fia. And stop actin' so odd." He still reached for the bag. Her heart jumped into her throat. If he found the crown missing now, he would send his men out to look for it. And if he figured out that Lorraine had it, he would be asking a lot of questions that could get them both in trouble. She had to distract him quickly. Therefore, she did the only thing she could think of that would stop a man in his tracks. Moving in between him and the bag, she stood on tiptoe and pressed her lips up against his in a passionate kiss.

"Mmm," he said with a satisfied moan. Her distraction worked beautifully. His hands lowered to her waist as he forgot all about the bag. Pulling her closer against his chest, he kissed her deeper, letting his tongue enter her mouth.

It triggered off a reaction in her, causing a tingling sensation between her thighs. Fia couldn't stop thinking that Alastair had entered her body! She was a virgin, and this was the first time a man had kissed her in this way. It was invasive, yet at the same time erotic. She liked it.

His open palms grazed over her hips and slowly slid down her thighs, rounding her bottom as he kissed her again. His hands cupped her rear, and he gently squeezed, sending a shiver of delight through her. Then, as she was warming to him and welcoming his touch, he did something that scared her. He pulled her up against him, surprising her when she felt his hardened length against her stomach. She gasped and quickly backed away.

"What's the matter, lass?"

"I – I'm no' sure. But I dinna think ye should be doin' this to me."

"Ye were the one to start it. Dinna start somethin' unless ye are willin' to finish it." In one sweeping motion, he lifted her off the floor and carried her in his strong arms over to the pallet. His lips caressed hers as he walked and he didn't break the connection of their kiss at all. Gently laying her down, he positioned himself atop her. His palm cupped her breast right through her clothes, causing her to close her eyes and arch her back, wanting even more. A warning flashed through her mind that she should stop him, but her heart urged her to let him continue his exploration.

"Alastair, what are ye doin' to me?" She opened her eyes slightly, barely able to breathe she was so excited by his touch.

"Relax, Fia. I assure ye I willna hurt ye. Ye might even enjoy it."

His hand slipped down under the edge of her bodice, his

fingers hot against her bare skin. And when he fondled her breast, his thumb grazed over her nipple. She jerked, feeling herself going taut at his touch.

"I have the idea ye need a man's touch. Ye are so tight ye are about ready to snap."

"I – I have a lot on my mind."

"Then close yer eyes and try no' to think of anythin' else but what is happenin' right here, right now."

She did close her eyes, wetting her parched lips with the tip of her tongue. A passionate fire burned out of control deep within her. To her surprise, his lips closed over her nipple. Then, his tongue swirled around in slow, sensuous circles. Her eyes popped wide open. Was this really happening? And was she letting him do these intimate things to her when she barely even knew him? She was about to protest when he started suckling at her like a babe, gently pulling and releasing her taut nipple, making her squirm. He ignited a fire deep down to her core, causing Fia to crave more intimate actions found between lovers. His lips suddenly released her with a slight popping noise that about drove her from her mind.

"Mmm, ye taste even better than ye look," he said, his voice sounding low and sexy.

"Alastair," she managed to say through ragged breaths. "I think – I think we should stop now."

"Nonsense. This is only the beginnin'. The best is yet to come." His hands slid up and under her gown to cup her womanhood next. Her eyes closed and she released the breath she'd been holding, as his actions caused her to feel moist between her thighs. He excited her in every way, making her want to experience the act of coupling. However, she didn't want her first time lying with a man to happen like this. It wasn't the way a lady acted! She had to stop it now before it went any further.

"Nay," she said, pushing against his shoulders, causing him to sit up in bed. He looked down at her with confusion in his eyes.

"Nay? What do ye mean?"

"I dinna want this," she said.

He looked down to her taut nipple and chuckled. "Aye, ye do. Yer body doesna lie."

"Nay, I dinna!"

He shrugged his shoulders and held his hands, palms up, in the air. "Then why the hell did ye kiss me?" He slid off of her and sat on the edge of the pallet, cradling his head in his hands.

She couldn't tell him the truth and wasn't sure what to say. Her actions, she realized, had deceived him in more ways than one. Now, she was sorry she hadn't figured out another way to distract him instead.

"I – I'm sorry," she apologized, knowing her words were not going to make the situation any better. The damage had already been done. "I didna mean to lead ye on."

"Nay." He rubbed the back of his neck. "It's fine." Standing up, he straightened his plaid and made his way to the door.

"Are ye leavin'?" she asked, not wanting him to go.

"I left my bottle of whisky downstairs. I think I need a dram right now." He opened the door, stopping to glance back over his shoulder. "I'll have Niven sit outside yer door tonight and I will be back first thing in the mornin'."

Fia watched him go, feeling her heart break. Her body still vibrated from their foreplay, and her cheeks were on fire. What had started as a means to protect her secret, turned into an act of betrayal in a way. She could tell by the disappointment in his eyes that she had hurt his manly pride. And now that she'd turned him down and pushed him away, she wasn't sure if he would ever try to kiss her again.

She rolled over on the pallet, fixing her clothes, telling herself that it didn't matter. He was only her captor and as he said – her enemy. She did what she had to in order to protect her secret. That was the most important thing of all. If her plan worked, she would have the chance of saving hundreds, mayhap thousands of lives and protecting those she knew and loved.

But if her plans fell through, she would have nothing to show for her actions. And then, she will have made the biggest mistake of her life. Because when Alastair found out the truth, he would never want her again.

# CHAPTER 12

The traveling party arrived at Cluny Castle just after nightfall the next day. Fia felt exhausted, and her body ached from riding a horse for so long. It wasn't easy traveling with Alastair's arm wrapped around her waist the entire time. They'd barely spoken to each other. This concerned her. What bothered her even more was that Alastair had done nothing to try to kiss her or touch her intimately again.

Had she made a mistake by pushing him away? Niven told her that Alastair drank the entire bottle of whisky and then fell asleep over one of the tables in the tavern last night. She had missed sharing a bed with him like she thought they would have done. Actually, she was sure they would have if she hadn't teased him and then turned him away.

Thankfully, he hadn't even tried to look in the travel bag. That, at least, took a lot of pressure off her.

"Here is my castle," he mumbled as they rode over the drawbridge and into the courtyard. There were a few rushlights but, for the most part, it was very dark. She could barely see a thing. The castle seemed large and foreboding, but there weren't many people around at all. To her knowledge, she'd only seen a few sentries on the wall walk and one stable boy in the courtyard. Mayhap there were more people inside.

"Where is everyone?" she asked.

"When I'm no' in residence there is no need to spend money housin' staff. They will be here tomorrow when the word gets out that I've returned."

"I see."

They entered the great hall that was dark and very cold since no fire lit the hearth.

"Niven, see that the stable boy tends to the horses and then return and light a fire since the men will be sleepin' in the great hall and it is quite chilly. I want them to be comfortable." He had a caring side to him. Fia liked that.

"Yes, my laird," answered Niven. "Shall I see to a fire in yer solar as well so we'll be warm tonight, too?"

"Nay. Fia will stay in the solar with me. Ye will stay in the great hall."

"Again?" complained Niven. "But my laird –"

"I'll no' hear another word. Och, I forgot the travel bag. Bring that as well as my hound to the solar right away."

"Of course, my laird."

"Yer hound?" Fia asked, curious to know more.

"Laird Alastair has a hound from hell," Niven told her with a grin.

"Hound from hell?" She chuckled at the thought.

"Dinna laugh until ye meet Cerberus for yerself." He took her arm and guided her through the dark. She held on to him tightly, not wanting to fall since she couldn't see where she walked. It impressed her that he moved with purpose as if he had light guiding his way.

"How can ye see where ye're goin' and why dinna ye light a torch?"

"I could walk these corridors with my eyes closed. I dinna need to waste a torch that will serve me no purpose at this point."

She tripped on the toe of her shoe and would have fallen if he hadn't grabbed her. He was probably aiming for her waist, but his hands came up under her armpits, his fingers brushing against the sides of her breasts. It warmed her instantly, bringing back memories of their playful time together. She was sure her face flushed from the thought, making her glad there was no light so he couldn't see the blush rising to her cheeks.

"I think Cerberus is a horrible name for a cute dog."

He snorted.

"What?" she asked.

"I have never heard anyone say my hound is cute."

"I think all dogs are."

"I assure ye, he's no'."

"I dinna understand why ye say that. Does the wee thing have three heads or somethin'?"

"Fia, I wouldna call him wee. And some might say he has three heads the way his mouth is always open and nippin' at somethin' or another."

"I like dogs," she said, missing her two hounds back home with her family. "I canna wait to meet him."

"Be careful what ye wish for." They approached the solar to find a small stream of light coming from the partially opened door. Alastair opened the door wider with a push of his large hand. A dark shadow lunged out of the room, causing her to scream. She heard a thud and realized something had landed on him. His body went crashing to the ground.

"Oomph," she heard as a whoosh of air left Alastair's lungs. Then she heard what sounded like a licking noise and panting. "Get off of me, ye crazy mutt!"

Fia giggled. Alastair's dog had barreled out of the solar and knocked him over.

After a string of curses, Alastair managed to remove the hound from atop him and get to his feet. He stepped into the room and lit a candle. The room lit up in a soft glow, enabling her to see the dog finally.

It was a Scottish deerhound with long legs, a small head and lots of gray, scraggly hair. It stood on its back legs and put its paws on Alastair's shoulders. In this position, the dog was as tall as him. Then, it started licking his face.

"I guess ye're happy to see me. But what the hell are ye doin' in my solar?" Alastair talked to the dog.

"My laird, I'm sorry about that." A man with a rope in his hand ran into the room after them. "I tried to keep him in the kennel, but he chewed through the rope so many times wantin' to come back to yer solar to wait for yer return. I can take him if ye'd like me to."

"Dinna bother." Alastair pushed the dog's paws off his shoulders. Cerberus started barking and running around the room in crazy circles. "He'll only sneak out and return."

"Aye, my laird, if ye're sure. I'll return to the kennels then."

"Thank ye, Johnston," said Alastair, guiding the man to the door. Just as he left, Niven popped his head into the room.

"Oh, I see ye found yer hound," he said, entering the room. "Here is yer travel bag, my laird."

"Put it on the chair and get back to the great hall to tend to the fire."

Niven bent over, calling the dog to him. In one wild leap, the hound sprang into the air, barking, knocking him to the ground as well. Niven laughed, rubbing his hands through the dog's fur. Alastair didn't think it was funny.

"Damn it, Cerberus, what did ye do?" growled Alastair.

"He's only playin'," said Fia, leaning over to pet the dog, thinking Alastair was overreacting.

"No' that. This," he spat.

She turned around to see the pallet pulled apart with straw spewed everywhere. A table was overturned on its side, and the edge of a hanging tapestry was chewed up and frayed. Clothes were scattered around the room, and some of them looked to be shredded.

"Oh, my," she said, holding her hand to her mouth. She was unable to believe what she saw. "Is the hound a puppy by any chance?"

"Nay, it is a full-grown monster that needs a lesson in manners." Alastair crossed his arms over his chest and glared at the panting dog.

"If ye dinna like the hound, why dinna ye get rid of it?" asked Fia.

"I canna." Alastair walked over to the torn pallet and sat on it, pulling off his boots.

"Why no'?"

"No reason. I just canna."

"He canna give it away because even though it drives him mad, he has lost his heart to the blame thing," explained Niven.

"I see." Fia's heart melted. The gruff, angry, Scottish laird had a soft side after all. "So ye hate and love the dog all at the same time."

"It's just a hound," he said, throwing his boot across the floor. The dog thought he was playing and hurried over and picked it up and ran in circles, knocking into everything again.

"Niven, stop him," Alastair commanded.

"I would if I could," said Niven, running after the dog and trying to catch it. The dog thought it was a game and barked even with the boot in its mouth. It got down low but left its rear high in the air. As soon as Niven got close, the dog sprang up and ran around the room.

Alastair complained. "Ye chew up another pair of my boots and I'll –"

"Here ye go," said Fia, reaching over and taking the boot from the dog and handing it to him.

. . .

ALASTAIR LOOKED up in amazement to see Fia petting the dog with one hand and handing him his boot with the other. The last time the troublesome hound stole his boot, he spent half a day chasing it before he finally found it shredded and floating in the well.

"How did ye do that?" he asked, unable to keep his jaw from dropping.

"Do what?" She shrugged her shoulders, acting as if she didn't know what he meant. "All the dog needs is a little love and attention."

"We'll see about that."

"Look," she said, pointing across the room. "He's over in the corner lyin' down and bein' guid."

Alastair stared in disbelief to see the dog lying down quietly and with its paws atop his travel bag. Whose dog was this? Certainly not his! He had never seen anything like this from Cerberus in his life. Fia seemed to bring out an obedient side of the hound without even trying.

"Shall I take the dog back to the kennel or down to the great hall for the night?" asked Niven.

"Nay, leave it here, please," begged Fia, looking at Alastair so forlorn that he couldn't say no. He hadn't had much sleep in the past few nights, staying awake to watch over her. He was counting on a good's night rest tonight, but with the dog in the room, that was going to be nearly impossible.

"My laird?" asked Niven, holding on to a rope to put around the dog's neck.

The dog sighed as if on cue, to make matters worse. Alastair looked over at Fia again. He swore her bottom lip became fuller in such a seductive pout that all he wanted to do was suck on it. "The dog stays," he said, falling back on the ripped pallet, so tired he didn't even care that there was straw sticking out and poking him in the back.

"Aye, my laird. I will go then." Niven left and closed the door.

"Thank ye," said Fia, running over to him and throwing her arms around him in a hug. "This makes me feel like I'm home with my two dogs that I havena seen in years."

With her breasts pressed up against his chest and her head lying on his shoulder, he couldn't stop from putting his arms around her and nuzzling his nose to the top of her head. Damn, she smelled good, like wildflowers mixed with a gentle summer breeze. This wasn't going to work. He pushed her away and turned onto his side. "Dinna touch me unless ye plan to carry it through because I willna be tempted and then be turned away again." He closed his eyes, longing for sleep. But now that she'd hugged him, he had a feeling it was going to be a sleepless night once again.

# CHAPTER 13

*A*lastair awoke the next morning to his hound licking him in the face. He had been dreaming about licking Fia and had hoped it was her kisses he felt. But alas, it was not.

"Cerberus, stop it." With his eyes still closed, his hand went out to push the dog away. When it wouldn't leave him alone, he rolled over and tried to continue sleeping. But then the hound nudged him in the back three times. The last time was so hard that he rolled off the bed and hit the floor. "All right. I'm awake," he grumbled, sitting up to realize he had fallen asleep with his clothes on last night. He looked across the room to see Fia sleeping on a chair by the window.

The early morning sunlight peeked in from the partially opened shutter, bathing her face in hues of orange and gold. It made her hair look like locks of angelic fire. Long, wavy strands fell over her chest, molding to her curves. How regal she seemed, like a princess mixed with an angel. Now, all she needed was to be wearing her crown. How the hell was he going to trade her to his enemy, not knowing if they were going to harm a hair on her head? For all he knew, they might rape her or beat her. After all, she said they wouldn't want her since she was from the Lowland sept. This decision was eating him up from inside. He had no choice, he told himself. He had tried for years to rescue his father, and this was his best and, mayhap, last chance. He had to do it.

Alastair let out a sigh and got to his feet, brushing the rushes off his plaid with one hand, trying to keep the dog from barking with his other.

He walked over to the door and opened it, letting the hound run out. "Go find Niven," he said, closing the door, knowing the dog's nose would lead him to the great hall since the meal would be served soon.

"Alastair?" came Fia's soft, gentle voice from the other side of the room.

"Go back to sleep. It's early." He headed back to the bed, hoping to get a few extra winks himself.

"Nay, I want to talk to ye." She slid off the chair and padded across the floor in her bare feet, daringly sitting on the edge of the bed next to him.

"About what?" he asked, pushing up to a sitting position, curious to know what she had to say. He made sure not to get too close, or he would be tempted to kiss her again.

"I wanted to apologize."

"Whatever for?" He straightened out his plaid that had ridden up his bare thighs.

"I wasna tryin' to tempt ye and then push ye away. It's just that I . . . I am a virgin, and yer actions frightened me."

All of a sudden, Alastair felt like a fool. Of course, she was a virgin. Why hadn't he thought of that? His lust had gotten in the way and turned his mind to mud. He should never have acted the way he did with the granddaughter of a king, even if she was spawned from naught but a bastard.

"I'm no' proud of the way I acted with ye," he admitted. "I – I let my feelin's for ye get in the way."

. . .

"Ye have feelin's for me?" Fia was surprised to hear Alastair admit it. She never expected this from a man like him.

"Well, I mean, I just got excited since I havena been around such a bonnie lassie in a long time. That's all it was, nothin' more."

He was lying again, and Fia knew it. He made it sound like he thought it was a mistake, but his body actions betrayed him. He sat on the bed with his knees out to the sides, nearly exposing his crotch to her under his plaid. And he leaned forward as if he didn't want to miss a word she said. His eyes quickly fell from her face, scanning down her body and then moved back up again. She watched as the pupils of his eyes grew two sizes larger. She smiled, knowing now that he was genuinely attracted to her.

"Tell me about yerself," she said, hoping to find out more about his life within the clan.

"What do ye want to ken?"

"Do ye have siblin's? And besides yer faither who is imprisoned, is yer mathair still alive?"

A dark shadow covered his face. He shook his head slightly. "I dinna remember much of my mathair. Somethin' happened long ago that I dinna understand. She left my faither when my brathair and I were just lads. My brathair, Toran, disappeared after a battle with the English a few years ago. I guess he is dead."

"Ye dinna ken for sure? Perhaps he was taken prisoner, like yer faither."

"I dinna think so. I found his sword on the battlefield and barely made it out alive myself. I was wounded and would have died if a mysterious woman hadna picked me up and helped me onto my horse."

"A mysterious woman? Who was she?"

His eyes flashed upward and to the side as if he were reliving a past event. "I dinna ken. Through my blurred vision, she looked to me like an angel."

"Mayhap you imagined her."

"Nay!" He sat up straight and his hands closed. "My faither thinks the same thing, but I didna imagine her at all."

"Then who was she? And what was she doin' on the battle-field?" asked Fia curiously.

"I dinna ken. I couldna see her face under the hood of her cape. The only thing I remember was that she wore a small heart brooch on her cloak just like the one ye wear." He gingerly reached out and ran the tip of his finger over her heart pin in a reverent manner.

"Are ye sure?" she asked. "Perhaps it was one similar to this, but no' the same at all."

"Nay, it is exactly the same. I'll prove it to ye if ye dinna believe me."

"How can you do that?"

"I have the brooch. The woman gave it to me before she sent me off on my horse, tellin' me to accept anyone I'd ever meet who wore a pin like it and no' to turn them away." He jumped out of bed and hurried over to a shelf, pulling down a small chest. Opening it, he plucked up something in two fingers and held it out for her to see. It was a heart-shaped pin that looked identical to hers. There was no doubt in Fia's mind that it came from one of the members of the queen's secret group. "What does it mean?" he asked her.

"Mean? I dinna understand."

"Aye. I noticed that ye wear one and so did Imanie and so do yer cousins. Lorraine from the Iron Eagle has one, too. I asked her about it once, but she wouldna tell me where she got it. It is no' a coincidence that so many women are wearin' the same brooch.

"It's just a brooch," she said, trying to make light of the situation so he wouldn't ask more questions.

"I noticed it on ye the first time we met in the woods. It star-tled me to see it. I have to ken what it means."

"Is that why ye let me go and allowed me to keep my crown? I always wondered about that," said Fia, finally understanding his odd action so long ago.

"Aye, I thought ye were special, and now I ken that ye are. I didna want to tempt fate by hurtin' or stealin' from a lassie who might be connected to the woman who saved my life."

"Interestin' that ye say that, yet ye are so willin' to keep me as yer prisoner and trade me to the enemy. Mayhap, that will be temptin' fate as well."

"Aye." He fingered the brooch while pacing the room, staring at the floor. "Mayhap it is, but it is what I have to do to bring my faither home."

"I'm sure there are other ways to rescue yer faither," Fia told him, trying to get him to change his mind.

"Nay. I've tried everythin', and yet the Grants still hold him prisoner."

"Did they demand a ransom?"

"They did no'. Instead, they hold it over my head that if we attack or even try to rescue him, they will kill him on the spot."

"The Grants said that?" This surprised Fia since Hamil, the clan chieftain, seemed to be such a reasonable man. He had even accepted her father, Reed, knowing he was the English king's bastard. But since Reed was married to Maggie, and Hamil liked Maggie, he made the exception. Fia didn't doubt that Laird Hamil would not want anything to do with her and that she would be far from a good trade for the captured laird of the MacPherson Clan.

"I dinna want to talk of my troubles anymore. Tell me, why were ye bein' fostered by an English earl if ye are a Scot?" He walked over and set the brooch on the bed.

Fia wanted to tell him about her family, but this was one question she couldn't answer without revealing the queen's secret group. So, instead, she decided to take the conversation in a different direction.

"I have a younger sister, Morag, who ye've already met."

"Aye, the inquisitive lass with the long, strawberry-blond hair."

"She is always gettin' into trouble."

"Why is she bein' fostered in Northumberland as well?"

Fia didn't answer. "Then I have twin brathairs named Conall and Dugal. Conall is quiet like my mathair, but Dougal is showin' signs of possibly endin' up a warrior just like my faither."

"So, are yer brathairs still livin' in Scotland? Or are they bein' fostered out to the English as well?" He kept up with his persistent questions.

"I also have an Uncle Duff who my mathair raised like her son instead of her brathair, after her parents and siblin's died in Burnt Candlemas."

"Fia, ye are tryin' yer hardest no' to answer my question. Now tell me what I want to ken. Why are ye and yer sister bein' fostered by an English earl and where did ye get the heart brooch? Matter of fact, why do ye have the late Queen Philippa's crown?"

"All right, I'll tell ye," she said with a sigh, planning on giving him just enough information to satisfy him without divulging too many secrets. "Queen Philippa was my grandmathair. Though I was only three when she died and never really kent her, she left crowns to the eldest daughters of the king's bastard triplets. She was the one to give us the heart brooches as well." Her hand covered the pin as she spoke.

"Really?" he asked. "Then, that means the queen must have given the heart pin to Lorraine and the mysterious woman on the battlefield, too."

Fia groaned inwardly, realizing she had probably just made matters worse. The last thing she wanted to do was to get Lorraine in trouble. Alastair asked too many questions and was very sharp. If she didn't stop this conversation soon, he was bound to figure things out on his own.

There came a slight knock at the door. Niven poked his head inside. "My laird, yer hound is causin' trouble in the great hall."

"What?" He turned on his heel. "Now what did Cerberus do?"

"He stole a chicken from the kitchen and is runnin' around the great hall with it in his mouth."

"Let him eat it, I dinna care," said Alastair with a wave of his hand.

"Ye dinna understand, my laird. The chicken is still alive and squawkin' like the devil. The hound keeps droppin' it at the feet of all the lassies and is scarin' the bairns every time he picks it up and throws it in the air."

"God's eyes, I am goin' to strangle that hound." Alastair stormed toward the door.

"Nay, let me take care of it," said Fia, quickly putting on her shoes and running toward the door. "Our dogs used to steal chickens back home as well. I ken how to stop it." She quickly left the room.

ALASTAIR WATCHED Fia hurrying down the corridor, liking the fact she stepped in to handle problems, almost as if she were Lady of the castle.

"I like havin' her around," said Niven, smiling like a fool.

"Dinna get used to it. Because as soon as I contact Clan Grant, she is goin' to be gone and my faither returned."

"Are ye sure ye want to do that?" asked Niven.

"I have no other choice. Niven, clean up this room and have my pallet repaired. That bluidy hound did a number in here."

"Aye," said Niven, walking to the other side of the room, starting to pick up a few things. "It also looks like Cerberus chewed up yer travel bag." He stared at the bag on the floor.

"Och, no' the travel bag," said Alastair, hurrying across the room. "Fia's crown is in there. I had hoped to use that as part of the trade. I hope it isna ruined."

"I dinna see a crown." Niven picked up the mangled bag and peered inside.

"What do ye mean?" Alastair snatched the bag from Niven. "I ken the hellhound eats everythin', but I highly doubt he could have devoured a jeweled crown." Alastair dug through the bag, realizing that what Niven said was true. The crown was missing.

"Where do ye think it is?" asked Niven, looking around the floor. "Mayhap it fell out and is in the rushes."

Remembering how Fia had clutched the bag and not wanted him to touch it made Alastair suspicious. He pulled out a half-eaten round of bread as well as a metal tankard that he recognized as one from the Iron Eagle. "Fia," he growled, throwing the drinking vessel down.

Niven laughed. "My laird, I am sure the girl didna eat the crown. Cerberus might have taken it and buried it somewhere. Perhaps I should check outside in the garden."

"Dinna bother." He dropped the bag in disgust, his hands balling into fists. It all made sense now in some crazy way. Fia wanted to be alone with Lorraine. And when he followed her outside of the tavern, Lorraine was nowhere to be found. He wasn't sure why she did it but he knew now that Fia had given the crown to Lorraine and replaced it with a dirty tankard and an old trencher to deceive him. "I'm goin' to wring her neck," he spat, hopping on one foot as he donned his boots.

"Who?" asked Niven.

"Fia."

"Why? I dinna understand. Do ye think perhaps Brohain or Rhodric stole the crown?" Niven picked up the bag and inspected the inside again. "After all, they had their eye on it since the first time we met Fia in the woods. Plus, ye said yerself that ye couldna trust them."

"Nay, I dinna think they took it at all. I think our angelic wee prisoner is no' as innocent as she wants us to believe." He strapped on his weapon belt. Feeling his blood boiling, he reached for his sword.

"Ye think Fia stole her own crown?"

"She gave it away, ye fool. And now I have less leverage for the return of my faither."

"Are ye goin' to ask her what she did with it?"

"I am goin' to get the truth if I have to shake it out of her to do it. The lyin' wench is keepin' things from me. I need answers." He walked back to the bed and scooped up the heart pin and slipped it into the pouch attached to his belt.

"Why would she do somethin' like that?" asked Niven, scratching his head. "I dinna understand."

"I'll make her tell me." Alastair stormed toward the door.

"But will she? Or will she only keep more from ye if ye demand answers she is no' willin' to give ye?"

Alastair stopped in his tracks. Niven was usually naught but a dimwit but sometimes he made sense. This was one of those times.

"Ye're right," said Alastair, touching the outside of the pouch thinking about the heart brooch. If he pushed Fia too hard, he would never find out what he wanted to know about the pin. Therefore, he would never find out whom the mysterious woman was who saved his life. He closed the door and came back into the room. "We have to trick her into tellin' me."

"We?" Niven's palms slapped against his chest and his brows arched. "Are ye sayin' ye want me to help ye?"

"Why no'? Ye were the one who came up with the idea."

"I did?" Niven's eyes opened wide, and bewilderment showed in his features. "I mean . . . I did." He stood up straighter and fixed his plaid. "So what do ye think we should do next?"

"I have an idea that might work. But ye have to keep it a secret, do ye understand?"

"I'm good at keepin' secrets," said Niven. "My lips are sealed." He pressed his lips together tightly.

All Alastair could think about was his last birthday and how Niven told him months in advance that the clan was getting him a dog. Niven had come up with the idea and also chosen the hellhound for him, he reminded himself. Alastair groaned inwardly, realizing this whole plan was probably going to backfire and blow up in his face.

# CHAPTER 14

"That's a guid boy," said Fia, taking the chicken from the dog, giving the hound a piece of dried meat in its place. She handed the chicken to a serving boy. The bird flapped its wings, trying to get away. "Ye need to be a guid dog or Alastair is goin' to get angry." The dog jumped up and tried to put its paws on her shoulders, but she turned to the side and stepped out of the way. "Off," she said, not rewarding the dog for bad behavior. "Sit," she told it several times. Finally, the dog sat at her feet. "Down," she told it, noticing the dog needed love and attention. It whined, but lay down, putting its head between its paws. "Now ye'll be rewarded," she said, getting down on the ground and petting the dog, kissing it atop its head. Cerberus wagged its tail happily, sending rushes from the floor flying in all directions. She laughed, thinking the dog reminded her of Alastair, responding so excitedly to a little attention.

"Get up," she heard from behind her. "The floor is no place for a noblewoman."

Fia looked up, but stayed on the floor, continuing to pet the dog. Alastair stood there holding something behind his back.

"Alastair. Did ye see what Cerberus did? He no' only gave me the chicken but sat and even laid down."

"If only ye were as obedient. Now, I said, get off the floor." His hand came under her arm, and he pulled her to her feet.

"He only wants attention. That is why he is so naughty. I think with a little trainin', he can turn out to be a verra obedient dog."

"Fia, forget about the dog."

"His fur is matted, and he is pretty dirty and could use a bath."

"Then I'll throw him in the moat."

"The moat? Nay! That water is so dirty."

"Leave the dog and come to the dais with me. I have an important announcement to make." He dragged her to the dais and from behind his back held out and dropped the travel bag atop the table. An instant knot twisted in her stomach. So, he had found out that the crown was gone after all. She was not looking forward to this.

"Quiet, everyone," said Alastair, raising his hand in the air. "I have an important announcement to make. Please, gather around."

The great hall was quite packed this morning, reminding Fia of a typical castle. She wasn't sure where all these people had been last night, but perhaps there were cottages spread out over the laird's demesne where they stayed when Alastair was not in residence. From the corner of her eye she caught sight of Niven lurking in the shadows at the back of the hall.

"What is it, my laird?" asked Rhodric as everyone gathered around the long, raised table.

"Have ye heard word of the ambush on the English yet?" asked Brohain excitedly.

"Are we goin' to fight as well?" asked another clan member.

"Earc should be back by tomorrow. We'll ken more about the ambush then," said Alastair. "For now, I want to say that someone has stolen from me and I will no' take it lightly."

"What's been stolen?" asked Fearchar.

Alastair held up the travel bag for all to see. Fia noticed it looked as if the dog had been chewing on it. "Fia's jeweled crown is missin', and I will no' only imprison, but hang the person who stole it from me."

"The crown is gone?" growled Brohain. "I told ye we should have sold it."

"Did ye take it?" asked Alastair. "Or was it Rhodric? After all, we all ken ye two were the ones who wanted it the most."

"If we were goin' to steal it, we would have done it long ago," snapped Rhodric.

"That doesna instill a lot of confidence in me," Alastair told them. Then he looked over to Fia. "What do ye have to say about yer crown bein' missin'? After all, ye dinna seem verra surprised or upset."

"I – I think it's awful," said Fia, trying her best to look upset. "I want my crown back."

"I agree," said Alastair. "I want it back, too. Where do ye think it is?"

Fia looked out at the crowd of people all staring at her. Mayhap, she should tell Alastair the truth, but this wasn't the place or time. Perhaps, if she could hold him off a little longer, Richard's troops might retreat, and the Scots' lives be spared. Mayhap, he'd be happy instead of angry. Nay, she couldn't tell him now with everyone in front of her. She would wait until later. "I – I dinna ken where the crown is," she said, not lying completely. The crown could be with Richard, then again, mayhap the courier was attacked in the woods, and the crown stolen by bandits. She had no idea.

"The way I see it, there were only three people who had contact with this bag," Alastair announced. "I ken I didna take it. And since Lady Fia doesna ken where it is, then that tells me that Niven was the one to steal the crown."

Shouts went up from the crowd.

"There he is!" Alastair pointed to the back of the great hall.

"Men, get him and throw him in the dungeon. He will be hanged tomorrow at sunup."

"Nay, leave me alone. I dinna take it," cried Niven as Brohain and Rhodric hauled him away.

"We should kill ye right here and now, ye traitor," spat Brohain, pulling his sword from the sheath.

"Nay! Put him in the dungeon only. I will see to his execution in the mornin'," commanded Alastair. "Now, take him away."

"Nay!" cried Fia. "Dinna accuse Niven. I am sure he didna steal the crown."

Alastair looked over to Fia thinking that now he would have his answer. His little plan was working beautifully.

"How can ye be sure?" asked Alastair. "Unless ye ken who took it. If no', I would say Niven is the only other one who could have stolen it. After all, I left him to attend to ye in the Iron Eagle."

"Perhaps it was stolen by someone when we werena watchin', but I ken Niven would never do somethin' like that." Fia's worried gaze shot over to Niven and then back to Alastair. "Please, Alastair, dinna kill Niven. He is innocent."

"I have no idea where the crown could be!" shouted Niven.

"The bag has been chewed on by the dog," she said, pointing at the travel bag. "Mayhap the hound stole it and – and buried it somewhere."

"Really," he said in a low voice. "I hardly think anyone would miss a huge mutt walkin' through the courtyard with a jeweled crown in its mouth."

"M-mayhap Cerberus did it when it was dark," she stammered.

"I dinna think so. Take him away." With a wave of his hand, Alastair sat down on his chair. He hoped to hell Brohain and Rhodric wouldn't take the matter into their own hands and kill

149

Niven. After all, this was only a setup to corner Fia into telling him what she did with the crown. "Fearchar, come here," he said, calling over one of his loyal men.

"Aye, my laird?" The man approached the edge of the dais.

Alastair leaned over and whispered to him. "Take two men with ye and go to the dungeon. Then, stay there and watch over Niven until I tell ye otherwise. Make certain Brohain and Rhodric dinna harm him."

"Aye, my laird," said Fearchar, hurrying away to do as instructed.

"What did ye tell him?" asked Fia, looking very worried.

"I told him to guard the prisoner since he is dangerous."

"Dangerous? Niven isna any more dangerous than yer hound!"

"Hah!" he snorted. "That doesna say much considerin' Cerberus tore apart my solar and caused a lot of damage."

"Alastair, ye canna mean to tell me that ye think Niven is a thief."

"I can unless ye tell me otherwise. Can ye?"

Her eyes fell to the table, and she wrung her hands. "I – dinna ken."

"That's what I thought." He raised his hand in the air. "Servers, bring the food. I am hungry."

"How can ye eat at a time like this?" she asked. "Ye have just sentenced yer best and loyal friend to death without even havin' evidence of the crime that ye accused him of commitin'."

"I am laird and have to do the right thing, no matter if Niven is my friend or no'. Now, sit down and eat," he said, pulling her into the chair. He figured it wouldn't be long now until she caved and told him everything he wanted to know.

\* \* \*

Fia finally had a moment to herself when she took Cerberus for a walk in the castle orchard later that day. She still wasn't outside the castle walls, but now she couldn't even think of escaping before she did something to help set Niven free. How could this have gotten so out of hand? She didn't think Alastair was such an ogre that he'd condemn his friend to death. She wondered why he would do such a thing over a stupid crown that wasn't even his to begin with.

"Come here, Cerberus," she said, calling the dog over, but it wasn't listening. The hound seemed to have a squirrel or something cornered behind the apple tree. Cerberus kept barking and running in circles. "How am I goin' to think of a plan when ye keep actin' like that?" She went over to the dog, thinking she'd find a squirrel or rabbit, but was instead surprised when she found a young woman hunkered down behind the tree, crying.

"Down, Cerberus," she said, pulling the dog away from the girl. "Go on," she said, throwing a stick. The hound tore out of the garden to fetch the stick. But instead of retrieving it, it lay down and gnawed on the wood.

"Please, dinna hurt me," said the girl, looking up with tears in her eyes. She seemed to be a few years younger than Fia. She had long black hair, gray eyes, and was dressed in the MacPherson plaid.

"I willna hurt ye," said Fia, sitting down on the ground next to her. "Who are ye, lass, and why are ye cryin'?"

Before the girl even answered, Fia noticed her eyes were the same color as Alastair's. Her features looked similar to his as well. "Are ye related to Alastair?"

"He is my brathair," she said, sniffing back her tears.

"He is?" Fia put her arm around the girl and pulled her closer. "Alastair told me he had a brathair but said nothin' about havin' a sister, too."

"That's because we have different mathairs."

"I see," said Fia, reaching out and wiping a tear from the girl's cheek. "What is yer name?"

"I am Caitlin. And I miss my faither."

"Oh, that's right. Yer faither is Alastair's faither who is imprisoned by the Grants."

"What is yer name?" she asked.

"I'm Fia. Fia Douglas." She decided not to tell her right now that her mother was a Gordon. It might make the girl even more fearful if she knew the Gordons and the Grants were aligned.

"Are ye a friend of my brathair?"

"Hah!" she spat, meaning to tell her she was his prisoner. Then, she realized that would be no way to gain the girl's trust. She wanted to help her, not scare her away. "I guess ye could say that. For now, at least. Tell me, why are ye hidin' in the garden and why havena I seen ye in the great hall?"

"Alastair doesna like me, so I try to stay out of his way."

"I canna believe anyone wouldna like a sweet lass like ye."

"He blames me for his mathair leavin'."

"Oh," she said, understanding this now. Alastair's father had an affair, and his mother must have found out about the bastard child. That was why she left. "Where is yer mathair?"

The girl wiped away more tears. "She died givin' me life, and I have no siblin's. My faither was the only one who ever cared for me. But since he's been gone, I feel so alone."

"Well, ye are no' alone as long as I am here." She pulled the girl to her feet. "I am goin' to be yer friend, Caitlin."

"Ye are? But we just met."

"It doesna matter. I can tell ye have a guid heart and that ye need a friend and that is enough for me."

"Thank ye, Fia." The girl actually smiled.

"That's better now, isna it?"

"Fia? Fia, where are ye?" bellowed Alastair from the entrance to the garden.

"It's Alastair," said the girl, fear showing in her eyes. "He will be angry if he kens ye are my friend."

"I dinna care," she said, patting Caitlin on the shoulder. "Leave him to me. He is already mad at me so it willna matter."

"Fia, there ye are." Alastair walked up and stopped in his tracks when he saw her with Caitlin. "Caitlin, what are ye doin' here with Fia? I thought I told ye to stay in yer chamber."

"It's a beautiful day, and no one should be confined to their chamber, nor the dungeon," Fia boldly interjected.

"The dungeon?" asked Caitlin in surprise.

"Aye. Alastair put Niven in the dungeon and has condemned him to die in the mornin'."

"Ye are goin' to kill Niven?" Caitlin's eyes filled with tears. "How could ye be such a monster? If faither were here, he would stop ye." Caitlin ran from the garden crying.

"Caitlin, wait," called out Alastair, but the girl kept on going.

Cerberus thought it was a game and ran after her.

"Cerberus, leave her be," shouted Alastair, causing the dog to stop and turn and run over to him instead. He lunged for Alastair, but he stepped aside. Instead of hitting him, the dog barreled into Fia, knocking her to the ground. The hound started licking her face.

"Nay. Get off of her, ye mangy mutt!" Alastair yanked the dog off of Fia, but Cerberus still thought he wanted to play.

Fia got up and brushed off her skirt, not minding that the dog did that, but it seemed to upset Alastair.

"Go on, get out of here," said Alastair, touching the dog to push it down every time it jumped up and put its paws on his shoulders.

"Sit, Cerberus," Fia commanded. The dog sat at her feet. Alastair looked at the hound and shook his head in disbelief. "Guid dog," she said, pulling a piece of dried meat from her pocket and petting Cerberus on the head. "Now, go on and play." The dog saw a squirrel and took off across the garden kicking up dirt on Alastair as it left.

"Let's go," he said, directing her with his hand at her back.

"Where are we goin'?"

"Somewhere – anywhere where the hellhound canna find us."

Alastair led her to the mews and entered, closing the door behind them.

"Where are all the birds?" she asked, looking around to see that the place was empty.

"I no longer have falcons since my faither is gone. They take a lot of care and are expensive. I am no' in residence often enough to care for them, so I sold them."

The sunlight streamed in from between the cracks in the walls, giving just enough light to see each other. "Ye are a spy, and that is why ye are no' here often. Am I right?"

"What difference does it make?"

"I'm curious."

He sat down on a wooden bench, picking up a piece of straw and twirling it in his fingers. "Aye, I am a spy from the Highlands, though I wasna always."

"Well, I ken ye were a spy three years ago when I first met ye in the woods."

"Aye. That was just after my faither was captured and I took over as laird. The clan was restless. I thought if we traveled they would be far more apt to stay together. No' all of them wanted to follow me."

"Like Rhodric and Brohain?"

"Aye," he admitted. "Rhodric and Brohain are older and dinna like followin' someone so much younger. I kent they'd be trouble, so I volunteered my clan to be spies for our country, comin' over the border to find out the plans of the English."

"It's a risky task," she said, sitting down on the bench next to him.

"I figured it would bide me time until I figured out how to free my faither."

"I see why Caitlin is so upset. After all, that is her faither, too. Why dinna ye like her?"

His head snapped around, and his brows dipped. "Who said I dinna like her?"

"She did."

"Well, that's a lie."

"Really? Then why do ye tell her to stay in her chamber? And why didna ye mention to me that ye even had a sister?"

"She's a half-sister. That is different." He threw down the straw and wiped his hands on his plaid. "I tell her to stay in her chamber to protect her."

"Protect her?" Fia laughed. "From what? Ye? After all, she is inside the castle walls."

"Ye dinna understand. Caitlin is like an orphan. After her mathair died givin' birth, she was a baby raised by servants. My mathair left when she found out, and my faither hardly ever paid any attention to Caitlin."

"Neither did ye."

His eyes lifted to hers. "Would ye, if ye were in my position? She is the reason my mathair left. My heart aches every day, as I long to see her again."

"Where did she go?"

"No one kens. I think she went back to her home from childhood."

"I'm sorry," said Fia. "But ye canna blame Caitlin for yer mathair leavin'. She is just a victim of circumstance."

"That's no' the way I see it." He stood up and paced the floor.

"Mayhap ye should try to be kinder to her. After all, ye are both sired by the same man."

"Dinna tell me what to do."

She stood as well. "Does no one mean anythin' to ye, Alastair MacPherson?"

"What do ye mean?" he asked, as if he were clueless as to what she meant.

"First ye shun yer own sister, and then ye condemn yer best friend to death, accusin' him of doin' somethin' he didna do."

"Ye dinna ken that. Or do ye ken what happened to the crown?"

"Stop it, Alastair," she said, getting very upset with his obstinate behavior. "We arena talkin' about the crown. I am referrin' to somethin' that is much more important than a piece of metal."

"What do ye mean?"

"I am talkin' about feelin's for those people who mean somethin' to us in our lives. I am talkin' about love – somethin' ye just canna seem to understand."

"Love makes a man weak," he told her, continuing to pace. "And what I do is none of yer concern."

"Is that right? After all, I am yer prisoner to be traded away like naught more than an object. Well, let me tell ye, Alastair MacPherson, ye are a cold, cruel man to treat people this way. I thought our kisses meant somethin' between us, but now I see it was only part of yer plan to benefit yerself. Everythin' is all about ye. I am tired of it. Ye need to think of others for a change."

"I am thinkin' of others. How can ye say that? I do things in the best interest of my entire clan."

"Do ye?" she asked, crossing her arms over her chest. "Is it for the better of yer clan that ye shun yer sister and condemn an innocent man to death?" She turned and headed toward the door.

"Fia, wait!" he called out from behind her, but she didn't stop. "Ye dinna understand."

"Nay, I guess I dinna, and never will." She stopped with one hand on the door and tears filling her eyes. "When ye saved my life, I thought I owed it to ye to save yers in return. But now I see it was a mistake. Had I kent I'd be in this position, I would have left ye to bleed to death in the secret garden and never batted an eye."

Fia ran from the mews, wanting to be alone, wishing more than anything to be back with her sister and cousins once again.

She entered the stables and threw herself down in the hay of an empty stall. Feeling weak and helpless, she cried herself to sleep.

"Fia, you need to concentrate," said Imanie, snapping her fingers in front of Fia's face. "Don't let situations and hardships distract you."

A cloud surrounding Fia diminished and Imanie came into full view.

"Imanie, ye're alive," said Fia, not understanding how this could be.

"No one can consider themselves alive when they are only going through the motions of life and doing nothing about it."

"I dinna understand." Fia wasn't sure if this was a dream. But if it was a dream of the past, she didn't remember Imanie ever telling her this before. "Am I asleep?"

"You are asleep as well as everyone else who considers themselves a victim of circumstance."

"Are ye talkin' about the fact I am Alastair's prisoner and canna escape?"

Imanie rolled her eyes and let out a deep sigh. "Did you learn nothing at all during our training sessions these past three years?"

"Imanie, ye ken I did. I learned how to read people and how to notice things that others dinna."

"Aye, you have the ability, but yet when you are around Alastair, it seems all sense flies out of your head."

She looked to the ground and blushed. "I suppose ye are right in sayin' that. Alastair intrigues me, yet he angers me at the same time."

"Then do something about it, Fia."

Fia's eyes snapped upward. "Me? What can I do? I am naught but a prisoner."

"And so is Niven."

"Niven doesna deserve to be imprisoned." She shook her head. "I dinna want him to die for a crime he didna commit."

"Then take control of the situation. That's what I am trying to say."

"What can I do?"

"What can't you do? You were smart enough and brave enough to send the crown to Richard to try to stop a war. So, don't tell me you are *going to sit back and do nothing as injustice is carried out right inside the castle walls."*

"I canna tell Alastair I was the one who took the crown." Guilt ate her up from the inside. "No' yet. Once I find out what happens with the battle, then I'll tell him."

"Will you?"

"Imanie, ye ken as well as I do that this is the only chance to save the lives of so many Scots as well as English. My own faither's life is at stake, as well as the lives of my uncles. I will no' stand by and do nothin' to change things. I had to do somethin' – I had to try."

"There you go. That is exactly what I mean."

"Do ye mean I should try to sway Alastair's decision?"

"No one can change a man's decision but himself. Or so he thinks." Imanie smiled. "Isn't that the root of the training for those in the queen's secret group?"

"That's right," said Fia, feeling awful that she let the situation come to this. "When Queen Philippa didna want the burghers of Calais to die, she talked the king into sparin' their lives."

"Every situation is different, Fia. Alastair is a proud man who is looking to restore the clan's faith in him as well as rescue his father. He will not be swayed easily. It will take time."

"We dinna have time," she told Imanie. "Niven is supposed to die at sunup. I have to do somethin' now – tonight."

"Then do it," said Imanie, fading into the cloud and disappearing.

Fia's eyes popped open, and she sat up straight to find she was still in the stable. She needed to get to the dungeon to save Niven. If there wasn't time to change Alastair's mind, then she had to help the poor lad escape. But there was a guard at the dungeon door that would never let her enter. Nay. She needed help to do this, and there was only one person she could think of who would go against Alastair.

Jumping up and brushing the hay from her gown, she took off at a run to start her plan in motion.

# CHAPTER 15

Fia hid in the shadows of the courtyard with Caitlin that evening, waiting for the opportunity to sneak into the dungeon to help Niven escape.

"Here comes Alastair," whispered Caitlin.

Alastair emerged from the door that led to the dungeon, talking with Fearchar. Fia couldn't hear what they said, but she saw Alastair rub his eye.

"He doesna even feel remorse that he put Niven in the dungeon," spat Caitlin. "How can he be so heartless?"

"Perhaps we're wrong," said Fia.

"What do ye mean?"

"I mean, his words say he thinks Niven is guilty, but I am no' so sure anymore. He rubbed his eye, so there is somethin' he doesna want to see."

"Hrmph," sniffed Caitlin. "He probably doesna want to see how mean he is toward others."

"Alastair doesna seem to want to hurt anyone intentionally," Fia observed. "Still, he did condemn Niven to death, so mayhap I am wrong. Are ye sure ye can distract the guards so I can sneak in and talk to Niven?"

ELIZABETH ROSE

"Of course, I can. Just watch."

As soon as Alastair left, Caitlin emerged from the shadows and went right up to the door leading to the dungeon. Fia watched as she talked to the guard, pointing up at something on the battlements. When the guard stepped out and walked over to look where she pointed, Caitlin gave Fia a quick nod of the head. This was her cue.

Fia hurried, sneaking through the dungeon door and down the stairs to the cells far below. It was dark and wet, and she almost slipped twice. One lone torch emerging from the wall cast enough light for her to see that all the cells were empty except one.

"Niven?" she whispered, seeing her breath in the cold air. She heard the sound of water dripping from overhead.

"Fia? What are ye doin' here?" came Niven's voice.

She ran to the cell, stopping in shock when she not only saw the door open but Niven inside gnawing on a roasted chicken leg with Cerberus sitting at his feet, begging. There were tapestries on the floor for warmth, a bed with a thick down blanket, and a feast spread out on the table that included stuffed rabbit, roasted chicken, honeyed mead and even sweetmeats.

"I think the question is . . . what are ye doin'?" She stepped into the cell looking around.

Cerberus hurried over to greet her.

"I – I'm a prisoner," said Niven, throwing the chicken leg to the dog and wiping his hands on his plaid. He stepped in front of the table to try to hide the food.

"I'm no' blind," she spat. "What is goin' on here? I am sure this isna the way Alastair treats his condemned prisoners that are to be executed in the mornin'."

"Would ye believe it's . . . a last meal?" he asked sheepishly, raising his brows.

"With the door open and the laird's hound at yer feet? No' likely. Now, tell me what is goin' on."

"Oh, all right," he said, plopping down atop a wooden stool. "I'm no' really a prisoner, but ye canna tell Alastair ye saw me or he will be furious."

"I dinna understand. Why would ye two try to deceive everyone this way?"

Cerberus whined and hunkered down, wagging his tail and waiting for Niven to throw him another scrap of food. When he didn't get anything, the dog started gnawing on the leg of the stool instead.

"I'm supposed to keep it a secret," Niven explained. "Alastair thinks ye had somethin' to do with the disappearance of the crown and he wants to flesh ye out."

"He does, does he?" Fia crossed her arms and narrowed her eyes.

"Fia, did ye have somethin' to do with the missin' crown?" asked Niven. "Because I would hate to think ye did and didna say anythin' and were goin' to let me go to my death."

Fia suddenly felt horrible. In trying to protect so many, she did something that might have ended in the death of an innocent man. Still, she couldn't tell Niven. If she admitted she took the crown, she would have to include Lorraine and others in the story. That wouldn't be right to endanger their lives when they already were at risk trying to help her.

"I wasna goin' to let ye die," she explained. "I came down here to set ye free."

"Then ye didna have anythin' to do with the disappearance of the crown?"

"I think at this time it is better if I didna answer that."

"Ye had better say somethin' to Alastair about it. If ye dinna, he is goin' to have to execute me in the mornin'." Niven got up, walked over and collapsed atop the bed, grabbing an overstuffed pillow, holding it to his chest.

"I highly doubt he will do that. But just the same, dinna say a word about me bein' here." She turned to go and saw the dog eating the food off the table. "Cerberus, nay!" She clapped her hands, scaring the dog.

"Why no'?" asked Niven. "What are ye goin' to do?"

"Alastair MacPherson is no' the only one who can play this game," she said, already devising a plan that would not only put the man in his place but teach him that he should never underestimate the power of a woman.

* * *

"WHAT DO ye mean ye dinna ken where Fia is?" Alastair asked his guard, pacing the floor of his solar as he spoke.

"I'm sorry, my laird. I didna ken I was supposed to watch her."

The last Alastair had seen of Fia was when she ran off to the stable, crying. First, he was responsible for making Caitlin cry, and then he somehow did the same to Fia. Why did he feel like such a cur? He hadn't meant to hurt anyone – except for mayhap his hellhound. He'd purposely left Cerberus with Niven so he could have a break from the beast. He told Niven it was so that the dog would protect him, but hell if that hound had ever protected anyone or anything in its life. Clan Grant could march in the front gate, and Cerberus would probably be happy, thinking the attack was just a game.

"Well, find her!" commanded Alastair.

"Yes, my laird." The guard opened the door to leave only to find Fia standing there.

"There ye are," said Alastair, making it across the room in three strides, pulling her inside. "Get in here, and dinna even think of disappearin' on me again. Where were ye?"

"I went for a walk in the courtyard with Caitlin," she said. For some reason, she was smiling when the last he'd seen of her, she'd been crying. The guard left, and Alastair closed and barred the door.

"Ye are lockin' me inside the solar? Just like Niven is locked in the dungeon?"

He looked up sharply at the mention of Niven. "Niven doesna have to be imprisoned. That is, if I find that he is innocent after all. Do ye have somethin' ye want to tell me?"

"Aye, I do." She walked over and looked out the window as she spoke. "I was thinkin' about the crown."

"And?" He hurried over to her, feeling as anxious as Cerberus with a table full of food.

"And I think ye are right."

"Right? About what?"

"About Niven being guilty."

He took a step backward, watching her in a leery manner. "But ye said he isna guilty."

"I've changed my mind." She waved her hand through the air and glided over to the bed next.

"How so?" he asked, not liking the sound of this.

"That crown was a present to me from the late queen. It is costly and holds sentimental value since it is the only thing I had by which to remember my late grandmathair."

"Ye didna even seem to care that it was missin' before now."

"I dinna like to show my emotions in front of the clan but, yes, I am verra upset about this. I think hangin' Niven for the crime isna a fit punishment. Mayhap, ye should have him drawn and quartered instead, or perhaps stabbed in the heart and thrown from the top of the battlements into the moat."

"Nay!" shouted Alastair, not understanding what had gotten into her. "How can ye even think of hurtin' Niven like that?"

"Now it is my turn to remind ye – that is no' what ye said earlier in the great hall. I think ye should execute him tonight instead of waitin' till the mornin'."

Alastair paced back and forth with his hand on his chin. This was not what was supposed to happen. "I'm sure there must be an explanation. Mayhap I should give him another chance."

"Do ye think so?" She looked up and batted her eyes, running her finger over the spindle of the bed.

"I – yes, I think so." He cleared his throat, realizing he had to get out of this or he'd be in a position in the morning to kill his good friend – something he would never do. "I suppose I could hold off on the execution until I ken more facts."

"Will ye release him and then keep a close eye on him? After all, that way if he is the thief, he might lead ye to the wherever he hid the crown."

"Yes," he said with a nod, thinking this would work well. "I will release him and follow him. That's what I'll do."

"Wise decision." She stretched and yawned before leaning over to pat the bed. "This new pallet seems much better. I think I'll test it out." She started to unlace her bodice, then stopped and cocked her head. "Please turn around while I undress."

"Undress?" Had he heard her correctly? Was she going to remove her clothes and sleep in his bed? He quickly turned around.

"Ye dinna expect me to sleep in my daily clothes do ye? After all, just because ye sleep in yer plaid doesna mean that I want to act that way."

"I dinna sleep in my plaid." He turned around to find her under the covers, smiling like she was happy about something.

"Really." She eyed him up and down. "It doesna look that way to me."

"I just didna want to frighten ye by undressin' since we will be sharin' the same bed."

"Is there somethin' about yer body that is frightenin', my laird?" She giggled as she said it.

"Nay, there is no' and I'll prove it to ye." He dropped his plaid and removed his tunic, satisfied by the way her mouth hung open, and her eyes skimmed down his naked form.

. . .

FIA PLAYED THE GAME, and it had worked like a charm. Alastair was going to free Niven tomorrow. But mayhap she'd taken things too far when she not only undressed and climbed into bed, but talked him into removing his plaid as well. She'd been told the men back in her clan wore braies beneath their plaids, but that wasn't so with Alastair. He not only took her challenge but dropped his clothes and now stood before her as naked as the day he was born.

"Frightenin', isna it?" he asked with a sly smile. The more she looked at his naked manhood, the more he grew before her very eyes.

"Guidnight," she said, turning over and squeezing her eyes closed. If she didn't fake sleep, she was going to end up making love with Alastair. And until she had the chance to tell him the truth about the crown, she didn't think that was a good idea at all.

# CHAPTER 16

*F*ia awoke the next morning feeling warm and comfortable and like she'd had the best night's rest in years. It took her a moment to remember she was sleeping dressed only in her shift and in Alastair's bed. He had his arm around her, and his mouth pressed up against the back of her head.

By the sound of his deep, even breathing, she realized he was still asleep. Trapped under his heavy arm, she could do nothing to move until he awoke.

"A-hem," she said, clearing her throat, wanting him to move.

He did move, but not in the direction she expected. He threw his long leg over her next, hugging her like a pillow. In the semi-darkness of the room, this seemed very intimate. Especially since she knew he was naked.

"Alastair," she whispered, not sure what she was going to do or say once he awoke.

"Mmmph," he said into her hair, followed by a puff of air from his mouth that sounded like a half-snore. It tickled her ear and made her giggle.

"Alastair, I want to get up, but yer leg and arm are over me."

"Hmm?" he asked, nuzzling his mouth against her ear. Then she felt the evidence of his arousal protruding against her back. She had gotten herself into a very interesting position.

"Alastair," she whispered again. This time his hand came up to brush a lock of her hair behind her ear.

"Ye are beautiful, Fia," he said in a deep voice. It was followed by a caress of his hand against her cheek. "I am verra attracted to ye and want to kiss ye again."

She turned her head and looked up at him. He was now staring right at her mouth. Why did she feel like a princess wrapped in his arms, safe from the world? Alastair MacPherson put on a gruff appearance for his men. But when he was like this, he seemed as gentle as a kitten. She liked this side of him.

"I – I would like to kiss ye, too," she admitted. Fia hadn't been able to stop thinking of their last intimate time together. She had left him wanting more and had also hurt his pride. It didn't feel right to her, so she figured it felt even worse to him.

His lips caressed hers ever so gently, erasing all thoughts of worry from her mind. She raised her chin to meet him, welcoming his kiss.

"I didna think ye'd let me do that again."

"I'm sorry – about the last time, Alastair. It's just that I dinna ken ye well and ye scared me."

"Dinna be afeard, Fia." His words calmed her nervous disposition. "I would never hurt such a gentle, bonnie lassie such as ye." His fingers trailed down her neck, lingering on her chest. Her anticipation grew.

"I am curious about making love to a man," she whispered, watching the rise and fall of her own chest as she became anxious just thinking about it. "However, I ken it is wrong unless I am married."

"Ye dinna need to worry, Fia." His finger made lazy circles right over one nipple. "Now that I ken ye are a virgin, I will no' take from ye what only yer husband should have."

"What do ye mean?" She turned and pushed up on one elbow to look directly at him. "Dinna ye want to make love to me?"

"I think my body speaks for itself." He waggled his brows. His eyes darted over to his erection. Her eyes followed, and she gasped. The sunlight streamed in through the crack of the shutters, falling right on his engorged form. He looked ready, willing, and very able.

"I dinna want to tempt ye and then leave ye hangin'," she said, not sure what to say or think. His manly beauty was arousing and alluring. If she didn't move away from him soon, they would end up doing something that she might later regret. "I suppose it is time we get up." She started to sit up, but he pulled her back down.

"No' so fast, lassie. There is no reason we canna share intimate time without actually couplin'."

"Do ye think so?" she asked, wondering how that would work. Her attention moved to his manhood again that seemed to have grown even more.

"Fia, I have never met a woman like ye before. Everythin' about ye intrigues me. Ever since the day I met ye in the woods three years ago, I have no' been able to stop thinkin' about ye."

"I have been thinkin' about ye as well." She held her hand against his chest, feeling the rapid beating of his heart. Her heart, she was sure, was beating even faster. "Alastair, I feel in some ways as if I've always kent ye. I did no' feel comfortable livin' in England and never wanted to be the ward of Lord Beaufort. I like bein' around the Scots."

"Like me? A Scot who has kidnapped ye?" He pushed away and sat up, holding his head in his hands.

"Are ye really goin' to trade me to the Grants in exchange for the release of yer faither?"

"Aye, if they'll agree to it. Fia, I have no choice. It is the only thing that will get my faither returned."

"Perhaps we can think of somethin' else instead," she suggested, not wanting to be a part of this deal.

"There is nothin' else that will work. I have tried for years. Please understand, I dinna want to trade ye, but I am only thinkin' of the best interest of the clan."

"What about my interest?" she asked. "I dinna want to be yer prisoner. Neither do I want to be traded away as part of some ridiculous deal that all came about because of a silly feud. Ye dinna have to do this, Alastair."

"Aye, I do, Fia. Ye dinna understand. Sometimes, we have to do things to benefit the masses rather than just one."

"I think savin' yer faither is only benefitin' ye."

"It is helpin' Caitlin and also the entire clan," he pointed out. "My faither was the best chieftain this clan ever had."

"Then are ye sayin' ye dinna want to be chieftain anymore?"

"I didna say that." By his body actions of opening and closing his hands, Fia could tell he was torn. "But tell me, where does a man's loyalty to his clan and also his family end and his pride and self-esteem begin?" He got off the bed and started to dress.

"I think I ken what ye mean," she said, scooting to the edge of the bed and putting on her gown. "I recently was in a situation like that as well."

"How can ye understand?" he asked, donning a tunic and wrapping his plaid around him. "Ye are only a lassie."

"Only a lassie?" She put on her shoes and stood. "So, are ye sayin' that women are no' capable of makin' decisions and doin' things the way men are?"

Before he could answer, there came a knock at the door. "My laird," called out a familiar voice.

ALASTAIR HURRIED across the room and pulled open the door. Cerberus jumped up, almost knocking him over. "Get down!" he growled. The hound shot across the room, over to Fia, sitting obediently at her feet although she hadn't said a word.

"Guid boy," Fia said, rewarding the dog by running her hand over his head.

Alastair bit off an oath and directed his attention back to the door where one of his clan members stood waiting patiently to be acknowledged. "Earc, ye've returned."

"I have, my lord, and have brought news of the battle," responded the man.

"Guid, come in."

Earc stepped into the room and stopped short when he saw Fia. "Oh, I didna ken ye were with a lassie."

"It's just Fia," he said, getting a nasty stare from the girl in return.

"Perhaps we should speak out in the corridor."

"Nay, there is no reason to do that," said Alastair, reaching for his weapon belt and fastening it around his waist. "Whatever ye say can be said in front of Fia as well."

"Are ye sure, my laird?"

"God's eyes, spit it out already, Earc. What do ye have to tell me?"

"It is Richard's army, my laird."

"Ah, so the ambush is in progress. Guid." Alastair chuckled as he checked his weapons. "How surprised was Richard when his troops were met by the Highlanders, the French, and our king?"

"I'm afraid it wasna Richard and his troops who were surprised, my laird."

"Huh? What do ye mean?" Alastair strapped his sword to his back. "There were no surprises on our end. What happened?"

"Richard pulled out his troops and sent them back to England early this mornin'. They never even made it to Fife."

"Didna make it to Fife? Why no'?" asked Alastair, not liking the sound of this at all.

Earc's eyes darted over to Fia and then back to him. "Rumor

has it, Richard got word about the ambush, and didn't want to risk the lives of his men after all. Therefore, the English retreated, and there was never a battle."

"Retreated? Nay, that canna be," spat Alastair. This news was making him angry. "That means all our work spyin' on the English and reportin' back to our king was for naught. How could they have found out? No one in this clan would be a traitor and tell those bluidy Sassenachs our plan. Besides, we had word that John of Gaunt was pushin' to keep goin'."

"King Richard made the final decision," said Earc. "Our informant said he had a visitor with somethin' in a bag last night though no one kens what it was. This mornin' he suddenly changed his mind about attackin'. Richard claims he turned back because the Scots burned the crops and there was no' enough food to feed his troops. However, no one can prove why he really turned around."

Alastair's eyes roamed over to Fia. She was hunkered down, pretending to tie her shoe, but he didn't believe it. She was not only listening but also acting like she wasn't even interested. That made him very suspicious.

"Thank ye, Earc," he said. "Meet me in the courtyard with the rest of the men and I will give them the news."

"Aye, my laird."

"And bring Niven from the dungeon and tell him he is free to go."

"Niven isna in the dungeon, my laird. He is in the great hall," said Earc.

"He is? Are ye sure?" Alastair asked quietly, hoping Fia wouldn't hear him.

"I saw him just minutes ago," Earc whispered back. "He asked me if Fia had told ye yet that she had seen him last night."

"Interestin'." Alastair glanced back at Fia. She was watching but quickly looked in the other direction. "Thank ye, Earc, ye can go."

As soon as Earc left, Alastair closed the door. He put his hand to his chin and paced the floor. "I wonder why Richard would even consider turnin' and runnin' with his tail between his legs back to England."

"I'm sure he had his reasons." Fia stood up and made her way across the room to open the shutter.

"I wanted to tell ye somethin', Fia."

"Really?" She turned around and smiled. "What is it?"

"I was dishonest with ye. I told ye I imprisoned Niven because I thought he stole the crown. Actually, I was only tryin' to flesh out the culprit."

She paused for a long moment, but then answered, "I ken." She busied herself weaving her long hair into a braid as she stared out the window. "I saw him in the dungeon last night, and he told me yer plan."

"Then . . . ye kent all along that I didna mean to harm him. That's why ye told me to kill him?"

She smiled and nodded. "That's right. I wanted to see what ye were goin' to do, just like ye did to me."

This surprised him. He admired her wiles and didn't think a woman could be so cunning without the help of a man. Aye, she really impressed him. He should be furious but, instead, he found a new respect for her.

Alastair strolled over to the window, not knowing what to think or what she was capable of doing anymore. Could she have also somehow had something to do with the English army turning back? He pondered the thought and then shook it from his head. That was ridiculous. How could one person have that much power and influence over a king? And, indeed, not a woman. He dismissed the idea altogether. Fia might have done something to keep her crown out of his hands, but she certainly didn't have the ability to figure out how to stop a war! It was all just a coincidence and naught else.

He walked up and slipped his hands around her waist,

nuzzling her behind the ear. "Ye are a bad lassie. I should turn ye over my knee for that." He kissed her on the cheek and then turned her and kissed her hard and long, claiming her as his own. Damn this woman excited him. If he hadn't already promised he wouldn't take her virginity, he'd throw her down on the bed right now, and couple with her hard and fast.

She reached up and took his head in her hands, looking deeply into his eyes. "Would ye do that?"

"If I bared yer bottom and turned ye over my knee would ye object?" Heat soared through him at the erotic thought of the action.

"Alastair MacPherson, I'm surprised at ye. Ye scold me one minute and excite me the next. Now, which one is it goin' to be?" She smiled coyly and tilted her head.

"Dinna tempt me, vixen. I will no' put up with yer flirtatious games anymore. I will let my actions speak for me instead."


ONCE AGAIN, Fia had pushed him too hard. She toyed with him, trying to be flirtatious the way her cousin, Willow, was with all the men. Fia only did it because she wanted Alastair to like her. Plus, she didn't think anything would happen since he promised to leave her virginity intact until she was married. Well, she was wrong.

Alastair scooped her up and threw her over his shoulder and headed back to the bed. She squealed, being surprised and excited, wondering what he was going to do next.

He sat on the edge of the bed. And, to her surprise, he did turn her face down over his lap. She couldn't stop laughing. She figured he only did it to scare her, but when he pushed up her gown and pulled down her braies, her laughing stopped.

"Alastair . . . what are ye doin'?"

"Ye will no' call my bluff again, Fia." His palm cupped her bare bottom end, and she heard him moan. He tapped her ever so gently.

"It is like two ripe peaches callin' out to me to taste their sweet nectar." He squeezed her cheeks, causing her to jolt.

"Taste?" she asked, not knowing where he was going with this. After rubbing his hands over her bottom, he leaned forward. Then, to her surprise, he kissed her on her rear end. A playful nip of his teeth followed.

It was a sensuous act that made her squirm. "Alastair, this isna appropriate," she said in a breathy whisper, turning over. His actions aroused her and were causing her to come to life.

"I have never been appropriate, and I willna start now."

"What in heaven's name are ye doin'?"

"Heaven is the word for what ye'll be experiencin' in a minute. Now close yer eyes and relax."

"Close my eyes? Why? What are ye goin' to do?"

"Just trust me, Fia."

She did trust him, and closed her eyes, surprised when he pulled her to the edge of the bed and spread her legs apart. Then his hands slid slowly up her inner thighs until his fingers fondled her most private part and played with her womanly folds.

"Oooh," she said, breathing deeper, falling back slightly to her elbows. And when she felt something wet between her thighs, she realized it was her own liquid passion. His fingers continued to do magic as he stroked her, petting her like a kitten. She found herself almost purring by his action. When she heard him move off the bed, she opened her eyes to see the top of Alastair's head between her legs. She sat up sharply, but his hands roamed to her knees. Then he reached out and gently pushed her backward.

"Relax, lassie. This is the part I think ye are goin' to love."

"I – I dinna ken about this, Alastair. It seems . . . so naughty."

"Sometimes, it's all right to be a naughty girl. Now, dinna fight me, Fia. I promise ye will enjoy this."

His tongue shot out, and he looked up at her as he licked her inner thigh. Shocked by his action, she couldn't bring herself to say a word. Then his hands slid up her legs, slipping around her bottom. He licked her again, but this time the action was longer, trailing up even higher.

"Ye – ye're are no' goin' to –"

"Shhh," he said, smiling and winking. The next time his tongue trailed over her skin, he got so close to her womanhood that she felt his hot breath at her door. And before she could object to what she figured was coming next, he pulled her closer, burying his head between her thighs, licking her somewhere else. Her body tingled and her eyes closed. His tongue traced her nether lips and after a few passes, she felt his wet, hot heat enter her body.

"Oh!" she cried, feeling vibrations she had never felt before. He flicked his tongue and teased her, taking her sensitive nub between his lips, making her cry out in unbridled passion. Her back arched and she gripped his hair as her womanhood came to life. She was so hot she thought she'd melt. Never had she experienced anything like this before. It honestly felt heavenly, just as he'd promised. Fia needed and wanted more.

"Do ye like that, lass?" he asked before continuing to stroke her with his hands as well as his tongue. He was driving her mad with lust. She wanted him so desperately that she no longer cared that she wasn't acting like a lady. Naughty was exciting and made her feel randy and very much alive.

Her senses reeled and her legs spread apart further on their own as she accepted his intimate actions and longed for more. "I – do," she said, just as his tongue dipped into her again, making her scream out in pure passion. Then he lifted her legs up and over his shoulders, burying his face against her. She gripped his hair, moaning and trying to hold back her screams of passion.

"Cry out," he told her. "Let me hear yer release."

She did scream, letting her senses take control of her actions. "Alastair, oh, Alastair," she cried as she climbed higher and higher to the top of the precipice where she had never been before. Her back arched off the bed, and her knees closed in around him as she screamed out in ecstasy one more time when he managed to bring her to completion with just his mouth.

In total exhaustion, she removed her legs from around him and fell back on the bed. Alastair leaned over her, kissing her, caressing her, and making her still feel strong with desire. Then he lay down next to her, taking her hand and guiding it up and under his plaid.

"Alastair, what are ye doin'?" she asked.

"I told ye I would keep yer virginity intact and so I will. But now that ye have been satisfied, I need to be sated, too."

With her hand in his, he closed his fingers around his erection and guided her to stroke him in much the same way that he had done to her with his tongue. And when he covered her mouth with his, her lips tingled from the vibrations of his moans of pleasure. Faster and faster he guided her hand, stroking his hard length. He felt like satin over steel. She reveled in the feel of having his arousal pressed into her palm. It didn't take long before his breathing labored and he cried out as he released his seed.

Then they lay in each other's arms, breathing heavy, and not saying a word. No words would be appropriate right now because they would only ruin the magic she'd experienced and she didn't want to ever forget the feeling.

Things had just changed between them. She no longer felt like his prisoner or his enemy. Nay, she felt as if they were lovers. It was going to be harder for him to trade her to the enemy now . . . and even more difficult for her to ever tell him the truth of what she did with the crown. She had no idea where this was going to lead. All she knew was that even if she never saw Alastair MacPherson again, she would always remember this intimate time they shared together. It would be her new secret – her secret of the heart.

# CHAPTER 17

*A*fter spending two nights of holding and kissing and pleasuring each other without actually coupling, Fia was starting to think Alastair had forgotten all about using her as a trade for his father. But she was wrong.

This morning, Alastair had left the solar before Fia even awoke. And when she went out to the courtyard with Caitlin, they found Alastair's men saddling their horses and collecting weapons as if they were preparing for battle.

"What is happenin'?" Fia asked Caitlin.

Cerberus picked up Alastair's waist pouch and ran in circles.

"Bring that back here," growled Alastair, trying to catch the dog. Every time he got close, the dog barked with the pouch in its mouth and ran further away from him, making him angrier.

"They are preparin' for battle," Caitlin told her.

"Are ye sure?" asked Fia in disbelief. "Richard's troops went back to England. There is no one to fight."

"It is no' King Richard they are preparin' to fight. They are goin' to bring back my faither."

"Yer faither?" Fia's heart jumped into her throat. If they were going to confront Clan Grant, that meant Alastair did not forget about the silly feud after all.

"Fia, that means ye'll be leavin' with them, and I'll never see ye again," said Caitlin. "I will miss ye. Ye have been my only friend."

"Dinna say that." Fia took the girl's hand in hers to comfort her. "I'm no' goin' anywhere."

"But if ye dinna go – my faither will never come home." Caitlin's eyes filled with tears. Fia looked over to Alastair. He managed to get his pouch from the dog and was pulling on one end while the hound pulled on the other. She would miss Cluny Castle and Caitlin and even the dog. And most of all, she would miss Alastair. The time they had spent together was special to her. She had lost her heart to him, and now he was about to break it. She had thought possibly of hiding or running or convincing Alastair to let her stay. But now, after seeing the tears in Caitlin's eyes, she realized it would be selfish for her to refuse to go. Caitlin needed her father. So did Alastair. Like Alastair said, sometimes you have to do things for the good of the masses and put your own needs aside. That is what she had to do right now.

"I will find a way to get back to Cluny Castle, I promise. And I will see to it personally that the Grants return yer faither." She pulled Caitlin to her in a hug, thinking of her sister and cousins back in Rothbury. They were probably frightened, wondering what happened to her. She was also sure, in time, her father would hear about this and come looking for her. If she was with Clan Grant, she could hopefully contact her parents and let them know where to find her.

She walked over to Alastair still struggling with the dog. When the dog saw her, he brought her the pouch. "Guid dog," she said, handing the waist pouch to Alastair. He shook his head and took it, tying it onto his belt.

"I'm ready to go," she told him.

He adjusted the leather harness that held his sword on his back, not looking at her. "Go where?"

"I ken ye are goin' to meet with the Grants."

"That's right I am. But ye are stayin' here with Caitlin."

"Nay, I am to be the trade for yer faither. Ye need to take me."

"Niven, let's go," Alastair shouted, mounting his horse. "Fia, go back to the keep."

"Ye said I was the only leverage ye had. I need to go with ye."

"I changed my mind." He turned his horse, riding over to join Brohain and Rhodric and the other men of the clan. "Guidbye, Fia."

Fia stood there not knowing what to do. She had been the one fighting him all along, but now he was telling her that she was staying behind. Determined not to let him leave without her, she ran after him. From his side, she spoke while he rode atop his horse.

"Alastair, ye need me. What will ye use for a trade if I am no' there?"

"Well now, I was hoping that fancy crown of yers would have served as a backup but, then again, we dinna have it any more, do we?"

"I took it," she blurted out, thinking he would get so angry with her that he would bring her along after all.

"I ken," was all he said, looking forward.

"Dinna ye want to ken why I did it or where it is?"

"Ye told me that ye dinna ken where it is."

"I really dinna ken where it is right now, and I am sorry, Alastair."

"It's all right, Fia. It was yer crown. If ye didna trust me and wanted to hide it to keep it secure, ye had a right. Now, please go back to the keep. I have business to attend to."

"Nay! Dinna leave without me, Alastair," she called out as he and his men rode away. Her heart ached. The Grants were a fierce clan and outnumbered Alastair and his men. If they approached the Grants at their castle to fight, there was no chance of winning, let alone coming back alive. She had to do something to help him, and she had to think fast.

Niven rode by next, followed by a covered supply wagon being pulled by one horse.

"Niven, take me with ye," she said.

"Nay, Fia. Alastair wants ye to stay here." Niven rode on.

She stood staring after him as Caitlin ran up to join her.

"Fia, what are ye doin'?" asked Caitlin.

"I need to help Alastair. I canna let them leave without me."

"What are ye goin' to do?"

Fia spied the back of the cover of the supply wagon flapping in the breeze. This was her only chance, and she had to take it. Aye, she would risk it all for Alastair and Caitlin and the good of Clan MacPherson.

"I'm goin' with them, Caitlin. And I will keep my promise to ye that yer faither will return, no matter what I have to do to make it happen." Fia darted after the wagon with Cerberus running and nipping at her heels. She jumped onto the back and slipped under the canvas, hoping this wasn't going to be the biggest mistake of her life.

* * *

"WE'LL STOP HERE to refresh the horses," Alastair called out three hours later as they neared Grant Castle.

"My laird, Cerberus is barkin' again and willna leave the food and supply cart alone," Niven told him.

"Bid the devil, why didna that blame hound stay back at the castle? He is only goin' to cause trouble."

"I'm no' sure, my laird. Did ye want me to tie him up?"

"No need. I'll do it myself." Alastair headed to the back of the wagon where Cerberus was nipping at the canvas flap and barking. "Leave it," he called out, almost wishing Fia were here to calm the dog. She had a way with Cerberus that demanded respect. He admired her for not only her expertise with animals but also her patience. Patience was something he was short on at the moment.

"My laird," said Rhodric, heading him off. "Why didna ye bring the girl along? She was our only means of gettin' yer faither released."

"I decided against it," he said, knowing there would be repercussions because of his decision. For three long years, they had waited for something that would tempt the Grants, and they finally had it. A daughter of not only a legendary bastard that they were already aligned with, but a granddaughter of the late English king was something they wouldn't be able to turn down. If naught else, the Grants could get a pretty ransom from King Richard for the return of his cousin.

However, after spending several sleepless nights thinking about it, Alastair decided he could not offer up Fia like a sacrificial lamb, even if it meant he would risk not having his father returned.

Something about her touched his heart, and he couldn't put her in the path of danger. He would give his life to protect her instead.

"Aye, what's this all about?" snorted Brohain, coming to join them. "Without a trade, approachin' the Grants on their own land will be nothin' short of a massacre. What were ye thinkin', Alastair?"

The dog continued to bark and pull at the tarp. When Alastair walked over to stop it, he saw inside the wagon, and his heart dropped.

"Fia," he said, surprised to see her there.

"There's the girl," said Rhodric. "Guid. Now we have a chance."

"Go see to the horses," Alastair told the men. "Tell the others to sharpen their weapons. We're no' ten minutes' ride from

Grant Castle. Let's get this over with so we can head back home."

"Aye, my laird," said Brohain. He glared at Fia. "Guid thing ye showed up. I woulda came and hauled ye here myself if I had to."

"Go!" commanded Alastair, sending them all away. "And bid the devil, Cerberus, stop yer infernal barkin'." Alastair could barely think straight because of all the noise.

"Here, Cerberus, go chew on this." Fia gave the dog a piece of dried meat from inside the cart, sending Cerberus away happy.

"What are ye doin' here, Fia?" It took all of Alastair's strength not to strangle the girl for sneaking into the wagon. This was the worst situation he could be in at the moment. In trying to protect her, he had caused her to do something that put her directly in the line of fire. "I told ye to stay back at the keep."

"I am sorry, but I couldna do that." She slid out of the wagon and stood, brushing off her gown. "I ken I disobeyed ye, but I did it for the guid of the entire clan."

"God's eyes, what are ye talkin' about?"

"Alastair, ye said yerself that sometimes we need to make decisions that concern others and no' just ourselves."

"I said that when I still had a mind to trade ye to the Grants."

"I think ye still should."

"Fia, what are ye sayin'?" Alastair realized most of his men stood watching, so he took Fia's arm and guided her to the edge of the forest to speak in private.

"Alastair, ye have no choice. Ye have to use me as a trade so the Grants will release yer faither."

"I am no' nearly as worried about my faither as I am about ye and what Clan Grant might do to ye."

Fia straightened her back and flipped her long braid over her shoulder. "I am a Gordon and am aligned with them. Plus, I am a granddaughter of the late King of England. They willna harm me. If they do, they will have to deal with my faither."

"And do ye think that scares them?"

Her green eyes opened wide. "I think it does. Everyone is afeard of my faither as well as my uncles. They were once kent as the Demon Thief. They are the Legendary Bastards of the Crown. No one wants to anger bastards of the king."

"A dead king," he reminded her. "Fia, no one cares about legends or bastards of a king who is no longer in power. Dinna ye see how dangerous this is? Ye might be hurt. I would never forgive myself if anythin' happened to ye."

"Ye are bein' ridiculous and over-cautious, Alastair. Without me, yer entire clan might be killed. Now, let's go before anythin' happens to yer faither."

Alastair grabbed her arm to keep her from moving. "He's been imprisoned for three years, another ten minutes isna goin' to make a difference. I want to talk to ye, Fia."

"It's no use. I've made up my mind." She shook loose from his grip. "There is nothin' ye could say that would make me stay behind." She turned to go.

"I love ye," he blurted out before he lost the nerve to say it. She stopped in her tracks and slowly turned around.

"YE WHAT?" Fia could barely believe her ears. No man had ever told her he loved her before. The last person she would expect to hear it from was her captor.

"Ye heard me, Fia." He stepped forward and cradled her hands in his. "I care for ye. I dinna understand how this happened so quickly, but ever since I saw yer heart brooch I kent we were destined to be together."

"Alastair, I am flattered." She looked up into his eyes and smiled. "I have feelin's for ye as well. But we canna let our feelin's get in the way of makin' important decisions that involve the lives of others."

The dog ran over to join them. It looked as if it were going to jump on Alastair, so she reached out and pulled it away.

"My laird, the horses are watered, and the men are ready to approach the castle," said Niven interrupting their conversation. "Hello, Fia. I didna ken ye were here."

"Of course, I'm here," she said, noticing Alastair's stance. His arms were crossed, and his hands were in fists. He was closed off from even listening to her. A deep crease was prominent between his furrowed brows. She had put him in a very awkward situation.

"So, ye are to be the trade to the Grants for Laird Duncan?" asked Niven.

"Aye," she said at the same time Alastair said, "nay."

"I'm confused." Niven shrugged his shoulders and looked from Fia to Alastair and back again. "Are ye goin' with us or no'?"

"Nay, she is no'," snapped Alastair. "Niven, take Fia on yer horse and return to Cluny Castle anon."

"Back to the castle? But we just came from there."

"Just do it."

Niven shrugged his shoulders and held his hands in the air. "All right, even though I dinna understand what is goin' on."

"Take the bluidy dog with ye, too," Alastair called out. "And whatever ye do, dinna let Fia out of yer sight for even a minute. If anythin' happens to her, I swear I will have yer head. Do ye understand?"

"Aye, my laird," said Niven, taking Fia's arm and leading her away from Alastair with the dog following.

Glancing over her shoulder, Fia saw Alastair mount his horse and lead his men toward Grant territory. Everything happened so quickly that she didn't have time to tell Alastair anything. Her heart ached because she hadn't told him that she thought she was falling in love with him as well. And now, he marched right into the midst of trouble. For all she knew, she might never see him again.

## CHAPTER 18

"*N*iven, I need to use a bush," Fia said, already planning a way to get back to Alastair. She had to do this. She'd told Caitlin she would make sure her father returned, plus Fia wanted to use herself as a trade to help Alastair. Clan Grant, to her knowledge, liked to fight. The Gordon sept where she grew up in the Lowlands liked to bargain to get what they needed. It had taken her father a long time to realize that fighting was not always the answer.

"All right," said Niven, coming to a stop. He got off the horse and helped her dismount. Cerberus watched anxiously, thinking they wanted to play. "The horse could use a break. I'll wait here for ye, but dinna go far. I am supposed to keep an eye on ye every minute. Cerberus, ye'd better go with her."

The dog whined and lay down with its nose between its paws.

Fia took off, hiding behind a bush, wondering how she was going to get back to Grant Castle on foot. She needed the horse, but Niven was standing there with the reins in his hand. So, she decided she would have to cause a little distraction. And who better to help her than the king of distraction himself?

"Cerberus," she called softly, but the dog was wandering

185

around sniffing the ground and didn't hear her. She picked up a rock and threw it. It landed right in front of the dog's nose. His head sprang up. When he saw her, he ran over. She reached out and petted him, at the same time spying a squirrel up in the tree. "Look at the squirrel," she said, knowing the dog would go crazy. Sure enough, Cerberus started to bark, trying to get up the tree to get to the squirrel.

"What's goin' on?" Niven called out, but Fia didn't answer. "Fia?" he said, tying the reins to a branch and venturing over. She hid behind a tree and waited. When Niven got close to the dog, she raced out, mounted the horse and rode away.

"Fia, come back here," shouted Niven from behind her. "Laird Alastair is goin' to have my head."

"Dinna worry, I'll talk to him," she said, waving a hand through the air. "Take care of the hound now."

Fia picked up the pace, heading back in the direction from which they'd come. If luck were on her side, she would get to the castle right after Alastair and his men and, hopefully, be able to do something to make a deal and save his father.

* * *

"MACPHERSON, dinna cross my bridge unless ye want a fight," called out the laird of Clan Grant.

Alastair gripped the hilt of his sword tightly, knowing the time had come. He was out of options. The best chance of saving his father at this point was to do it forcefully. "I've come for my faither. If I have to fight to bring him home, then I will. But I will no longer put up with yer antics."

"If ye want yer faither, ye need to give us somethin' in return," called out their chieftain, Hamil.

"How do I even ken my faither is still alive?"

"Fingal, bring the prisoner," said Hamil with a nod of his head. "MacPherson, enter my courtyard so we can make a deal."

"Dinna do it," Brohain warned him. "He will trap us inside his castle walls and lower the gate. We will have no way out."

"It's a chance we have to take, although I dinna think he'll do it."

"Why did ye send the girl away?" growled Rhodric. "We could have used her as a trade and been out of here by now."

"Let me see my faither," shouted Alastair. "And we arena comin' inside the walls. Ye will bring him out here to me."

Conversation passed between the Grants. Finally, a man appeared holding Alastair's father. Duncan MacPherson looked gaunt and pale and had his hands tied behind his back.

"Faither," Alastair shouted. "What have they done to ye?"

"Dinna fret about it, Son. Have ye brought a ransom?"

"They didna request a ransom," Alastair told him.

"Then did ye bring somethin' to trade? Son, I have been here a long time and am more than ready to come home."

"We want ye back, Chieftain." Brohain rode forward with Rhodric at his side. "However, yer fool son let the girl go who was to be the trade."

"That's right," added Rhodric. "She is the daughter of one of the Legendary Bastards of the Crown."

"The late English king's granddaughter?" asked Hamil with a soft chuckle. "Aye, that might have been somethin' I would have considered. So, ye have nothin' of value to trade then?"

"Nay," admitted Alastair.

"Slap him back in the dungeon and, this time, throw away the key," growled Hamil. "Actually, ye'd better hold on to the key because I'll have more prisoners momentarily. Attack," he cried with a wave of his arm.

"Wait!" shouted someone from behind Alastair. The crowd parted. Fia rode down the drawbridge sitting atop Niven's horse.

Alastair groaned. "Canna that lad do anythin' right?" He never should have left Fia in Niven's care. "Fia, turn around and go home," Alastair said in a low voice.

"Home?" she asked. Her eyes held deep sadness within them. "I am a Gordon and an alliance of Clan Grant, Alastair. I am home."

"Fia, nay. Dinna do it," he begged her.

Fia dismounted and walked over to Hamil. "Laird Grant, do ye remember me? I am Reed's daughter."

"Fia?" asked Hamil. "What are ye doin' here with the bluidy MacPhersons?"

"I was taken as Alastair's prisoner, and he is usin' me to trade for his faither."

"Guid job, Son," said Duncan. His eyes were half-closed, and he looked tired and broken.

"I admit I kidnapped Fia, but it was only to save my own life," Alastair explained. "I am sorry, Faither, but I refuse to use her in this manner again. I am no' tradin' her for yer release."

"Then who or what will ye trade?" asked Hamil. "After all, unless ye have somethin' of value to offer, yer faither is no' leavin' here now or ever."

"I offer myself." Alastair put his sword back into his scabbard and dismounted. Holding his hands out so they could see he had no hidden weapons, he walked over to join them.

"Son, dinna be a fool!" snapped Duncan, using all his energy to say it. "Use the girl instead."

"I willna." He took Fia's hand in his. "I would die to protect ye, Fia."

"That can be arranged," mumbled Hamil. With just a nod, Hamil's guard drew his sword.

"Put away the sword," someone shouted as an entourage of men on horseback barreled over the drawbridge and joined them in the courtyard.

"Da?" asked Fia, looking up in wonder. "What are ye doin' here?"

"Fia." Reed approached on horseback. "As soon as I got the

message from yer cousins that a MacPherson abducted ye, I figured the cur would show up here sooner or later."

"Nay, Da, Alastair is no' a cur. He did kidnap me, but didna go through with tradin' me for the release of his faither."

Reed got off his horse. His men sat watching, still mounted, hands on the hilts of their swords.

"Really. Then why is he here?" asked Reed, glaring at Alastair. The man was tall and foreboding with a sturdy build and arms as thick as tree trunks. Alastair had never met any of the bastard triplets but could see now how intimidating just one of them was. Reed's shoulder-length red hair was the same color as Fia's. Dressed in the Douglas plaid, he stood proudly with his sword in hand. Here was a fierce warrior that would do anything to protect his daughter.

"I am here for the release of my faither," Alastair explained. "I told Fia to stay back at the keep where she was safe."

"It's true," admitted Fia. "I came here of my own accord. I offered myself as a trade so Alastair's faither would be released. This feud has to end."

"I would never harm her," said Alastair, wanting Reed to know he was no threat to Fia. "I have come to care about yer daughter, and that is why I could not carry out the plan."

"He offered himself up to replace his faither, and I think we'll take it." Hamil shoved Duncan forward. The man stumbled and fell at Alastair's feet.

"Faither," said Alastair, helping him to stand, untying his hands as well.

His father looked up with weary eyes. "Kill them, Alastair. Kill every bluidy last one of the Grants for what they've done."

The Grants overheard and suddenly the scraping sound of metal echoed through the courtyard as they drew their swords, preparing for a battle. Alastair noticed Brohain and Rhodric and the rest of his men pulling their weapons as well.

"Nay, put away your weapons," he called out. "We arena here to fight."

"Men, collect my new prisoner and bring him to the dungeon, anon," Hamil commanded.

"Nay!" shouted Fia, hurrying over to Alastair and throwing her arms around him.

"Stay back, Fia. This is no' yer battle."

Duncan leapt forward, pulling Alastair's sword from the scabbard on his back. Swiping it through the air, he lunged for Hamil. Hamil jumped backward, using his sword to block the blow.

"Stop it!" Fia cried. "No more fightin'."

"No one comes into my courtyard and threatens my men or me," snarled Hamil. "This calls for battle."

"Hold it," said Reed, stepping in between Duncan and Hamil. His men surrounded him on horseback, drawing their swords as well.

"Reed, have ye gone daft?" spat Hamil. "Ye are married to a Gordon and aligned with us now. Ye should be on our side, no' the side of the enemy."

"My daughter is involved. I think we need to hear what she has to say first. Now, lower yer weapons, all of ye," commanded Reed.

"Ye have one minute, and then I am goin' to run Duncan MacPherson through with my sword just for the satisfaction of seein' him die." Hamil begrudgingly lowered his sword.

"Faither, give me the sword," said Alastair, holding out his hand. "We have been enemies with the Grants for far too long. Fia is right in sayin' this has to end."

Duncan lowered the sword but did not give it to Alastair.

"Fia, did MacPherson hurt ye in any way?" asked Reed, lowering his sword slightly, taking a step toward his daughter.

"Nay, Da," answered Fia. "Alastair kidnapped me only because the English threatened to kill him. Things have changed since then. He told me he loves me."

"Loves ye?" Reed cast a sideways glance to Alastair. "Is this true, MacPherson?"

"Aye," admitted Alastair, putting his arm around Fia's shoulder. "Yer daughter has made me rethink my ways. I came here only for the return of my faither, no' to fight."

"I – I think I am fallin' in love with ye, too, Alastair," Fia told him, making Alastair's heart soar. How he longed to hear her say this. "Da, make this feud stop. I want to be with Alastair."

"This fight is far from over," snarled Duncan. "No one is goin' to keep me as a prisoner for three years and then just walk away like nothin' happened." Duncan let out a war cry and lunged once again for Hamil, sinking the sword into the man's side. Hamil raised his sword and did the same to Duncan. Fia cried out and Alastair pulled her to the side, blocking her with his body to protect her. He felt as if his world had just come crashing down around him.

"Faither, nay!" he screamed, rushing forward to stop him from killing the chieftain of the clan. Hamil's men grabbed Alastair, thinking he was attacking as well. Reed nodded, and his men apprehended Duncan. Reed then went over to help Hamil.

"Enough!" shouted Reed. "What is the matter with all of ye? Thousands of Scots' lives were just spared when the English turned back and headed home, yet here we are still fightin' amongst ourselves."

"Stay out of this, Reed," warned Hamil.

"I will no'," he snapped. "This is my daughter, and she is in love with a MacPherson. I say we stop the silly feud between clans and concentrate on what really matters."

"And what might that be?" asked Hamil.

"Let's join forces instead of killin' each other," said Reed. "Together, we can be strong. And next time the English invade, we will no' let them retreat."

"Fine, comin' from a bastard of the English king," sneered Fingal.

"I say we kill the Grants for keepin' our chieftain prisoner," came Brohain's suggestion from behind Alastair.

"Nay," said Alastair. "But what if we make an alliance?"

"Aye," agreed Fia. "That would be the right thing to do, just like Alastair said. We can get married and seal the deal."

Alastair was surprised to hear that Fia thought this is what he meant. While he was going to suggest an alliance of some sort, he hadn't even considered the way to do it was by marrying Fia. Or had he? Now that Fia mentioned it, he liked the idea of her becoming his wife. Now, if only Hamil would agree, even though Fia wasn't directly from his clan. Still, she was a close alliance.

"Reed, I ask for yer daughter's hand in marriage," said Alastair.

"Son, dinna be a fool!" Duncan lay on the ground with his side bleeding heavily. "Her faither is the bastard son of the English king. She has Sassenach bluid runnin' through her veins! Ye will never be able to trust her – just like what happened between yer mathair and me."

"YER MATHAIR WAS ENGLISH?" asked Fia, surprised to hear this since Alastair had not made it clear that she wasn't Scottish.

"She was English, just like my faither said," Alastair told her. "I dinna care what ye say, Faither. I love Fia and want to marry her. Laird Grant, if Reed agrees to let me marry his daughter, will ye release my faither and accept an alliance between our clans instead?"

"I agree to the marriage if it is what Fia wants," said Reed, holding the tip of his sword out as if he were ready to strike down the next person who attacked, no matter what side they were on.

"It is what I want," answered Fia. "I want this verra much." She turned and looked directly into Alastair's eyes. "This will be the best for all concerned. We will do it no' only for us, but for the guid of all the clans involved."

"I agree," said Alastair, still not able to move because of the guards holding him.

Hamil held his hand over his bloody side, conversing quietly with Fingal and several of his men. Finally, he looked up and nodded. "Reed, if ye are willin' to have yer daughter married to a MacPherson, then I accept the alliance between our clans and set Duncan MacPherson free."

"Then it is done," said Reed, putting away his sword. "Release him," he told the guards holding Alastair. Alastair gave Fia a quick hug and kiss atop the head and then ran over to help his father stand.

"Faither, ye need to get back to camp. Yer wound bleeds heavily. Someone, bring the supply wagon quickly."

"There is a healer here," offered Reed. "Perhaps he can look at yer faither's wound."

"Nay," complained Duncan. "I would rather die right here than to stay another minute within the walls of Grant Castle."

"Get him out of here," Alastair commanded. Brohain and Rhodric stepped forward to help their chieftain to the wagon.

"Come on, Fia," said Alastair, helping her mount his horse.

"Where are ye takin' my daughter?" asked Reed.

"We are goin' back to Cluny Castle. Ye are welcome to come along," Alastair told Reed. "My faither needs healin', and I would like to discuss the marriage with ye as well as with Fia."

Reed nodded to his men. "Let's help them in any way we can. If my daughter is goin' to be a MacPherson, then I want to see where she will be livin'. Let's get a move on to Cluny Castle."

# CHAPTER 19

Three days had passed, and still, Duncan MacPherson's wound was not healing. Alastair was so upset by this that Fia had hardly seen him. He spent most of his time at his father's bedside.

Her father, Reed, left days ago to collect the rest of their family and bring them to Cluny Castle for the wedding that was planned to take place as soon as they returned. A message had also been sent to Castle Rothbury to tell Fia's sister as well as her cousins the good news.

Fia walked the grounds of the garden with Caitlin, trying to calm the girl since she was afraid her father would die. Having seen the man's wound, Fia realized it didn't look promising. An infection had set in. And in his weak state, she was sure Duncan MacPherson didn't have long to live.

"I am so frightened," said Caitlin, sitting down on a bench. Fia sat next to her and put her arm around the girl.

"Everythin' will be all right, Caitlin. Dinna worry."

"Do ye think my faither will live?" Caitlin looked up and dabbed at the tears in her eyes. Fia didn't want to give the girl false hope. If her father was dying, she had a right to know.

"Only God kens for sure, Caitlin. The most we can do is pray. But I want ye to realize that no matter what happens to yer faither, I will always be here as yer friend. Alastair will, too."

"Thank ye, Fia, but I dinna think Alastair will ever accept me. He will always see me as the reason his mathair left."

"I dinna want ye to worry about that. Now, go back to yer chamber and wash yer face and put on a smile. Ye need to be strong."

"Thank ye," she said, heading toward her chamber.

Fia followed Caitlin inside. She caught sight of Alastair in the great hall and approached him, noticing the way he sat with his ankles crossed, closing himself off. Something was troubling him even more so than before. "Is yer faither any better?"

"Nay, he's no'," he said cradling a tankard of ale. "I think he will no' live until the mornin'. I am goin' to get the priest to bless him one last time and hear his confession before he leaves this world."

"Oh, Alastair, I am so sorry." She sat down and leaned against his chest. "I also feel saddened for Caitlin because she is havin' a tough time with the thought she might lose her faither and have no one."

"I feel no remorse for that girl." His hands balled into fists. "She is the reason my mathair left me when I was only a lad. Now she'll ken how I felt."

"Stop it, Alastair. Yer anger is misplaced. It is no' Caitlin's fault what happened between yer mathair and faither."

"How can ye say that?" he asked her. "Ye have only been with the MacPherson Clan a short time. Ye dinna ken the way it used to be before I lost my mathair."

"It has been long enough to see that ye are actin' like an ass." His eyes opened wide, and his mouth turned down into a frown. Cerberus ran over, jumping up on Alastair, barking as usual. The hound took hold of Alastair's sleeve and tugged, ripping his tunic.

"I dinna have time for this." Alastair shot up off the bench, pushing the dog. "Get away!"

"Ye are always pushing away those that love ye," she pointed out.

"The hound is always aggravatin' me, Fia. I have things botherin' me. I dinna need this in my life right now."

"If ye paid more attention to the people or things that are important, instead of holdin' on to yer grudges of the past, ye would see how much happier ye'd be."

"My faither is dyin'. My clan is upset, and half of them think I did the wrong thing by makin' an alliance with the Grants. I dinna have time to be befriendin' a troublesome hound."

"Is that what ye think? That ye did the wrong thing?" she asked, not liking what he said.

He stopped and pulled her up next to him, gathering her in his arms, holding her tightly. "Nay, Fia. I didna do the wrong thing. I will marry ye no matter what anyone thinks because I ken we were meant to be together." He kissed her tenderly on the mouth, making her want to spend intimate time with him alone. Her heart went out to him because she knew how troubled he was with all that had transpired lately. "I promise ye things will be different soon. But right now, I need to get the priest and go to see to my dyin' faither."

As soon as Alastair left, Niven came to find her.

"Lady Fia, Laird Duncan calls for ye at his bedside," said Niven.

"Me?" That surprised Fia. She didn't understand it at all. The man didn't even seem to like her. Why would he call for her?

"Aye, he asked me to fetch ye right away."

"I'll wait until Alastair returns with the priest."

"Nay," said Niven. "Laird Duncan stressed the point he wanted to see ye while Alastair was away."

"He did?"

"Go on," Niven told her. "Dinna be afeard of him, he willna hurt ye. He hasna enough strength left in his body to hurt a flea."

"I'm no' afeard." Fia headed to Laird Duncan' s solar. Outside the door she paused, feeling anxious about talking with the man. Why did he call for her and why did he request to speak with her alone? She had no idea but had the feeling he wanted to say something that he didn't want his son to hear. Fia raised her hand and knocked softly. The door opened and the healer, an old Scotsman, nodded and let her in.

"Leave us," said Duncan from his bed.

"Aye, my laird," answered the healer, slipping from the room and silently closing the door behind him.

"Come forward, lass."

Fia ventured closer, feeling awkward being alone in the room with the dying man and wishing Alastair was there with her. "Ye wanted to see me?"

"Sit," he commanded, talking to her like he would a dog. She didn't like it but, in respect to a dying laird, she sat on the edge of a chair next to the bed. Just a sheet covered the man's thin body. His eyes were sunken on his face, and she swore he was not much more than skin and bones. His midsection was wrapped with a bloodstained cloth.

"How are ye feelin' my laird?" She tried to make casual conversation to ease her nerves.

"Stop with the pleasantries. I didna ask ye here to inquire about my health. We both ken I am dyin'." His voice was rough and low. The dank, dark room smelled musty. Burning sage smoldered from atop a copper plate next to the bed. It thickened the air, making her feel as if she were going to choke. She coughed into her hand, wanting to rip open the shutter for fresh air.

"Why did ye summon me here?" she finally asked him. "Ye have never even spoken to me before today."

"Ye are a brash lassie, and I dinna like it." Even in his dying

197

moments, Duncan MacPherson was a crude and intimidating man.

Her hand covered the heart brooch on her bodice as she thought of Imanie and tried to be strong.

"That brooch," he said, closing his eyes for a second, struggling to breathe.

"What about it?" she asked, surprised he had even seen it in his condition.

"I noticed it at Grant Castle. Where did ye get it?"

"It was a present, my laird." She didn't feel as if she owed him any more of an explanation.

He nodded slightly. "A present from the late Queen Philippa of England." As he said the words, he stared at the ceiling.

"Aye. How did ye ken?"

"Alastair has a brooch just like that."

"Aye, he showed it to me," she said, running her fingers over her pin. "He said it was given to him by a mysterious woman who saved his life on the battlefield. He also said ye dinna believe him."

"Fia, I am dyin'. The reason I called ye here was because ye will soon be my son's wife."

"Aye, I will. But I dinna understand what ye want."

The man turned his head and coughed before continuing. "I never doubted Alastair's story for a minute."

"Really? Then why did ye tell him ye didna believe him?"

"It was a choice I made to keep him from findin' out more."

"More? About what?"

"About the queen's secret group of women kent as the Followers of the Secret Heart."

Fia gasped. "Ye ken?" she asked, almost falling off the chair. She repositioned herself and pushed back further to regain her balance.

"My wife was English, and I should have kent trouble would come from it. I am no' proud to say I beat her when she wouldna tell me about the heart brooch and where she got it. I thought it was from another man. When I found out the truth, I wished it were from a man because at least then I coulda killed him."

"Alastair's mathair was a member of the group?" she asked in amazement.

"I didna like the fact then, and I dinna like the fact now that my son is goin' to marry and make the same mistake I did."

She sat up straighter in the chair. "I dinna believe by any means that bein' a strong woman is a mistake."

"That's no' the mistake I meant." He released a breath and closed his eyes. His breathing became shallower. She almost thought he fell asleep, but then his eyes opened and he continued. "I was talkin' about the mistake of sendin' her away and tellin' her that if she returned or even tried to contact our sons . . . I would kill her."

"Och, ye dinna say that!"

"I did. I even took a mistress. We had a baby because I thought if I had someone else, she would never try to return."

"Caitlin," mumbled Fia.

"Aye, Caitlin is my daughter. Her mathair died givin' birth. It was my punishment for sendin' away the only woman I ever loved."

"Ye loved yer wife and yet ye beat her? And ye never tried to find her again?"

He coughed, sounding much weaker than before. "The more time passed, the harder it was for me to admit my mistake of no' tellin' Alastair and his brathair, Toran, the truth."

"And now yer wife and son are dead."

"I'm afraid Toran died on the battlefield three years ago, although I could never find his body to prove it. But my wife, Oletha, is still alive."

"How do ye ken?"

"The mysterious woman on the battlefield that saved Alastair's life – I believe it was her watchin' over him."

"The brooch," said Fia, understanding everything now. "Why didna ye tell Alastair? Ye need to tell him."

"I'm afeard if I tell him, he will never forgive me. I wanted to confess to someone before I died, but I couldna bring myself to tell him."

"And ye're tellin' me because ye want me to relay the story to him?"

His eyes closed again. His skin became even whiter. "Ye are a strong lassie; I can see that. I will leave it up to ye if ye tell him the secret or no'."

"Nay! Dinna dump yer deceitful problems on me. Besides, ye ken as well as I that I am sworn to secrecy and canna tell Alastair or anyone about the Followers of the Secret Heart." Fury raced through her as well as confusion. She glanced back at the door, hoping Alastair would return during their conversation. He had to. There was no way she wanted to try to explain all this to him. There had to be another way.

"It is up to ye now, Fia, whether Alastair ever . . . kens the truth . . . or . . . no'." His breathing stopped. And when it did, his haunting eyes stared into her very soul. He died, therefore making his problems hers. She didn't need this, nor did she want it.

"Laird Duncan," she said, reaching out and shaking him but, of course he didn't respond. Tears filled her eyes. "Laird Duncan wake up! Dinna leave yer secrets on my doorstep. I already have enough weight on my shoulders. Please, dinna do this to me!"

"Fia!" Alastair rushed into the room with the priest and the healer right behind him. "What are ye doin'?"

"He's dead," she said, with tears streaming down her face. "Alastair, why didna ye come back five minutes sooner?"

"Nay! Faither!" Alastair leaned over and stared into his father's open, lifeless eyes.

"Let me check him," said the healer, stepping in between Duncan and Alastair, holding his hand to the man's neck and then his wrist. He reached out with one hand and closed Duncan's eyes. "I'm sorry," he said, shaking his head solemnly. "Alastair, the infection has taken the life of yer faither."

"Let me give him a final blessin'," said the priest, stepping up to the bed and opening his book.

Fia's body shook while tears streamed down her cheeks. Alastair's arm slipped around her shoulder. Lovingly, he pulled her closer. "It's all right, Fia," he said, thinking she was crying over the death of the man.

The fact that Alastair lost his father saddened her, but what the man told her with his dying breath is what really had her upset. She now held the secrets that could end all Alastair's searching for answers, yet at the same time could expose her and make him hate her. She had a decision to make that could alter the course of both their lives and didn't know what to do.

In another day or two, she and Alastair would marry for the sake of an alliance between two clans that had been enemies for years. If she told Alastair the story his father had relayed to her, would it bring to his mind more questions? What if he found out she was the one responsible for the English army's retreat, hence spoiling the surprise ambush by the Scots? Would he be angry that she ruined their plans, or happy since she'd saved so many lives? And the question that bothered her the most was would Alastair react to her the same way his father responded when he found his wife was a member of the late queen's secret group? If so, a marriage that had not yet even started could be over before it began.

With her eyes transfixed on the dead man, she listened as the priest recited prayers that she was not sure would benefit the man's soul and get him to heaven. Duncan MacPherson had made mistakes that she wasn't sure could ever be forgiven. And now he'd laid his troubles at her doorstep. It was all up to her now. She was the only one who could right the wrongs of the past. But in doing so, she could hurt a lot of people and, perhaps, even bring about a war. If the Scots knew the English retreated because of a warning from a woman, her cousin, King Richard, would be made a laughingstock to even his own people. How much could she tell Alastair and how long could she continue to keep secrets? She longed to be a loyal wife, securing her marriage to Alastair and maintaining peace between the clans. Fia never felt such turmoil in her life.

Where were her cousins, Maira and Willow, now that she needed them? She couldn't make this decision alone. She needed someone to guide her, and she needed it fast.

$\mathcal{A}$lastair held the burning torch, ready to light the funeral pyre that would send his father's soul on to either heaven or hell. Every day lately had been mentally exhausting. Finally, he'd managed to free his father from Clan Grant's prison, only to end up seeing him die in the end.

"Go ahead, Alastair," said the priest, giving him a nod to light the fire. Fia stood at his side, seeming almost more upset than he was if that was at all possible. He'd yet to have a chance to ask her why she was alone in his father's room when he'd died. Niven told him that Duncan had called for her right after he left to find the priest. Odd, since his father didn't even seem to accept the fact that he was going to marry Fia.

"My laird, everyone is waitin'," said Niven, urging him to do the one last deed that would finalize the fact Alastair would never see his father again. He nodded and stepped forward slowly, touching the fire of the torch to the dead branches and twigs under his father's dead body. Flames shot up, licking at the air. He threw the torch into the fire and stepped back, watching as fire consumed his father.

"They are waitin' for ye to say somethin'," Niven reminded him.

Alastair wondered what he could possibly say to his clan that would bring any of them peace. He felt turmoil wracking his body and rattling his nerves. If he hadn't looked over to see his beautiful bride-to-be, he didn't think he'd be able to speak at all.

"Come, Fia," he said, holding out his hand. She walked forward to take his hand and join him. "Ye are my strength that will get me through this hard time."

"I am?" she asked, sounding as if the thought disturbed her.

"We are gathered here to say our last guidbyes to a man who I have idolized my entire life," Alastair told the crowd. "My faither was strong through all the troubles in his life. Duncan MacPherson was my rock when my mathair left us because of the jealousy of another woman who had claimed my faither's heart."

Fia coughed and pulled her hand from his. He looked down at her, wondering if the smoke was bothering her. "Are ye all right, my love?"

"Aye," she said, forcing a smile. "Go on."

He turned back to the crowd. "I will continue to be chieftain of this clan, and I will follow in my faither's footsteps. My actions will be the same as those of my faither when he walked the earth."

Fia started coughing more now. He figured he had better finish quickly and take her away from the funeral pyre. She seemed to be having a very hard time with the death of his father.

"I dinna want to dwell on anythin' upsettin' anymore, and that is why I will be married first thing in the mornin' to the beautiful Lady Fia."

Clapping and cheers went up from the crowd. Still, Fia didn't seem very happy. Alastair realized that she had been through a lot lately and that, after tomorrow, things would be better for everyone.

"Cheer up, Fia," he whispered in her ear. "In the mornin' we will be married. And I canna wait to claim ye as my wife – in all ways."

* * *

RUNNING her hand over the heart brooch that Alastair kept in the wooden box, Fia couldn't stop thinking about what Duncan had told her. Had this pin once been worn by Alastair's mother and was she a member of the queen's secret group? And had she been the one to save him on the battlefield? It was too much to be just a coincidence. The brooch looked exactly like Fia's. Besides, there was no way Alastair's father would have been able to make up such a story.

Secrets ran rampant at Cluny Castle, and Fia was now the keeper of them all.

She heard the door open behind her, and slammed down the lid and replaced the box on the shelf. "Alastair," she said, taking a deep breath and faking a smile. Why did she feel like such a traitor when she hadn't done anything wrong? Or had she? She no longer knew.

"Fia, why did ye leave the great hall right after the meal? I thought we would have time for a dance or two before retirin'." Alastair entered the room with Cerberus sneaking in right behind him before he closed the door. He walked over to the shelf and put what looked like a small box behind the chest that held the brooch.

Her stomach clenched. It seemed difficult to breathe. After hearing Duncan's story early this morning, she sent a messenger boy to the Iron Eagle with a note to Lorraine that she needed to talk to her right away. She had hoped the boy would be back by now, but it wasn't a fast trip. For all she knew, he might not even return until the morning.

"I wasna feelin' well," she said, laying her hand on her stomach.

"Ah, ye are nervous about the weddin' in the mornin'. I am a little fidgety myself." He removed his sword and weapon belt and hung them on a hook on the wall. Then he kicked off his boots. The hound picked up a boot and started running in crazy circles around the room, knocking into everything. The dog jumped up in the air, hitting things and acting possessed.

"Cerberus," she said, trying to still the dog.

"Nay." Alastair stopped her with his hand on her arm. "I have this." He whistled. Immediately, the dog came running, stopping in front of him and dropping the boot. Alastair pulled a dried smelt from his pocket and flipped it to the dog. The dog snatched it right out of midair. "Guid boy, but ye have to leave now. I need to talk with Fia." The dog followed him over to the door. He took another smelt from his pouch and threw it into the corridor. The deerhound ran after it, and Alastair quickly slammed the door. He turned around with a huge smile on his face, and a sense of pride in his stance. "How's that?" he asked, brushing off his hands.

"Ye gave the dog a smelt?"

"Aye. I figured there are barrels of them in the larder. Since I canna stand the taste, I willna miss them. I took a lesson from ye and started rewardin' the dog for bein' guid instead of yellin' at it for bein' bad." He pulled her into his arms and kissed her. The dog scratched at the door and barked, trying to get back in.

"I think he needs a little more trainin'," she told him.

"He'll calm down and head to the great hall for scraps of food once he realizes I am no' goin' to open the door."

"I'm impressed, Alastair."

"I took yer words to heart, Fia. Now that my faither's funeral is over, I had time to think and realized ye are right. I need to start concentratin' on my family – and even the bluidy dog."

"What about Caitlin?" she asked. "Are ye goin' to be nice to her or continue to blame her for yer mathair's departure?"

He groaned and released her, moving over to the bed where

he started disrobing. "What would ye do in this situation?" he asked, surprising her to answer that way.

"I would take the girl under my wing and treat her like the sister she is if I were ye."

"Really?" He pulled off his tunic and threw it next to his plaid and climbed into bed naked, pulling the covers to his chest. "If it wasna for my faither's roamin' eye, my mathair would still be here today."

"Ye dinna ken that."

He looked at her oddly. "Fia, ye are actin' strangely. And why were ye lookin' at the heart brooch when I walked in?"

Damn, he'd seen her actions, and now she was going to have to say something to satisfy his curiosity. She still didn't know what to tell him about her conversation with his father. Perhaps as soon as Lorraine got there, or her cousins arrived on the morrow, she would talk to them and figure out her answer.

"I was thinkin' about the woman who saved yer life on the battlefield," she said, fingering her heart brooch for strength.

"What about her?"

"Do ye ever wonder who she was and why she was – wearin' that pin?"

"Now that I think about it, she might have been a nun."

"A nun?" That surprised her.

"Aye. After the battles, the nuns from the convent walk the fields lookin' for wounded to help."

"I dinna think a nun would have any jewelry of her own. They take the vow of poverty if I'm no' mistaken."

"Ye're right," he said with a shrug of his shoulders. "Perhaps she stole the pin off a dead body on the battlefield and then felt guilty. That is why she gave it to me."

"Alastair." She put her hands on her hips. "Nuns dinna steal. Besides, it is a lady's brooch. The dead on the field are all men. Tell me again, what she said to ye when she gave it to ye?"

Alastair's eyes glanced up and to the side and he relived the memory from the past. "She said I should be kind to anyone I ever saw wearin' a brooch like that. But I think she felt guilty about somethin', and perhaps that is why she wanted to give it away."

"Nay, I dinna believe that. There must be another explanation."

"Mayhap there is, but tonight I dinna want to think about it." He held out his arms. "Take off yer clothes and come here, Fia. I am feelin' randy."

Her body stiffened. She couldn't intimately lie with him while she was harboring so many secrets. It wouldn't feel right.

"Alastair, ye ken we decided ye wouldna take my virginity before we were married."

"Losh me! We are marryin' in the mornin', Fia. How much longer must I wait?"

"At least until the morrow," she said, walking to the door.

"Fia? Where are ye goin'?"

"I am worried about Caitlin. I am goin' to spend the night in her chamber to comfort her since she just lost her faither and is all alone."

"I just lost my faither as well." The hurt in his eyes about broke her heart, but she couldn't stay with him now. He was only going to make this harder. She needed to talk to Lorraine or her cousins and figure out what to do before she lost her head and did something crazy like making love to Alastair before they were married.

"Ye are a man, Alastair. Be strong. I will see ye in the mornin'."

Fia made her way down to the great hall where she found Niven laughing and having a tankard of ale with Brohain and Rhodric.

"Niven, have ye seen the messenger lad named Finn?"

Niven waved at her, sporting a silly grin. "Hello, Lady Fia. Nay, I havena seen him since early this mornin'. Why do ye ask?"

"I sent him on an errand and was curious if he'd returned yet."

"Well, what do we have here?" asked Brohain. "The little bride-to-be is all alone and lonely." He stood and staggered since he was so drunk.

"Why dinna we keep her company tonight?" Rhodric was at her side, just as well in his cups as Brohain.

"Leave her be." Niven stood up, but Brohain pushed him away, sending him crashing into a few knights talking by the fire.

"I'm surprised to see ye are no' by Alastair," said Brohain. "Perhaps he isna man enough to keep ye in his bed. How about ye try a real man like me instead?" He reached out and pulled her to him, kissing her hard on the lips. The rancid taste of his mouth on hers almost made her retch.

"I want a kiss, too," said Rhodric. "Or mayhap a squeeze of those perky little breasts." He reached out with both hands to touch her. She fought back, trying to push him away.

"Leave me alone," she cried.

Niven came to help her once again, and Brohain kicked him in the stomach and then turned back to her. "Why should Alastair have everythin' guid?" asked Brohain. "I think we'll help ourselves to a little taste of what the wench has to offer."

"I think no'!" Alastair appeared behind her wearing just his plaid, no tunic or shoes. However, he did have his sword in his hand, and it was pointed right at the men. The tip of it came up, scraping the skin under Brohain's chin. Brohain and Rhodric backed away with their hands in the air. "I should kill ye both for even thinkin' ye could go behind my back and try to assault my bride."

"I tried to help her, my laird," Niven called out, bent over and holding his stomach.

"Now that my faither is dead, I see no reason to keep the two of ye in the clan any longer. Brohain and Rhodric, gather yer things and leave right now. Ye are never to set foot back in Cluny Castle, or I swear I will kill ye both, do ye understand?"

"We were just havin' a little fun," complained Brohain.

"Ye canna blame a man for tryin' with a wench who looks like Fia," added Rhodric.

"Out!" Alastair shouted, nodding and bringing over two of his men. "Earc and Fearchar will see ye to the gate. And I warn ye; I never want to see yer ugly faces again."

"Come on," grumbled Fearchar pulling Brohain and Rhodric to the door. Earc helped him.

Fia threw her arms around Alastair and clung to him. She had been so afraid that she was about to be raped. "Thank ye for comin' to my rescue."

"No bride of mine is goin' to be roamin' the castle while I'm sleepin' alone in my bed. Now, I am here to take ye back to my bedchamber. I will no' hear any objections, and that is final."

# CHAPTER 21

*A*lastair awoke with a crick in his neck and pain in his calf, having slept in his plaid again. The damned chair was so uncomfortable that he should have slept on the floor with the dog instead.

He sat up and looked across the room. Caitlin and Fia shared his bed while his hound was also lounged atop the pallet, on its back and with its legs up in the air.

"Losh me, ye've got to be jestin'," he said softly to himself. Even the damned dog got to sleep with Fia while he fell off the chair three times trying to get comfortable – in his own room.

Needing some ale or mayhap something stronger like whisky, he got up, grabbed his tunic, boots and weapon belt, and tiptoed to the door. As soon as the door opened a crack, Cerberus bounded off the bed and pushed him down in his hurry to leave the room. Alastair dropped his things, looking up only to have his face washed with a long tongue.

"Stop it, ye fool." He got up and picked up his things and quietly closed the door. With the beast tripping him every step he took, he finally managed to make his way to the great hall to find Niven standing in the doorway stretching and yawning.

"Niven, take the dog," he said, needing a minute of peace. Seeing the great hall filled with drunken bodies from last night, he opted to go up to the battlements for some fresh air to clear his head instead.

"Come here, Cerberus," said Niven, trying to catch the dog. But it kept darting away from him. "Why didna ye have Fia show ye how to control him, my laird?"

"I dinna need a lassie to show me how to do anythin'." He put his weapon belt on the floor with his boots while he quickly pulled his tunic over his head.

"Speakin' of Fia, I'm sorry about last night." Niven lunged at the dog and landed on the floor when the hound stepped back and then jumped over him and ran like a possessed demon through the great hall. Rushes flew up in the air from the animal's feet, and Cerberus' tail knocked over a few empty tankards from last night's celebration. Several of the men complained and started cursing at the dog.

"It would have been better if ye werena in yer cups and could have watched over Fia for me, but it doesna matter since I saw to matters. If Brohain or Rhodric show their faces here again, I will keep my promise and kill them."

"Where is Fia?" asked Niven, getting off the ground and brushing the dirt from his palms.

"She's still in bed."

"Ah." Niven smiled from ear to ear. "She was so appreciative that ye saved her virtue from Brohain and Rhodric that she gave it to ye instead."

"Nay. She spent the night in my bed but not with me. She was consolin' my half-sister, Caitlin, all night."

"Caitlin? How did that happen?" asked Niven, scratching his head. "I swear I heard ye say ye were takin' her to yer bed when ye left the great hall last night."

"I did say that." Alastair strapped on his weapon belt. "But before I kent what happened, I agreed to let Caitlin sleep in my bed while I slept in the damned chair." He stretched his neck to the side and rubbed it with his palm. "Even the dog got a better sleep than me. I swear I dinna ken how Fia does it."

"Does what, my laird?" asked Niven with a yawn.

"She made me think it was my idea when I had somethin' different in mind."

"So it was her idea that ye let Caitlin sleep in the room with ye?"

"Nay. Aye. Hell, I dinna ken. I need to take a walk on the battlements to clear my head." He bent over and put on one boot. As he reached for the other, Cerberus ran up and snatched it from him, getting down on his haunches, looking up at him with playful eyes. "Give me the boot, boy." His hand shot forward, but the dog jumped up and started running around the room with the boot in his mouth.

"I'll get it for ye, my laird," offered Niven.

"Hell, dinna bother. I dinna even care." He limped away wearing only one boot, climbing the steps of the battlements, almost getting run over by Earc on his way down.

"Sorry, my laird, I dinna see ye there. It looks like Finn is back and I see a travelin' party approachin' as well. I'm goin' to open the gate."

"Finn is back?" he asked. "From where? Why? Who sent him anywhere?"

"Niven told me that Fia sent him out to the Iron Eagle yesterday."

"Why would she do that?" Alastair had a strange feeling that Fia was deceiving him about something.

"I'm no' sure, my laird. Did ye want me to send Finn up here to speak to ye?"

"Aye. Nay." He ran a hand through his hair in aggravation. The last thing he wanted to do was to go behind Fia's back checking up on her. If she was hiding something, he wanted her to tell him herself.

ELIZABETH ROSE

"My laird?" asked Earc in confusion.

"Send Fia up to the battlements to talk to me instead."

"Aye, my laird." He looked down at Alastair's feet. "Did ye ken ye are only wearin' one boot?"

Alastair glared at him. "Did ye ken the other boot is goin' to be kickin' ye in the arse if ye dinna get out of here right now?"

Earc hurried away while Alastair made his way up to the battlements. Leaning over the wall, he rubbed his stiff neck hoping the cool morning breeze would clear the confusion from his head. Ever since he found Fia alone with his dead father, she had acted strangely. Things had been so hectic that he hadn't even had time to ask her what she was doing in his father's chamber in the first place. He heard that his father had called for her, but he had no idea why.

The sound of the creaking chains and pulleys filled the air as the gate lifted. He looked over the wall to see Finn on his horse waiting to enter. Then, before he could even get inside, Fia ran out to talk to him. He couldn't hear what they were saying, but by the look on Fia's face, he could tell she wasn't happy.

"FINN, it's about time ye returned." Fia ducked under the moving gate and ran to meet the messenger. "Where is Lorraine? Didna she return with ye?"

"I'm sorry, my lady, but when I got to the Iron Eagle and asked for her, I was told by her husband that she never returned from her errand. Her body was found miles away. It seems she was attacked and killed on the road by bandits."

"Nay!" she shouted, feeling her heart sink in her chest. "Lorraine is dead? Are ye sure?"

"Her husband told me directly. He said the bandits took everythin', even her horse and only left the clothes on her back."

Fia reached out and laid her hand on Finn's horse, feeling as if Lorraine's death was her fault. If she hadn't asked Lorraine to

214

take the crown to Richard, the woman would still be alive today. She didn't even know now if Lorraine had met up with her contact and given them the crown. Then again, she must have been on her way back to the inn when it happened since the English did turn around and retreat.

"Fia," someone shouted, gaining her attention. She looked up to see her sister, Morag, approaching on horseback. With her was Fia's entire family.

"Morag," she called out, picking up her gown and running to greet her. Her sister was off the horse and in her arms before the horse even stopped moving.

"I was so frightened for ye," cried Morag, hugging her hard. "We thought ye were dead. Thank guidness Faither came to Rothbury to tell me ye were alive and gettin' married."

"Mathair," cried Fia, running to greet her mother who was riding in a wagon with Fia's thirteen-year-old twin brothers, Conall and Dugal. She greeted her mother and brothers as well as her father and looked around. "Where is Uncle Duff? Will he be comin' to my weddin'?"

"His wife is havin' another baby any day. He sends his regrets but wants to stay and tend to the other children to help her," said her mother.

"Ye are goin' to live in a castle?" said Conall, his red hair shining in the sun almost as bright as hers.

"Why dinna we have a castle, Da?" asked Dugal, the dark-haired twin.

"Boys, ye ken that we live simply in our clan because that is the way yer faither wants it," their mother reminded them.

"Maggie, it's time the boys ken the truth," said Reed. "I didna pledge my loyalty to the late King Edward like yer uncles did, or I would have had a castle as well."

"Why didna ye?" asked Dugal with a frown.

Morag answered for him. "Because then ye would all be livin' in England with Sassenachs the way Fia and I have been doin."

215

"Speakin' of that," said Fia, looking around. "Where are Willow and Maira? I need to speak with them about somethin' important."

"They're no' comin'," said Morag. "The earl wouldna let them leave his care."

"What? No' even for my weddin'?" asked Fia. "Why no'?"

Reed cleared his throat and looked the other way. "They'll be along later after yer uncles talk to Lord Beaufort."

"Da almost strangled the earl with his bare hands for lettin' ye be kidnapped when he was supposed to be watchin' over ye," tattled Morag. "Now the earl willna let Willow or Maira leave until he has written permission from Uncle Rook and Uncle Rowen."

"Da, how could ye?" spat Fia. "I am to be married this mornin', and I wanted them here."

"Ye'll just have to wait and talk to them when they arrive in a day or two," said Reed, leading the way inside the castle.

"A day or two? That is too long. I need to talk to them now." Fia followed her family inside the castle courtyard feeling as if she would never have anyone to confide in with her problem.

"Fia, ye have me to talk to," said Morag, leading her horse, walking at Fia's side.

"This is nothin' ye can help me with, Morag. It has to do with the Followers of the Secret Heart."

"I'm a member now, too, dinna forget." Morag tapped the heart brooch on her bodice. "Imanie made me a member so ye can talk to me about things as well."

"Imanie was also cursed by doin' that and died for it, unless ye forgot," Fia whispered. Before Morag could respond, Earc approached.

"Lady Fia, Laird Alastair would like to talk to ye anon up on the battlements."

"Now?" Fia's heart pounded in her ears. "But my family has just arrived."

"Fia," Alastair called down from the battlements. "Come up here, please."

Reed looked up and nodded a greeting to Alastair who nodded back.

"Yer family is welcome to refresh themselves in the great hall. I will be right with them," he told her.

"Aye, my laird," she said, climbing the steps to the battlements, feeling as if she were heading to the gallows instead.

"Fia, come here." Alastair turned and headed down the walk way. She noticed he limped and then saw why. "Ye are only wearin' one boot?"

"Dinna ask."

"I'll bet it was Cerberus who took the other. He is such a playful dog." She tried to talk about anything other than what she knew he wanted to speak to her about.

"Forget the dog. I want to ken why my faither called ye into his chamber."

"I was glad he did since I wanted to say guidbye."

"Ye didna even ken him nor did he like ye. Dinna lie to me, Fia. Now, tell me what it was that was so important that he found the need to tell ye with his dyin' breath."

Fia looked over the edge of the battlements, wishing she were anywhere but here right now. If only she had been able to talk to Lorraine or her cousins for guidance, she would be feeling much better at the moment. Now, this was all up to her. Duncan MacPherson could go straight to hell for all she cared, putting her in this position. Mayhap he did it purposely, trying to tear Alastair and her apart.

"He called me into his chamber to tell me that he always believed ye when ye told him a mysterious woman saved yer life on the battlefield."

"What? Why wouldna he say that to me instead? That makes no sense."

Fia could no longer hold back. If they were to be married, she had to be honest with him, or he would never trust her again. "He told me because he saw the heart brooch I wore, just like the one that the mysterious woman gave ye."

"And?" He tapped his fingers on the wall of the battlements and waited for her to continue.

"Alastair, he told me he thought the woman who saved ye on the battlefield was yer mathair."

"Nay. How could that be?"

"I dinna ken, but the woman gave ye the heart brooch. Yer mathair had one just like it."

"She did?" He stopped and pondered the thought, his eyes going up and to the side as he tried to recall. "Aye," he said with a nod as if suddenly remembering. "I was verra young at the time, but now I vaguely remember her wearin' a brooch just like that. What does it mean?"

Fia released a breath, closed her eyes and finally told him. "I belong to a secret group devised by the late Queen of England. Yer mathair belonged to it as well."

"Stop it, Fia. Ye're speakin' nonsense. My mathair never met Queen Philippa."

"Yer faither didna like the idea. He was the one to send her away," she continued, wanting to tell him everything before she changed her mind. "He beat her to get her to tell him about it."

"Nay." Alastair held on to the wall, gripping it so hard she saw his knuckles turn white. "If I had kent this, I would have fought my faither to protect my mathair."

"And that is why he could never tell ye. He took a mistress and told yer mathair if she ever returned or tried to contact ye or yer brathair he would . . . kill her."

Alastair's head snapped up, and his eyes bore fire. "Tell me ye are makin' this up."

"I would never make up such a horrid story. I am sorry, Alastair." She reached out and covered his hand with hers.

"What is this secret group?" he asked, staring out over the wall as he spoke. A muscle ticked in his jaw as he tried to hold back his emotions.

"It is called the Followers of the Secret Heart. It is a group of women chosen by the queen, trained to be strong and to help their country and their people in secret."

"Ye're sayin' my mathair did this?"

"I dinna ken."

"And ye and yer cousins? How could ye be trained or even chosen by the queen when she has been dead for years?"

"Imanie trained us. The queen chose us as children to be trained when we were of age. When my grandfaither was on his deathbed, he gave us the queen's crowns and these heart brooches because it was her wish."

"Fia, this is all so hard to believe."

"I'm sorry, Alastair, but it is all true."

"What about the crown? What did ye do with it? I ken ye had a hand in its disappearance."

This part wasn't going to be easy. Still, she couldn't keep it a secret any longer. "I gave it to Lorraine to give to a friend."

"Lorraine had a heart-shaped brooch, too. I want to talk with her." He stood upright as if he meant to go.

"Ye canna talk with her because Finn just told me she is dead."

"Dead?" A shadow covered his face. He looked down at her in a scolding manner. "What else are ye no' tellin' me, lass? Are ye in some kind of danger?"

"Lorraine was found dead on the road, and with nothin' at all but the clothes on her back. It is thought that bandits stole from her and then killed her. It is all my fault." Fia tried hard to hold back the tears, ready to break down at any moment.

Alastair must have noticed because his demeanor suddenly softened. "It is no' yer fault, Fia."

"But it is. I gave her the crown because . . . because . . ."

"I ken why ye did it."

"Ye do?" she asked in surprise.

"Aye. Ye were my prisoner, and ye did no' want me to have the crown. I canna blame ye. After all, Brohain had his eye on it for a long time. I had half a mind to hide it myself so he couldna find it."

"Alastair, that is no' exactly why I did it."

"It doesna matter. It is over now." He pulled her into his arms and ran a soothing hand up and down her back to try to calm her.

"Are ye angry with me?"

"I'm no' angry at ye, Fia, but I wish ye would have told me and no' kept it a secret."

"So – it doesna matter to ye that I wear this brooch and all that it stands for?" She looked down to the pin and rubbed her fingers over it, trying to find strength.

"Imanie is dead and so is Lorraine. Fia, I dinna want ye involved in things that are dangerous." He took her hands in his and looked her in the eye. "Promise me that as my wife ye will stop doin' anythin' in secret that has to do with this group."

Part of Fia wanted to rebel and tell him that she would never agree to this. But she hurt so bad from hearing that her actions caused Lorraine's death that she never wanted to feel this way again. In trying to keep harm from those she loved, her clansmen and both her countries, she lost a friend who was willing to risk her life for the good of so many others.

"I see now that things are no' as I thought they would be with bein' a member of this group. I mourn the passing of Imanie and feel as if Lorraine's death was my fault. I promise ye, Alastair, that as yer wife, I will give up livin' a secret life. I will no longer go behind yer back and do things that might endanger my life or the lives of others."

"Guid," he said, kissing her on the head. "That's what I wanted to hear."

"However."

He pulled back and looked at her from the sides of his eyes. "Aye?"

"Neither will I promise to be a subservient wife to be treated no better than a dog."

She held her breath, waiting for him to explode at hearing this. She had spoken out of line and no man she knew would ever put up with a woman talking this way to him. It was a risk to say this, but she didn't want to marry him if he was going to beat her the way his father did to his mother.

He was quiet for a few seconds, and then a grin spread across his face, and he started laughing! Taking her by her shoulders, he pulled her to his chest in a protective hug. "Dinna worry, Fia, I will never treat ye less than honorably. After all, ye are the grand-daughter of a king. Besides, ye should ken by now that the dog of this castle gets treated better than even me around here. Now, let's go greet our guests that are startin' to arrive for the weddin'."

"Alastair? Do ye think ye will ever see yer mathair again?"

"I'm no' sure. And I am no' convinced the woman on the battlefield really was my mathair."

"But are ye sure ye didna see the lassie's face who saved ye? Certainly, ye wouldna have forgotten the face of yer own mathair."

"Nay, I didna see it. Her face was in shadow, and she wore a long, hooded cloak."

"Then perhaps yer mathair is still alive. Now that yer faither is gone, mayhap she will have the courage to return."

"I'd like to think that, Fia, honestly I would. But in my heart, I feel as if she is watchin' over my deceased brathair instead. They are together wherever people go when they leave this life. Now, please, let's no' talk about death anymore. We are to be married and will start a new life together. What is in the past is gone and I willna be reminded of things that upset me on the most important day of my life."

# CHAPTER 22

Two hours later, Alastair paced back and forth in his chamber, not able to find the small box with the ring in it that he had bought for Fia. He tore up the room looking everywhere, but could not find it.

He picked up the box with the heart brooch in it, opening the lid and gingerly plucking up the pin to inspect it. Could this have been his mother's? And was she the one who helped save his life when he was wounded on the battlefield and left to die? It was a hard story to believe, not to mention the one his father supposedly told Fia. It wasn't that he thought Fia was lying, but he had trouble understanding there was a secret group of strong women that was chosen by the late English queen. The whole thing sounded like something made up by a drunken bard.

"My laird," said Niven, rushing in the door, out of breath. "Everyone is waitin' for ye in the courtyard. Fia's faither said if ye dinna come down there anon, he is goin' to come up here and get ye himself."

"Have ye found the ring?" He slammed shut the box and replaced it on the shelf.

"Nay. I looked everywhere for it. Where did ye leave it?"

"If I kent that, I wouldna be late for my own weddin'. I swear I put it up here on the shelf." He ran his hand over the shelf once more but found no ring.

"It looks like Cerberus has been in here again and just after I cleaned up from the last time he demolished the room," stated Niven, looking at the mess.

"Nay, most of this mess was done by me lookin' for the ring."

"Oh." Niven raised his brows in surprise.

"Well, I will just have to explain it to Fia and get her another ring later. I hope she can forgive me for bein' so careless."

They made their way down to the courtyard decorated with archways of flowers leading to a raised dais where the priest stood waiting with his book in his hand. Alastair stopped in his tracks when he saw Fia waiting for him to join her. She was even more beautiful than he'd ever seen her before.

"Alastair," she said with a smile as he approached, keeping her head down and looking up shyly, making her big, green eyes seem twice as large. Damn, she was alluring. Morag stood at her side, straightening the train of her long gown. It was made of dark green velvet with eyelets of white lace on the tippets and down the bodice.

"Ye look stunnin', my bonnie cailin."

She smiled and held out the sides of her gown. "My mathair brought this gown for me to wear."

"She made it years ago, hopin' someday Fia would marry," Morag blurted out.

Fia's long, red locks were loose and cascaded down her shoulders. It was a striking contrast to her forest green gown. The only thing that could have made her look more like a princess was if she were wearing her crown. In her hands, she held a bouquet of colorful wildflowers.

"Shall we start?" asked the priest, seeming anxious to have the wedding over. The sky started to darken, looking like rain.

"Wait! Wait for us," called out a female voice from the drawbridge. Alastair turned around to see Fia's cousins and their fathers – the other two Legendary Bastards of the Crown, riding in through the front gate.

"Maira! Willow!" Fia shouted excitedly, waving the flowers in the air. "Over here."

The girls dismounted and ran over to hug Fia.

"I DIDNA THINK YE WERE COMIN'." Fia's heart soared to see her cousins. Willow and Maira had arrived with their fathers in time for the wedding after all.

"We rode all night to get the girls here in time," said the blond-haired triplet, Rowen.

"Alastair, ye already ken my cousins, but I would like ye to meet my Uncles Rook and Rowen," said Fia.

"About time ye got here," Reed called out. "It took ye long enough." Reed went over to greet his brothers with a quick clasp of their hands.

"Are we ready now?" asked the priest, glancing up at the sky. A few raindrops fell around them. "I recommend I do the short version since it is about to storm."

"Make it quick," said Alastair, taking Fia's hand in his. "I canna wait a minute longer to make her my wife."

After repeating their vows, the priest nodded to Alastair. "Ye can put the ring on her finger now." He nervously glanced upward at the sky once again.

"Fia," said Alastair. "About the ring."

"Aye?" she couldn't imagine what he was trying to say.

Cerberus pushed through the crowd and leaped up at Alastair, putting its paws on his shoulders just then.

"Get down," he grumbled, having no luck at pushing the dog away.

"He has somethin' in his mouth," observed Fia.

"It's the ring," called out Niven from next to Alastair.

"God's eyes, ye're right." Alastair took the small box from the hound's mouth and opened it, pulling out a ring and holding it up in the air. "I couldna have trained the dog to do that," he said with a chuckle.

"And just in time," added Niven.

Alastair slipped the ring onto Fia's finger just as the sky opened up in a downpour.

"I pronounce ye man and wife, ye may kiss the bride," the priest said all at once, slamming shut his book and running for cover.

"Everyone to the great hall," called out Reed, leading the crowd out of the rain.

Fia didn't notice the rain drenching them because she was busy kissing Alastair and thinking of how excited she was to be his wife.

"Tonight is the night," he told her, picking her up in his arms to carry her to the great hall. Fia knew what he meant because she was anticipating their consummation just as much as he was. "Niven," Alastair called out as he placed her on her feet inside the keep.

"Aye, my laird?" asked Niven, rushing over with the dog at his heels.

Alastair stared into Fia's eyes as he spoke. "Tell the cooks to hold off the meal for an hour and have the minstrels and jongleurs entertain everyone until we get to the great hall."

"My laird?" asked Niven, pushing the dog away as it barked and continued to pull at his sleeve. "Ye are already here."

"Nay, we're no'," he said, picking up Fia and carrying her in the opposite direction. "And keep the damned dog out of the bedchamber because I am no' goin' to be in the mood for sharin' my bed with anyone but my new wife for the next hour."

"Alastair," said Fia as he kicked open the door and headed straight to the bed. "My parents are out there and so are my cousins and uncles."

"And that is where they will stay until we have consummated our marriage." He closed and barred the door and hurried back to the bed.

"Perhaps we should wait until after the celebration."

"I have waited long enough and will no' wait a minute longer." He started a fire in the hearth and was out of his clothes before she even knew what happened. "Let's take off that gown and dry it by the fire, shall we?" He pulled her over in front of the hearth.

"I – I – " She said nothing more because his mouth covered hers in a passionate kiss while his fingers expertly undid the lacing of her bodice. He slowly pushed the gown off her shoulders and slid it from her body letting it pool around her ankles.

"Ye are my wife," said Alastair, removing her shift and then untying her braies and dropping them to the floor as well. "Ye are my bonnie, bonnie wife." In one motion, he swept her off her feet, causing her to squeal in pleasure. He brought her to the bed and laid her down gently, covering her body with his.

His skin against hers felt hot. His manhood was already stiff and rubbed up against her belly as he held himself up on his elbows. He trailed kisses down her neck and over to her chest.

"Alastair, I have waited for this moment for a long time."

"No' as long as me."

"I am excited, but yet I am scared."

He lifted his head and gazed into her eyes with concern. "Fia, I would never hurt ye. Ye need to ken that."

"I do," she told him. "I trust ye, Alastair, and I love ye."

"I love ye, too." He rolled to his side and took his time making sure she felt at ease before he entered her. "Close yer eyes, Fia."

"Nay. I dinna want to miss a thing."

"Then kiss me and love me and dinna worry because I promise ye this will be enjoyable. I will make certain it is."

That was all she needed to hear to relax and live in the moment. They were together and alone. It felt wonderful. "I am ready," she told him, kissing him on the mouth and running her hands down his chest. She daringly let her fingers travel lower. When she felt his aroused form, her fingers closed around him, and she squeezed slightly.

"Bid the devil, if ye keep that up, I will no' be able to keep my promise to make sure ye enjoy this because it will be over before it begins."

"Kiss me, Alastair."

He kissed her again and let his hand slide seductively to her breast. His fingers expertly aroused her, causing one nipple and then the other to stand erect. Next, his mouth replaced his hand, causing her to arch up off the bed. Inquisitively, she reached out to touch his chest, feeling the crisp, dark curls of hair beneath her fingers. And when he slid his hand lower, past her belly and below her waist, she couldn't stop thinking of the last time he pleasured her using only his mouth.

Her hand trailed lower to feel the crisp circlets of hair below his waist. Her fingers brushed against the tip of his manhood where a drop of moisture wet her hand. She caressed him in her palm and flicked her thumb over his tip causing him to jerk and let out a low moan.

"Fia, ye are drivin' me mad. Why do ye do that when I told ye I wanted to excite ye first?"

"I'm curious how it'll feel," she told him. "Besides, I am ready. Ye need no' wait any longer."

"Let me check," he said, cupping her mound with his hand. "Ye are almost there, but I want to make sure." He slipped one finger into her and then two, causing Fia's anticipation to grow even stronger. A vibrant heat engulfed her, and she felt as if she didn't want to wait to consummate their marriage any longer.

"Please, Alastair, dinna tease me."

He opened her legs further and settled himself between her thighs. Then, ever so gently, he pressed the tip of his hardened manhood up to her, letting it enter just a little.

"Oh, my," she said in surprise since he was much bigger than using his fingers.

"I will be gentle, Fia. But in case I am no', I need ye to tell me. I want yer first time to be somethin' ye will remember yer entire life."

"I am sure it will be. Now, please, enter me fully, and dinna make me ask again."

She didn't need to beg him because he entered her, slipping inside her and then slowly pulling back out. She squirmed beneath him, wanting him to give her more.

"Do it faster," she said through ragged breathing, seeming to surprise him by her request.

"Are ye sure?"

"Aye. I want to ken what it feels like to be bedded by a passionate, randy man."

"Then I willna deny yer request." He thrust into her entirely, and she felt her maidenhead break away. His hands slip around her buttocks, pulling her even closer. She found the rhythm and also felt that same feeling she had when he'd brought her to climax before.

But this time, Alastair was inside her, and their marriage was consummated. Because of this union, there would be a chance that she would conceive a child. The thought of possibly giving Alastair a son or daughter excited her even more. She lifted her hips, wanting to make sure she took in every bit of her new husband. And when they both reached their peaks of total pleasure, finding release, she felt as if she had found the person she'd been looking for her entire life.

## CHAPTER 23

*W*hen Fia and Alastair entered the great hall sometime later, the crowd cheered and clapped knowing they were now, indeed, man and wife.

"Congratulations, Fia!" Willow and Maira rushed over to hug her. They pulled her to the side to talk to her while the men conversed with Alastair.

"What was it like?" asked Willow. "Did you scream when you found your release?"

"Was he fierce with his lovemaking or was he gentle?" Maira wanted to know.

Fia noticed Morag watching them from the other side of the room, looking very left out of the conversation. "Morag, come join us," she called out, watching her sister's face light up as she ran over to join them. Cerberus was on her heels thinking it was a game.

"Get outta here," complained Morag, trying to shoo the dog away. Fia was about to help her when there was a loud whistle from the other side of the room. The hound looked up and darted toward Alastair. Fia waited for it to jump on him as always, but Alastair stood tall and held out his hand and told the

229

dog to sit. To her surprise, it did. Then Alastair plucked a smelt from the tray of a server and tossed it to the dog, turning to get back to his conversation with Fia's father and uncles.

"Thank ye for includin' me in the conversation." Morag looked happier than she had in a long time.

"Ye are my sister, Morag, and I am sorry I have no' included ye in more things in the past," Fia told her. "I have somethin' to tell all of ye. It has to do with the queen's secret group."

"I am a member now as well," Morag reminded her, touching the heart brooch on her bodice.

"Aye, ye are, Morag and that is why I included ye."

"What do you want to tell us?" asked Maira.

"Where is your crown?" added Willow, straightening her crown as she spoke. "It seems you would want to wear it on your wedding day."

"Aye, I noticed that it was missing as well," said Maira. "Did the MacPhersons take it from you?"

"No," said Fia. "I gave it to another member of the secret group. Her name is Lorraine. She was tryin' to get it to Richard with a message from me that the Scots were waitin' to ambush his troops."

"Ye did what?" asked Morag in shock. "If faither finds out ye went against the Scots, he will be furious."

"Morag, I only did it to try to save many Scots' lives as well as English."

"It must have worked," said Maira. "The English retreated and came home."

"And the Scots never had a chance to attack," added Fia. "Lots of lives were spared but, unfortunately, Lorraine died in the process."

"Nay," said Willow. "That is horrible."

"Alastair's mathair was a member as well," Fia continued.

"She was?" Morag's eyes opened wide.

"You didn't tell Alastair any secrets, did you?" asked Willow.

"I had to tell him. I also promised no' to be involved in the group any longer because it is too risky. I wish ye would all think about it as well." She touched the wooden heart on the bracelet she wore, silently apologizing to Imanie for her decision.

"But look at all the good you did, Fia." Maira did not like the idea of letting it go. "The queen thought this was important, and so do I."

"Me, too," said Willow.

"Same as me," added Morag.

"I canna tell ye what to do, but I want to ask ye to think before ye do anythin' that might be dangerous. Sometimes it is hard to see, but the best-laid plans can also come back to haunt ye."

"You aren't to blame for Lorraine's death," said Willow. "It could have happened to her at any time."

"That's right," said Maira. "You need to think of all the good you've done by giving up your crown to save the lives of so many others."

"Fia," said Alastair, hurrying over, looking like he'd seen a ghost.

"What is it?" she asked.

"Fia, God has answered my prayers. Look who is here." He held out his arm as a monk walked up next to him.

"Who is this, Alastair?"

"This is Brother Toran."

"Nice to meet ye," she said, still not understanding why Alastair seemed so excited to introduce her to the holy man.

"He's my brathair, Fia. He didna die after all. Toran was taken in by a nunnery when he was close to death. He has spent three years healin', but now he has returned."

"I've also joined the order to thank God for givin' me a second chance at life," said Toran.

"I see," she said, feeling happy for him.

"I am pleased to meet ye, Lady Fia." Toran took her hands in his. "And I am sorry to hear my faither has passed on before he found out that I was still alive."

Caitlin walked past, and Alastair called her over. "Sister," he said, putting his arm around her and including her in the circle. Caitlin looked up, confused. "Our brathair, Toran, is home." Alastair glanced over to Fia and winked. Then, he and his siblings walked off talking. Fia had never seen Caitlin smile as much as she was right now. Alastair seemed to take her advice to heart, and she liked the changes in him.

"Lady Fia," said Finn, coming to join them with a large canvas bag in his hands. "A woman just dropped this off at the gate and asked me to give it to ye."

"What is it, Finn?"

"I dinna ken. She said it was a weddin' present."

"Well, did ye ask her to join us? Where is she?"

"There she is," said Finn, pointing to a woman in a cloak standing in the shadows by the door.

"Ask her to come here, please. I want her to join the celebration. It's the least we can do after she arrived with a present." Fia took the bag from him and peeked inside. Her jaw dropped when she saw the contents.

"What is it?" asked Morag excitedly. "Take it out so we can see it, too."

With a shaking hand, Fia dug into the bag and lifted out her crown.

"It's your crown!" exclaimed Willow.

"I thought you said Richard has it and that is why he retreated," added Maira.

"I thought so, too." Fia's eyes fastened to the crown in thought. Suddenly, she had no idea if Lorraine delivered the message or if bandits stole the crown before it even got to Richard. Or had Richard sent it back to her in thanks? She turned toward the woman at the door, wanting to ask her, but saw Finn looking around in confusion and shrugging his shoulders when their eyes met.

"The woman. She's gone," said Fia.

"Who do ye think it was?" asked Morag.

Fia had a feeling it was Alastair's mother, coming to see that her sons were safe. But if it was, why hadn't she stayed? Was it because she was so devoted to the vow she'd made years ago to Queen Philippa that she gave up her own family to carry it through? Fia decided she would never know the truth.

She put on her crown, her eyes meeting her husband's from across the room. He pointed to his head and then hers, and smiled. She now felt like a queen.

"Fia, what do you think happened?" asked Maira.

"Was it your action that caused Richard to turn around and leave Scotland?" Willow wanted to know.

"I dinna ken. And I doubt that we ever will, now that Lorraine is gone and canna tell us." Fia almost wondered if it was better that she never knew the truth.

"Mayhap, ye should ask Richard," suggested Morag.

"Nay, Morag, I would never do that. Besides, he would never admit it even if it were true."

"What about Alastair?" asked Willow. "Will you ever tell him what you did to try to save the lives of thousands of men?"

Fia looked back at her husband who was smiling and laughing and had one arm around Caitlin's shoulder and another around his brother, Toran. He had found happiness today in more ways than one. Even if it was his mother at the door, it was her choice whether to make her presence known or not. Fia promised not to speak of things today that upset Alastair. She also promised not to be involved in the Followers of the Secret Heart anymore. There was no need to find out these answers because they no longer mattered.

Alastair waved her over. "Fia. Wife, come join us," he said. "I want my entire family together on this verra special day. And I want ye at my side every single minute from now on."

"I am comin'," said Fia, smiling and feeling a wave of joy flow through her. She looked forward to living a new life with Alastair. Hopefully, someday, she would raise a family with him as well.

She turned back to her sister and cousins. "I will no' mention the incident with the crown and Richard ever to Alastair and neither will any of ye."

"Why no'?" asked Morag.

"Because we dinna ken for sure if my actions had anythin' to do with the English army retreatin'. And as ye all said, we also have no proof that what I did had anythin' to do with Lorraine's death."

"Then you don't ever want to find out?" asked Maira, sounding as if she couldn't believe it.

"Nay," Fia answered, smiling at her husband, wanting nothing more than to be in his arms. She had one more thing to say to her cousins and sister, and then she would start a new life with Alastair, and never keep secrets from him again. "What happened in the past no longer matters. It is only the present we should be concerned with, and continue to move forward. By lettin' go, we truly learn how to live. So, my answer to ye three is nay, I never want to find out what really happened because it no longer matters to me. Those answers will, from this day on, be naught but *Highland Secrets*."

# FROM THE AUTHOR

I hope you enjoyed *Highland Secrets* and will take a minute to leave a review for me.

When I started this series, I did a reader's poll. I knew I wanted to do a series featuring some of the daughters from my past characters. However, I wasn't sure which characters from what series to use. Hands down, my readers wanted to hear about the daughters of the *Legendary Bastards of the Crown.*

This, being a next generation, took me into a new timeframe with a new king. During the series, you will see characters from some of the other books show up, especially the bastard triplets of King Edward, being Rowen, Rook and Reed.

King Richard was King Edward III's grandson who ruled after him, since his son, The Black Prince, died a year before Edward almost to the date. Richard was not the warlord that his father and grandfather were. In the Battle of Morranside that you read about in *Highland Secrets*, the Scots burned their crops to keep them from the English troops. King Richard was urged by his uncle, John of Gaunt, to keep raiding Scotland, but Richard decided to retreat and turned his men back home. No one really knows why he did it, and some theories say it is because he wasn't a warrior, or possibly that he didn't want his men to starve to death.

Of course, in my version, I give a third option. Since I like to write strong women into my stories, Fia and her cousins are part of a secret organization set up by the late Queen Philippa. Philippa was a strong woman in history and often influenced her husband's decisions as well as led the army while he was campaigning in France.

We know that women were not treated well at all in medieval times. But as a romance author and reader, I like my heroines to be strong. Therefore, I came up with the idea of a secret group of women led by the queen. And the queen's secret garden was inspired by my own secret garden where I lay in my hammock and write novels all summer long.

Fia's cousins, Willow and Maira, will have their stories told next in *Seductive Secrets*, and *Rebellious Secrets*. And because I can't let Fia's little sister, Morag, go without her own story, you will see her book, *Forgotten Secrets*, show up as the last book of the *Secrets of the Heart Series.*

Thank you,

*Elizabeth Rose*

# ABOUT ELIZABETH

Elizabeth Rose is a multi-published, bestselling author, writing medieval, historical, contemporary, paranormal, and western romance. She is an amazon all-star and has been an award finalist numerous times. Her books are available as Ebooks, paperback, and audiobooks as well.

Her favorite characters in her works include dark, dangerous and tortured heroes, and feisty, independent heroines who know how to wield a sword. She loves writing 14th century medieval novels, and is well-known for her many series.

Her twelve-book small town contemporary series, Tarnished Saints, was inspired by incidents in her own life.

After being traditionally published, she started self-publishing, creating her own covers and book-trailers on a dare from her two sons.

Elizabeth loves the outdoors. In the summertime, you can find her in her secret garden with her laptop, swinging in her hammock working on her next book. Elizabeth is a born storyteller and passionate about sharing her works with her readers.

Please be sure to visit her website at **Elizabethrosenovels.com** to read excerpts from any of her novels and get sneak peeks at covers of upcoming books. You can follow her on **Twitter**, **Facebook**, **Goodreads** or **Bookbub.**

*And more!*

Please visit http://elizabethrosenovels.com

*Elizabeth Rose*

Made in the USA
Coppell, TX
09 June 2021

57101609R10143